Borrowed Fantasy

By Joseph Mason

Edited by Greta Wink

Cover art by Audrey Webb

Special Thanks to

Scott Mertz

and

Logan Mertz

Part I:

For You, Brother

Chapter 1: An Unexpected Visitor

Pain was all the Earth felt. War and pestilence ravaged the land. Ignorance and fear filled people's minds. Savage beasts roamed the wilderness and plains. No place seemed safe from the horror of this age…except one.

Tucked away in the valley of a mountain range surrounded by impassable forest, the tiny village of Trow lived unnoticed by the outside world. The villagers had only a slight recollection of the outside. A secret kept them safe in Trow. A secret that would soon end.

"HARVEST FESTIVAL!!!"

"Yes, Aleese. You only said that a hundred times," Abram acknowledged his sister, knowing twelve years ago he was the tiny six-year-old screaming at the top of his lungs about the harvest festival.

Abram also looked forward to the harvest festival. The villagers bring their best dishes. Dancing and music fill the village. Even so, the best part was their Grandpa's Skyward Lights.

After dusk, Grandpa would walk up the mountain alone and create the most phenomenal light show. No one knew how he made the lights. Grandpa carried nothing but his walking stick up the mountain. Some thought he kept the secret to the lights hidden up the mountain, but all who traveled up the mountain could find neither hide nor hair of anything that could help him. Several would offer to aid him in his display, but he would sternly reject their offers, insisting that when the time comes, he would gladly unveil his secret.

"Grandpa. What if you can't make it up the mountain? Who will do the lights?" implored Aleese.

Grandpa, seeing the concern in her eyes, reassured her.

"I was thinking I might take your brother Levi up with me soon enough."

"Did you hear that, Levi!?! Grandpa is going to share the secret of the lights with you, and then you can share it with me!" squealed Aleese.

Abram could not help but feel jealous. His brother Levi had already mastered all the games they played. No one could beat him in a strategy game except Grandpa, but Grandpa stood no chance in the physical games. Although only two years older than Abram, the village council already considered Levi a pivotal member. Abram only had his brother beat in two areas; herbalism and farming.

When Aleese mistook poison ivy for a normal plant, Abram saved the day with a special salve. Abram knew the land and would put in the hard work to cultivate it. Villagers would often say there was no one more diligent than Abram in his farming. This was little consolation to Abram, who admired the work of his older brother. He always pictured himself as a cow and his brother as a majestic horse. Abram was stockier and shorter than his brother. His brother was nimble, light of foot, but immensely powerful. Abram knew he could take his brother in a game of brute force like tug-of-war, a game that required sheer strength and little skill. However, Abram had to concede to his brother on almost every other effort.

"Grandpa, Levi is already busy with his work in the village. Maybe you could take me instead," replied Abram, thinking that would show his brother who was truly important.

"I say he takes both of us and sees who does it better. Then everyone will know that I am the best," joked Levi, not being one to miss an opportunity to rib his younger brother.

"Maybe a friendly rivalry would spark some intrigue in this quiet village," Grandpa laughed.

Abram felt like the butt of the joke, but Grandpa's wonderful spirit was infectious, so he could not help but laugh as well.

However, all the talk about passing on the secrets of the Skyward Lights raised some questions for Abram. Is Grandpa going somewhere? Is Grandpa secretly ill? He could not stop thinking about it, so he had to take his questions to his mother.

He found his mother in the kitchen preparing for the festival.

"Mother, is Grandpa sick?"

"No. Why do you ask?"

"Grandpa was talking about showing Levi how to make the Skyward Lights. I just know he would not say something unless something was wrong."

"Listen, you are entirely too worried." His mother said, trying to comfort Abram, "You could put the plow on Grandpa, and he could till better than any mule."

Abram appreciated the joke.

"I still can't help but feel that something is wrong."

"Abram. Honey. When was the last time anything bad happened to this village? You know what you should be worried about? Getting some of your fruits and vegetables in here so you can prepare them for the feast."

His mother was right. Abram could not remember the last time something bad had happened in their village. He was not sure whether that fact should comfort or worry him. Still, he knew he had to hurry and get the fruits and vegetables. The merriment of the festival waited for no man, or woman, for that matter.

Abram picked his fruits and vegetables. He was always calmer when he tended his garden, and Abram almost forgot about the last ten minutes, and the concern they brought. Abram had to pick the best fruits and vegetables. The villagers would expect nothing less than that. Pleased with what he gathered, Abram headed back to the kitchen, half in a daze, thinking about all the fun of the festival. Abram thought about the singing and dancing, eating the delectable foods and especially Grandpa's Skyward Lights before something pulled him right out of his daydream.

"AAAAAAHHHHH!"

That was Aleese! Abram dropped his bundle of fruits and vegetables and rushed to help her. When Abram found Aleese, he spied an unusual beast.

"Get it away!" Aleese implored.

"What is that!?!"

"It's just a rat, Aleese," Abram stated matter-of-factly.

But this was not just any rat. It stood perched on its hind legs, staring at them with scarlet eyes. Abram had never seen a rat with red eyes. But what was more puzzling to Abram was how Aleese did not know what a rat was. How did he know what a rat was? He has never seen a rat in the fields or in town or in his house. What is this rat doing in his house now? Abram still could not get over the rat's eyes.

While Abram stared at the rat, Grandpa rushed in, and smashed the rat with his walking stick. Abram expected the rat to be dead after such a blow, but something odd happened. His grandpa whispered a few words, and the rat burst into flames. Abram stood dumbfounded.

Grandpa pulled them close.

"You know what? Why don't we collect everyone and have the Skyward Lights right now!"

Unfazed by the events, Aleese said, "It's daytime. We won't be able to see anything."

"Oh, Aleese, these will be special lights. You will see them clearly," Grandpa assured her.

Abram could not believe it. Did they not see what happened? A rat, something that had never been seen in their village, had appeared, with red beady eyes. When Grandpa muttered to it, the rat burst into flames. Now, Grandpa is displaying the lights at midday, and he said they will still be able to see them.

"Oh, Aleese, Abram. If you see your brother in the village, tell him to meet me at the foot of the mountains. It is time he learned the secret of the Skyward Lights," Grandpa zipped out of the room.

"Aleese, you gather the people in the village, and I will get the people from the fields."

Aleese nodded and skipped out the door.

Abram was still wondering how the two could be so levelheaded about the rat, but he did as Grandpa asked.

The abruptness of the Skyward Lights stunned most people. No one was ready for the festival, but everyone dropped what they were doing because they did not want to miss the lights.

Abram was walking back to the center of the village when he saw his brother.

"Levi, Grandpa told me to tell you to go to the foot of the mountains. He's going to reveal the secret of the Skyward Lights."

"So, Grandpa is going to teach me the secret of the lights. I'm glad he came to his senses and didn't choose you."

"Yes," Abram sighed defeated.

"It was just a joke, Abram. Still, maybe I won't be good at doing it, and he will choose you next time. I doubt that will happen, but who knows," Levi laughed his way to the mountains.

Abram slumped and made his way to the center of the village, where everyone had gathered-around Grandpa.

"Abram. Did you send your brother to the foot of the mountains?" asked Grandpa.

"Yes, Grandpa, but why couldn't you have chosen me?" Abram whined.

"You will know in time," Grandpa said, patting Abram on the back. Then Grandpa turned to the villagers and announced, "In a short while you will see one of the biggest and best Skyward Lights you have ever seen!"

Grandpa walked to the mountains. Abram sulked as he watched Grandpa leave. Ten minutes later, the show started.

A loud crack marked the start of the show. Then something different happened. Something no villagers had ever seen. A black spot appeared in the sky. The black spot alarmed the villagers because it was growing. Did this always happen? Could they just never have seen the black spot in the night? The villagers began whispering to each other words of dread.

The black spot overtook the sky so that not a bit of light showed through. They could see nothing, not their hands or feet, nor the person standing next to them. When the villagers were about to panic and ready to run in every direction, a gold ribbon of light cut the darkness, illuminating the sky and the crowd. The oh's and ah's rippled through the crowd.

The gold ribbon was only the first of many lights. Bursts of red and blue peppered the sky as the gold ribbon danced. A silver ribbon then appeared, glimmering next to the gold ribbon. Sparkles shimmered, falling to the ground. The crowd felt a titillating tingle from the Skyward Lights. This had never happened before. The Skyward Lights were always in the sky, but here they were dancing among them. The spectacle overjoyed the villagers. They heard the cracks and pops as the light danced around them.

But what unsettled Abram is he could hear Grandpa chanting something. He had never heard it before. He turned to Aleese. She was dancing about, giddy with delight.

"Can you hear Grandpa?" Abram asked.

Aleese shook her head and went back to twirling.

Abram definitely heard chanting, but no one else seemed to hear it or care about it. He could not make out the words, but Abram could feel it. He knew it was unhappy. The chant soured him. He was probably the only villager not smiling.

Just as everyone was saying this could not get any better, the sky lit up even brighter, and the light appeared in hues of their favorite colors.

One villager exclaimed "It's blue!

Another said, "No, it is red".

Suddenly, the sky turned black again and, as if it was never even there, the sky returned to normal.

The villagers whooped and hollered.

"Make the lights dance around us again!"

"Make it scary black again!"

Only Abram did not join in. Abram could not shake the sense of foreboding.

Grandpa made his way through the crowd all the while people were cheering his fine work. Grandpa came to Abram and Aleese.

"Grandpa, what were you saying during the Skyward Lights?" questioned Abram.

"You have a keen ear, Abram, but it was nothing you should worry about."

"Where's Levi, Grandpa?" asked Aleese.

"Oh, I sent him to collect some herbs."

"Why wouldn't you send me, Grandpa? I know herbs better than Levi."

"He was feeling sick after the lights. I told him to get the herb and go home to rest. He will be back in no time, I assure you. Just after a little rest."

It felt like Grandpa was avoiding the question.

Abram knew his brother would not miss the chance to gloat. The sun was high, and he knew it was only a matter of time before his brother would arrive with great arrogance. But he did not. Noon became afternoon, and afternoon became evening. Finally the night fell, but there was no sign of Levi. Abram was worried, maybe Levi was really sick. he thought.

Abram found Grandpa alone, leaning on a tree, nervously looking around.

"Grandpa, what happened to Levi? He was not at the festival at all. Was he hurt by the Skyward Lights? The Skyward Lights were loud down here. They must have been deafening where you were. Did he hurt his ears?"

"No, no, he's fine. I saw him not too long ago. He went off with some friends. You will see, he will be back home before long."

Grandpa was faking a smile. Abram could tell something was wrong.

"Well, I'm tired. I think I will go back to the house and sleep. I'm sure when I wake up, Levi will be there to rub in how he knows the secret of the Skyward Lights. Goodnight, Grandpa."

"Goodbye, Abram. I am sure he will have plenty to tell you in the morning."

And off Abram went, to go home and sleep.

Chapter 2: A Wicked Truth

Abram tossed and turned in his bed during a restless sleep. Between his brother being chosen to learn the secret of the Skyward Lights and Levi not showing after the festival, his mind was spinning. The image of his brother falling into darkness awoke Abram. Out of breath and sweating all over, he looked to Levi's bed, but Levi was not there. Abram knew he had to meet with Grandpa and, this time, get actual answers.

Abram crept out of the house quietly, not wanting to wake his family. He walked straight to Grandpa's house. To Abram's surprise, the house was lit. Abram thought for sure that Grandpa would be asleep and he would have to wake him. Abram stepped closer to Grandpa's front door. He heard something strange. Grandpa was crying. Abram walked in without knocking.

"Why are you crying, Grandpa?" Abram asked.

"Oh, I am a fool, Abram. I sent your brother alone outside the village and over the mountains. I am afraid he is lost or worse. But what I fear most is what I must do now."

"What is Levi doing over the mountains? I don't think anyone has ever gone over the mountains."

"You are right that no one has gone over the mountains since the day this village arose. I have taken steps to make sure no one wants to leave this village."

"Steps? What do you mean, Grandpa?"

"This village was founded over four hundred thousand years ago by me."

"Wait. What do you mean, Grandpa? I have lived here all my life, and I am only eighteen years old."

"You won't believe me, but you are 4 years older than the village."

"You're not making sense. How can this be?"

"I found you when you were three and brought you here with your brother Levi and your mother to the place that you know now as Trow. This was flat land before us. A barren desert before we came."

"Mountains do not come out of nowhere. How is this possible?"

"Listen to my story, and then I will ask something of you."

"This is all confusing, but for my brother's sake, I will listen."

"I am not your grandpa, though I so wish I could be. Before I met you, I lived the life of a warrior in the army of Ares. The priest of Ares found me to be an acceptable vessel for magic, so they enchanted me. With my new power, I had a unique ability. I could extend the life of Ares's men and my own. Before me, a mage's life was brief. The power aged the body faster.

I believed myself content with my life. Ares, who adorned me with this power, was very pleased. His soldiers now lived longer. Ares gave me wealth beyond my wildest dreams, but I wanted more. A wife, children. He gave me my choice of women, and I had many wives, but no children. My wives feared me more than they loved me. Worse still, magic users could not have children. Without progeny, I felt lost and angry at the one who gave me this power.

I confided in some other mages. They shared my woes, and with them I found a bond not only of spirit, but magic as well. A select few mages could share powers. We became our own army, wielding each other's magic. Now I could morph into animals, breathe fire hotter than the sun, and fly through the sky.

The power was intoxicating, but it did not go unnoticed. The Gods who gave us the power feared we would become too powerful, and we would be used against them. They began killing us one by one. We could only run and hide.

The Gods had eyes and ears everywhere, and they used them to kill us. However, we found something very odd. The magical force of the fallen strengthened our magic, but at an extreme cost: the magic ravaged our bodies. We thought our bodies could not take more power. So few of us were left alive, and we knew we had to do something. We decided we would build a haven where we would be safe.

We had no skills other than war-making. So, we had to find people to work in this new haven. We searched in secrecy, little by little finding people who wished to get away. Unfortunately, we found that those corrupted by the Gods were not safe for us to take. They unknowingly alerted the Gods leaving a precious few we could take.

We had the people. Now we needed to hide our power. The amount of magic needed to sustain a new land would not go unnoticed. We had to buy time. So, we set out into the desert thinking no one in his or her right mind would follow us. We created a small oasis to sustain life for a short while.

Our mages were so few when we made the oasis that we knew we would have to find a fast solution to hiding our magic. During my search, I found a tribe of creatures, the Tangfu. They could hide magic. They carried relics that seemed like ordinary objects when they held them. However, when they released them, the item was no doubt magical. In exchange for a longer life, they agreed to hide our magic and our secret land. They agreed even to defend it if necessary. I just had to lead them back to our secret location in the desert.

During the trip, I felt my magic growing stronger and my body withering. We were losing mages. I was losing friends. When I returned to the camp, I was the only mage who had made it back. There may have been a few more out in the world. I didn't know how many of us were left, but I knew I had to hide these people.

I used my magic to conjure a tangled forest. The Tangfu agreed to stay in the forest and protect the secret of the village. I used my magic to raise the land into a mighty mountain range. I parted the mountains to make a valley for us to live in. With my magic stronger than ever, I could encase this land in a bubble that bent time and could keep the villagers and the Tangfu alive indefinitely.

My last spell over the villagers was to ensure no one ever wanted to leave the valley. I cast a spell to make them forget the outside world. Their desire to see family or the riches of the world had to be severed. I could not stamp out their memories, but I could make them hazy.

I transformed the desert into a lush valley and forest, hoping that no one would notice. The Tangfu could hide the magic that this land possessed."

Grandpa's lament almost turned to pride thinking of how preposterous the idea was. How can you hide an entire forest and mountain range created in a desert? But there they were hundreds of thousands of years later.

Abram, feeling this was the end of the story, spoke up.

"So we were farmers you found: Father, Mother, Levi, Aleese, and myself?"

"Aleese was born in this valley a farmer, but when I found you, your mother, and Levi, you were not farmers. In my search for a way to hide our magic, I found two incredible children. My magic aura bent to them. They were perfect conduits for magic, and they were not afraid of magic. They ran to me and embraced me as if we were old friends. Their abilities would be found all too soon and would be used for evil acts. I had to take them. However, a problem arose. Their mother would not let them go, and I was not sure if I could take her. She had already been corrupted by the Gods. I felt my choices were limited. So, I did what I thought I had to do. I did my best to purify the evil in their mother so I could take all three, and I thought it worked. It was you, Levi, and your mother I took. You were the ones with the power.

On your birthday, I created the first Skyward Lights. I've preserved this town by rejuvenating the magic every year. No one from the outside world knew of this village for millennia, but the rat you saw was no ordinary rat. Something sent out the rat to ferret out magic. I do not know what purpose.

Yesterday, when I raised the Skyward Lights, I cast a protection spell over the land. I explained to your brother that the spell would keep out smaller creatures and slow down bigger beasts, but it would not stop a larger threat. Then I asked your brother to take my magic and find the source of the rat. I instructed Levi to find it and eliminate it. He accepted, knowing the consequences. I did not know whether he could share my magic like my friends. There is no way of knowing before the magic is taken. He could not share my magic, but he had already shown tremendous magical ability. I thought he had enough to survive the outside world and to eliminate the source of the rat. But he has not returned. It has been over forty years in the outside world's time. I fear he has been captured."

"Captured? By whom?"

"Abram, listen to me. I must ask of you the impossible. You must find the source of the rat and eliminate it and, if possible, bring your brother back. I will not ask you to take on magic. I have exhausted mine and have little stamina to do anymore. The protection spell takes too much of my magic to sustain. The only thing I can offer you is this pendant that I have enchanted. This pendant will ensure that you do not age normally outside of the village, and it will allow you to follow the trace magic that the rat left behind."

The pendant hung from Grandpa's hand. It was a golden circle with ivory embellishments.

Abram's mind was buzzing. Levi was given magic powers and followed the rat. Now he has gone missing.

What chance do I stand? Abram thought. My brother was taken even with his great power; how will I survive?

"Abram, are you listening!?"

"Yes! Yes, I will go!"

Abram had to find his brother.

"Before you go, I must cast a spell on you. If the Gods corrupt you, you can't come back. This spell will make you forget the way back if the Gods take hold of you."

"Do what you must, Grandpa."

Grandpa held his hands over Abram, and a light beamed down upon him. Then Grandpa spoke.

"Abram, you must leave before your family wake. Time will move so slowly here. They may not be up before you come back. Pack light because you must move fast."

Grandpa's face grew grim.

"Abram, the Tangfu are the protectors of this land. I have not spoken to them since I created the forest. They will know something is wrong because of the protection spell. They may see you as a threat and try to kill you. Your brother had the power to elude them. I can give you no such protection or assurance."

"Grandpa, I will find Levi!"

Abram snatched the pendant from Grandpa's hand and ran back to his home to get ready for the journey.

Chapter 3: The Trial

Abram walked up the mountain trail Grandpa walked for the Skyward Lights. Before he went over the mountain, Abram looked back at his home. He could not shake the feeling that he would not see it for a long time. Abram found it hard to believe his family might not wake up before he returned. Abram took a deep breath and went over the mountain.

The mountains were steep on the other side and offered no protection from the wind. He looked down and saw the forest. It was dark and foreboding with no visible trail, and Abram did not have so much as a knife to cut a way through.

Abram slowly crawled down the edge of the mountain, making very little ground. He hoped this would be the hardest part of the journey. After a few steps, the ground under his feet shifted, causing Abram to lose his balance. Abram toppled down the mountain. He felt powerless against the pull of the Earth. He made a loud cry and braced for a hard landing. Abram smashed his head at the foot of the mountain.

Abram saw stars and glared at the forest before him. As he looked at the forest, he swore he saw movement. Abram was not sure if it was the effects of the fall that made him see the movement or if he had seen a creature in the forest.

Well, if anyone didn't know I was here, they do now. Abram thought.

Abram collected himself and started moving towards the forest. As he approached the forest, the pendant pulled on him, almost begging him to move forward. The pendant felt alive on his chest. A throbbing sensation radiated from it.

"Yes, I know. We have to go," Abram said, as if talking to the pendant.

Abram listened to the forest. It was loud and menacing, but he knew he had to move forward. Abram pulled back some vines and stepped into the forest.

Silence. The forest went silent as if it were stalking him. No motion could be seen, and no sound could be heard. The only sound was his breath, which Abram could feel turning into a gasp.

Abram started questioning himself. Was he the right one for this trip? So many others in town would lay down their lives for Levi. No! He had to be the one to find his brother or he would never forgive himself. His brother was out there in an evil world, and Abram had to save him. Grandpa would keep Trow safe. All Abram had to do was find Levi.

The pull of the pendant was weak in the forest. Abram thought it must have been the magic of the forest that interfered with the pendant's pull. Abram could barely track the rat's path, and navigating the forest did not make it any easier.

Abram saw light on the other side of the forest. The end of the forest must be only fifty yards from him. A few feet from exiting the forest, Abram heard a snap. In a flash, a net caught Abram, whooshing him up into the air. Abram struggled to get free, but it was no use. He then felt a sharp pain in his leg. Before Abram knew it, he was fast asleep and at the mercy of his new captors.

Someone splashed water on Abram's face. When he came to, he was bound and sitting in a dark room. Abram could barely make out any figures in the room, but whoever they were, they were large.

A strange voice spoke out, "Ah, you are awake. We never had a creature so susceptible to our venom darts. Now we ask you, where does that magic trail you created lead?"

Abram felt eyes upon him, waiting for his response.

"Are you the Tangfu?"

The voice paused but then continued questioning, "Where does the magical trail lead?"

"I don't know where the trail leads. A rat came into our village and left it."

The voice became angry at his words and accusation.

"There are no vermin in this land, and there is nothing a magical rat would be drawn to. We cover the magic of this land and keep it safe."

It asked again, "Where does the magic trail lead?"

"I swear to you I am only following the trail left by the rat. I must follow it to find my brother. He is in trouble."

The voice became shrill and more agitated.

"Now you say there was another person who made it through our forest without us noticing! There is no one silent enough to elude us!"

"My grandpa gave him magic to get through the forest unnoticed."

"The only mage in that village is Alucca, and he has no heirs, liar."

"He is not my real grandpa. Alucca brought my mother, my brother, and me to this land to protect us. He did not want us to be used for evil."

"I can feel your aura. You speak the truth of one thing, but how do we know you are not a liar? Your brother may be a lie. How did he elude us? Did he fly over the forest?"

Abram did not know how Levi evaded the Tangfu.

"I must admit that I do not know how he got through the forest. I only know if he does not get help, he surely will die!"

His captors now seemed more intrigued. "You had nothing to help yourself out of our trap. You have nothing to help yourself now. The venomous darts were more potent because of your weak constitution. You are small and pathetic. What good will you be to this brother?"

Abram began to tear up.

"I do not know, but I must save him!"

His captors found pleasure in the results of their questioning.

"Take him to the Chieftain. He will know what to do with him."

They untied Abram and led him out of the room. This was Abram's first chance to see his captor's appearance. They were nothing like anything Abram had seen before. They were human in shape but had long tails, scaly green bodies, snouts, and claws. For their size, they were light on their feet, barely making a sound as they moved. Their grip was powerful. Abram felt their hands constricting his arms.

Abram's fate was now in the hands of The Chieftain.

The creatures brought Abram to The Chieftain. He had Abram's pendant. Abram had not even noticed it was gone. His only protection against the outside world was now in The Chieftain's hands.

The Chieftain spoke.

"This led you through the forest. What is it?"

Abram responded, "It is a pendant my Grandpa…Alucca gave to me. It will preserve my life outside of this land and will lead me to my brother's captor."

"And what did you expect to do when you met his captors? You have no weapons. No magic. Were you going to move them with your tears?"

The words hurt, but Abram knew they were true.

The Chieftain continued, "A warrior's spirit is not measured by the sharpness of his blade, but the grit in his being. You will be judged, but not by me."

The Chieftain reached for a chalice in front of him.

"This is Icimer Milk. You will drink this, and if you have the spirit of a warrior, you will be reborn. But if you do not have what you need for this journey, you will die."

Abram saw very few choices. They underestimated him because of his size. He thought he might be able to pull away and run for the door, but Abram considered his situation again. He did not have the pendant. His brother had been gone for more than forty years in the outside world. What if Abram needed fifty? He would never live to see his brother without the pendant. He had to get the pendant, and there was no way to get it without drinking the milk.

The Chieftain stepped in front of Abram, holding the chalice. Abram took the chalice from the chieftain and drank.

Nothing happened. Abram wondered if he had passed the test. The Chieftain smiled.

Then fire!!! Fire burned throughout Abram's veins. A searing sensation filled his eyes. His tongue burned as if it had dried from the heat. Abram passed out from the pain.

When Abram woke up, he was engulfed in darkness once again.

"Hello! Is there anybody out there?" Abram called out.

No one answered, and though Abram was in darkness, he still plainly saw himself. Abram noticed he was moving in waves, and a familiar creature moved from behind him. He felt the rat and knew he had to catch it. The rat led him to a see-through wall. There was a man trapped in the wall. Abram had no time to help him. The rat traveled through the wall and onto the other side. Abram pushed forward through the wall.

Once Abram was on the other side, the man trapped in the wall was now part of his party. The man seemed very grateful to him. The two followed the rat. No matter what speed they took, the rat remained out of reach. It eventually came upon a door and slipped through a crack.

When Abram opened the door, he saw Levi inside a bright room. Abram was happy to see his brother, but there was a chasm between them. Abram also noticed something odd. Levi was holding his own heart. Abram looked at the man in the wall to see if he saw the same thing. However, the man in the wall was pointing at Levi. Abram looked and a black liquid was dripping from Levi's heart. The black liquid crept up Levi's arms. The goo that fell to the ground crept up Levi's legs. In just a few moments, Levi became covered in the dark sludge. Abram heard his brother crying out in pain.

Abram looked at the chasm again. He didn't think he could jump over it. At that moment, the black liquid burst into flames. Screams of agony came from Levi.

What could Abram do? He looked to the man in the wall, but the man in the wall now had a staff and a sword. The flames grew larger and gave way to a dark figure and a menacing sound. Evil laughter filled the void, and from the burning goo emerged a giant red dragon. The man in the wall did not hesitate, firing balls of light at the red dragon. Abram stood there, unable to move.

Was it fear that held him fast? The man in the wall began shouting at Abram, but all Abram could hear was the red dragon's laugh. What should he do? Abram looked at the red dragon. The dragon tilted his head back and then leaned forward. A spray of fire escaped the dragon's mouth and encompassed the man in the wall. There was nothing but dust left where he had stood. At that moment, Abram knew what he had to do. Abram picked up the old man's sword, closed his eyes, squatted down and jumped as hard as he could towards the dragon's chest. He reared back his sword and stabbed for its heart. The dragon collapsed into a splash of black liquid. When Abram opened his eyes, he was standing over his brother Levi with a sword in Levi's chest. A blinding light came towards Abram.

He grew startled and woke in the Chieftain's hut. Abram paused and looked down with tears in his eyes and softly said, "I killed my brother…"

The Chieftain looked at Abram and assured him the test was over.

"You are ready for your journey, but you will need more than your wits."

The Chieftain and several of the Tangfu led Abram to a table. On the table were a sword in a scabbard, a small pouch, rope, a rod, a backpack, and two rings. The Chieftain picked them up one by one and handed them to Abram.

"This sword is the heaven's judge. It is holy and will glow when evil is present. The weapon will become more powerful with every evil creature it kills. The small pouch is full of Jaja beans. One bean can feed a man for days. There is also silver in the pouch that you will need to barter in the outside world. This rope will tie and untie at the owner's command, and you are now the owner. The rod carries a living flame, a small spirit. The spirit can light up the night or kindle a fire. Just speak your command, and it will obey. Feed the spirit flakes of wood and it will live indefinitely. This backpack is a Sack of Never-Ending Bottom. It can hold almost anything the size of the opening, but it will never feel more than a few pounds. These rings will protect you. One allows you to breathe underwater, and the other will protect you from burning. Know these rings need to be commanded. They are useless in the hands of those who do not have the will to wield them. They also grow stronger when the will of the holder is stronger. The Icimer milk has physically made you ten times more powerful. Use that strength to bolster your spirits, and you shall have no trouble commanding the rings."

The Chieftain put his hand out. "We will lead you to where the Aura you follow leaves the forest and where we can go no further."

Chapter 4: Following a Rat

Outside the forest, there was nothing in sight but a seemingly endless expanse of desert. Abram ate a Jaja bean and pushed forward into the sand.

The chieftain shouted out, "Remember the truth of your dream. This world will test you, and I pray you make the right decision."

With that, the Tangfu disappeared into the forest.

Abram had never felt more alone. "I'm coming, brother."

Abram followed the pull of the pendant through the desert. A few days went by with nothing but the desert. The heat messed with his mind. He saw a man waving in the distance.

"Brother, is that you? I'm coming, brother!"

Abram ran happily towards his brother. But when he got to the dune where he saw the man, no one was there. Abram doubted himself. Did Levi have this much trouble? Abram was at his wit's end when something caught his eye.

Trees! Abram had found his way out of the desert. He rejoiced and picked up his pace. When Abram got to the trees, he noticed they were not the lush green trees of his village or the jungle outside the mountains. These trees were drab, more brown than green. Abram paid no mind to it.

How lush can trees be on the edge of a desert? Abram thought, continuing his journey.

Going deeper, the forest did not give way to greener trees or grass. An infestation seemed to ail the vegetation. Something was wrong. Abram traveled miles into the forest, and the infection seemed to prevail. This disease seemed to affect the wildlife as well. The birds did not sing. Small creatures did not scurry about. It was too quiet. Abram could not help but feel on edge. "How hard is life outside our village?"

Lost in thought, something startled Abram from behind.

A fat, giant, almost human creature staggered up behind Abram with what appeared to be a small adult flung over its shoulder. The man on his shoulder wriggled but could not get free. Abram did not hesitate to pull his sword. The glow proved to Abram what he instinctively knew. This was an evil brute.

"Unhand the man, or I will strike you down," Abram commanded.

"Down," the grotesque creature said, laughing. The beast threw the man at Abram, knocking them down and out.

When Abram came to, he was tied up with his own rope. Abram saw this as a stroke of luck. He could just command the rope to untie itself and be free. Unfortunately, one beast had become five. They were talking busily and ignoring Abram and his new friend.

"So hungry. Give bag beans!" One of the creatures grunted.

The beast grabbed the bag of Jaja beans and poured them all into his mouth. To the creature's surprise, it was not hungry anymore.

Abram was aghast. All those Jaja beans could have fed him for months. Abram looked around and found only more to regret. The smallest of the creatures was throwing Abram's silver up into the air.

Wait, he thought. The pendant and the rings. Did he still have them? Abram could feel them. Abram was relieved that the beasts had not taken these magical items yet.

That's when he noticed the small adult next to him moving.

The small man was unusual to Abram. He had soft features and pointed ears.

"We've found ourselves in quite a pickle. We've got captured by ogres. The name's Fleck."

"I'm Abram. You're not human?"

"I'm an elf."

"An elf?"

"Yes. Now that we are done with our tête-à-tête, what do we do now?"

"I can untie myself, and if I get my sword, I may be able to fight them."

"As impressive as your sword fighting is, I think we should come up with a plan that doesn't involve fighting or getting eaten."

"They're going to eat us!"

"Shhh."

"They're going to eat us?" whispered Abram.

The largest of the ogres confirmed Fleck's presumption. The beast looked at them and said, "Tasty."

The ogre then pointed to two smaller ogres.

"You two! Wood!"

As the other two went into the woods, Fleck smiled.

"I think I have a plan, Abram. If you can close your ear holes, I recommend doing it now."

With that warning, Fleck sang. Abram could not believe how beautiful the song was. His town had some wonderful singers, but this was phenomenal. The more Abram listened, the more he liked it. Abram began yawning. His eyes were getting heavy. Abram was not the only one affected by the song. The fat creatures started yawning, and their bodies sagged. Before long, all the ogres in the camp and Abram were asleep.

Abram felt something sting his cheek.

"Pst, wake up, Abram. Wake up. These dim creatures will stay asleep for a while, but we don't know when their friends are coming back."

Fleck pulled at the knot tying Abram.

"These lummoxes aren't all that bright, but they can tie a knot."

"Untie." Abram commanded, and just like that, the rope unraveled.

"That is a nifty trick there."

Pleased with the results, Abram stated, "It's a magic rope that unties and ties at my command."

Abram looked around at what he could salvage. The Jaja beans were gone, but he had the rope. Abram spied the rod, sword, and backpack. The backpack was resting underneath one ogre. Abram thought that if he was careful, he could get the rod and the sword.

Abram tiptoed around the ogres, picking up the rod and the sword.

Fleck did not share Abram's confidence.

"What are you doing? Get out of there!"

Just then, the ogres getting wood came back.

The ogres exclaimed, "Get them!"

Fleck yelled, "Run!"

Abram ran as fast as he could behind Fleck.

Abram looked behind him and yelped, "I don't know how long I can run like this."

But when he looked forward, Fleck was nowhere in sight.

Abram shouted, "Fleck! FLECK!!!"

Something pulled Abram to the side, into the trees. A hand covered his mouth and shushed him. Abram watched as the ogres ran past them.

Fleck whispered, "You're not the only one with tricks. Cloak of invisibility."

"Fleck! You amazing elf!"

"Shhh! I don't see any movement. I think we can go now." Fleck confirmed.

"Wait. My sword detects evil. We will know they are gone when it is no longer lit."

Abram cracked his sword from the scabbard, and it shined brightly.

"We need to wait until this is not glowing," Abram assured

The two waited and waited and waited.

Fleck, not impressed, questioned Abram, "Are you sure the sword is not broken? I hear nothing. I say we go."

Abram begrudgingly put his sword away.

"I don't know what's wrong with it. The Tangfu said it was holy."

"Lizard people. You should never trust lizard people."

"By the way, thanks for saving me."

"Think nothing of it. I just might have a request for you down the road. Someone who would help an elf despite their reputation deserves some help themselves."

"Reputation?"

"As assassins and thieves. We kind of have a bad rep."

"Are you an assassin?"

"No! Heavens no. Don't have the stomach for killing."

"Are you a thief?"

"No…no. I prefer to think of myself as a master of reappropriation. If you don't have something and you want to have it, I make it yours for a fee."

"I saved a thief."

"Excuse me! This 'Thief' saved you! And rather than getting into the semantics of who saved whom, I say we get away before an ogre finds us. Come on, I know a town nearby."

"I can't believe I am doing this. I'm following a thief."

"Why were you out here so heavily armed anyway?"

"I am trying to find my brother. I'm following the trail left by a magical rat straight to him."

"If you didn't want to tell me, you could have just said Pass."

"No. That is actually why I am out here."

"You must follow the trail left by a magical rat to find your brother. Weird."

"No weirder than ogres and elves," Abram retorted.

"Where have you been? We're everywhere. By the way, how do you know where this magical rat is? Is it here? I can't see anything around here."

Abram did not trust Fleck. He thought that at the first chance, Fleck would steal the pendant. So, he did the first thing that came to his mind.

"I can see it. My grandfather gave me the power to see the trail the rat left."

"Your grandfather is a mage. Now that is rare. I heard mages can change ordinary things to gold. Is that true?"

Abram changed the subject.

"I wish I had those Jaja beans back. I'm so hungry."

"Those beans. Forget those beans. Stick with me, Abram. I'll get you fed. The only thing I ask is that you introduce me to your grandfather. Maybe he can make gold for me," Fleck nudged.

Abram sighed, "Following a thief…"

Chapter 5: A Hasty Retreat to an Unwelcome Reunion

Abram and Fleck walked into the town of Beterham. Cheap huts strewn about. Abram could not get over the poverty. This was nothing like Trow. But there was one thing in particular Abram could not get over.

"What is that smell? Do all towns smell this way?" Abram said in disgust.

"You get used to it."

To Fleck, this was a normal town. He walked straight to the local tavern and sat down at a table. Abram followed him to the table.

"Now Abram, I know we both lost our money to the ogres, but follow my lead and we will get some food."

Abram was willing to try anything at this point. Abram scanned the room watching all the food brought to the tables. Trow had nothing like this. Abram was so lost in his hunger that he did not notice the woman who walked up to their table.

"Welcome to The Walking Egg. We serve eggs, chicken, potatoes, and ale. What will you have?"

Abram was taken aback by the woman. She was possibly the most beautiful woman he had ever seen. She had red hair and gorgeous green eyes. Now, if she was as kind as she was beautiful, Abram knew he was getting fed.

Fleck laid out his story. "We seem to be short of funds today. But if you could get us some eggs and ale on the house, we would be greatly appreciative."

The server was not buying his story.

"A charm spell? We are tattooed with the sigil of Aphrodite. Charms spells won't work."

Fleck backtracked.

"I don't know what you mean. We are simply two victims of an ogre attack. We lost our money, but we are good for it."

"Look," the server leaned in.

"You're not from around here."

The two shook their heads no.

She continued, "I can take care of your meal, but I need a favor in return. I need protection going north on a journey to my family's home. I can't promise you money up front, but my family will show their appreciation to you. Are you in?"

The two were too hungry to say no.

"Alright. I'll see you two after the tavern closes at midnight."

Before she walked away, Abram spoke up.

"What is your name?"

"It's Sarai."

The two ate and wandered around the town, waiting for midnight.

"Well, that went rather well," Fleck stated. "It is a shame that she couldn't find anyone to help her get to her family."

Abram did not understand what Fleck was implying.

"She asked us to take her."

"Abram, open your eyes. She had desperation all over her face. That means that she is in over her head with trouble."

"You can't know that for sure."

"Why would you ask two strangers who can't even defend themselves against ogres to be your guide? Des-per-ation. And don't you have a quest to save your brother?"

"My gut tells me to go north." Abram did not want to explain the pendant. "I need you, Fleck. I don't know my way around this area."

"Not happening," Fleck said matter-of-factly.

"I'll give you the rope."

"The same rope that ties and unties at your command? You can give it to me, and I can command it?"

Abram did not know how to change ownership of the rope.

"Yes. It will be yours, and I can promise you more. The beans the Ogre ate when we were tied up, they are Jaja beans. One bean could feed you for days. All this if you follow me."

"And those Jaja beans you were talking about, you could get me a hundred of them?"

"Yes, of course. When I return home, I will get as many as your heart desires."

Abram did not know if he could get more Jaja beans.

"Well, you have a deal. I feel this is the beginning of a long and fruitful friendship."

Abram and Fleck waited until a little after midnight to return to the Walking Egg.

Out came Sarai. She seemed nervous and was looking all around.

"Sarai! We're over here," Abram said cheerfully.

Sarai responded, "Shhh. Were you followed?"

Abram looked perplexed. Fleck was quick to respond.

"Were you expecting someone?"

Sarai tried to brush it off like it was nothing.

"No. I was just concerned about your safety."

Abram chimed in, "You're right. Maybe we should hold off on this trip 'til morning."

Sarai quickly responded, "No!... I mean no. I want to start this trip as fast as I can. Let's go now!"

The three began their trip walking on foot into the night. Fleck was on high alert. He did not like the idea of leaving at midnight, but that rope was too tempting of a prize.

Sarai was also jumpy. Something was bothering her, but Abram and Fleck did not know what. The only calm one was Abram, but he really did not know what was lurking in the dark.

After a few hours, Sarai seemed to calm down.

"Thank you for taking this trip with me. I don't know if I could do it alone. I ventured out once before running away from the family farm, but I was ambushed. All my valuables were stolen. I wound up in Beterham at The Walking Egg, and I've been stuck there ever since. I just wanted to get away. Farm life isn't fun, but it is simpler. What brings you two here?"

Abram was the first to respond.

"I'm searching for my brother. He is in trouble, and my grandpa thought I would be the only one who can help him. I hope he is right."

"Helping damsels in distress is just what I do," Fleck answered.

Sarai questioned, "You don't seem like that type. However, your friend does."

She pointed to Abram.

Fleck acted hurt.

"You wound me, madam."

"You know what? I don't even know your names."

"I'm Abram, and my friend is Fleck."

"Pleased to meet your acquaintance. Have you two been friends long?" Sarai asked.

Fleck, wanting to sound important, responded, "We bumped into each other literally a few hours ago. I had to save him from an ogre attack single-handedly."

Abram laughed, "If by fending off ogres you mean running off and hiding from ogres, then we both fought off ogres. But why did you choose us to go on this journey with you?"

Sarai looked at her feet.

"You two had friendly faces?"

"Well, I am glad to be a part of your party, and I am sure Fleck is too."

"Enthralled," Fleck said sarcastically.

"So…what do you do for fun?" Abram asked.

"Working at the Walking Egg didn't give me a lot of time to do anything. It is a sunup-to-sundown, seven-days-a-week kind of thing. Occasionally, I would stop to listen to a singing minstrel, but later I would get lashed for lollygagging… Did I say lashed? I mean, scolded."

Sarai gave an awkward smile.

Abram was really concerned. Fleck was only half paying attention.

"He would lash you? What kind of boss was he?" Abram said compassionately.

Sarai said nothing back.

Abram, trying to get more out of Sarai, repeated, "I'm out to find my brother. He has been gone for many years. Grandpa and I don't know where he is. When I'm done helping you, I am going to go find him."

Sarai looked like she was going to speak.

Abram, anticipating it, said, "You want to say something?"

"Really, it's nothing. Maybe we should stop for the night," Sarai said.

Abram was all aflutter in the company of Sarai

"I'm fine. We can go farther if you would like."

Fleck retorted, "I was tired hours ago. I think it is a good time to sleep."

"I guess I will stay up and be look out," Abram responded.

Abram gazed up at the night sky and thought it had never looked so beautiful.

Fleck and Sarai quickly fell asleep. Abram stood watch like he said. A few hours into the night, Abram heard a growl. He checked his sword, and it glowed brightly.

Evil is afoot! Abram thought.

Abram whispered, "Fleck. Pst… Fleck. Wake up. There is something evil out there. The sword is glowing."

Fleck shooed Abram away.

"Are you sure your sword is not broken again?"

"I heard growling."

Abram saw a figure creep out of the woods.

"Fleck! Get up!"

Fleck looked at the figure.

"Troll!!!" Fleck screamed.

Seeing Sarai, the troll hissed, "You thought you could get away, Sarai. You know Jin would never let his prizes go. And if you think those two can stop me, you are sadly mistaken."

Fleck and Sarai dove behind the same tree, bumping heads. Abram ran after the troll, slashing at it, severing the troll's arm.

"Ah, that burns! But you can't kill me with that little toothpick."

Abram was dumbfounded. He just cut off the troll's arm. Why was the troll not running.

Sensing Abram's confusion, Fleck shouted, "You can't kill a troll with weapons. You have to burn him."

Abram then had an idea. He pulled out the rod and shouted, "Illuminate!"

Flames ripped out of the rod. The troll panicked. Rather than running away from the fire, the troll charged Abram, knocking the rod from his hand. The flames fell on the dry grass and blew up like a powder keg. Abram thought he could not reach the rod through the fire. Feeling the heat scared Abram, and he did not go for the rod. The troll ran away in fear of being burnt.

Expecting to be burnt to a crisp, Fleck screamed, "I think we should run!"

With no hesitation, the three raced away from the fire until their lungs burned.

"Are we safe?" Fleck asked.

"We are safe from the fire, but we are not out of trouble. My sword is still shining," Abram responded.

Flecked scoffed, "Your sword is always lit."

Sarai anxiously said, "The troll will not give up. Jin would never let him come back empty-handed. Better dead than upsetting Jin."

Abram was worried.

"Who is Jin?"

Sarai slumped.

"He is the man who took me in after I got mugged. He owns The Walking Egg and runs Beterham. When I met him, I thought he was nice. He let me work at the Walking Egg for tips. Then he got abusive and started taking the tips, saying I didn't deserve them. No one in town would help me get away because they were all afraid of him. That's why I asked you two to take me away. You are not from Beterham and wouldn't know his reputation. I'm sorry I was not truthful with you two."

Sarai's eyes filled with tears. She looked like she was about to cry.

"Well, good luck with that. I think it is about time Abram and I took off."

Abram, shocked, responded, "We can't leave her now!"

"My loyalty wanes when insane people are involved."

"You want the rope, don't you?" Abram inquired.

Fleck was stung. "Not fair, Abram. Not fair."

"You still want the rope? You have a job to finish."

Fleck threw Abram a cross look.

"If I must," he responded with a defeated tone.

"We're here for you, Sarai. Let's get you home."

Abram and Fleck followed Sarai. She started heading northeast, but Abram could feel the pendant pulling him west.

"Hold on just a little longer, brother. I'm coming for you," murmured Abram under his breath.

The three traveled for most of the night. They were almost through the forest and approaching a clearing.

"There it is. My home!"

Sarai took off running to her family's hut. Abram did not follow, noticing something was wrong. The fields were overgrown with weeds and grass. The roof of the hut had holes, and when he looked around, he noticed bones.

"Sarai, wait!" Abram cried, but it was too late.

Sarai had already gone inside. She screeched and ran out of the hut, decaying creatures following her.

"Zombies!!" Fleck exclaimed.

Without hesitation, Abram pulled his sword. The zombies reeked of evil, and the sword burned bright.

Abram focused his attention on the creatures. Five of them staggered towards Sarai. Abram charged the largest of the zombies. Abram slashed, cleaving the biggest zombie and another in half. Their legs buckled, and the torsos landed on the ground and turned to ash. Abram stabbed the last tall one in the stomach and ripped upward. Abram followed the blow with downward chops on the two smaller zombies. All that was left of the five zombies was the ash on the ground

"Five zombies, Abram! You just killed five zombies like they were nothing. It's amazing. I've never seen them turn to dust like that," Fleck shouted.

Abram was not in a celebrating mood. He saw Sarai slowly walking to the ashes the zombies left behind, crying.

"That was my father. He's dressed in his favorite shirt. Over there is my little sister. She always wore that necklace. This was my family." She dropped into the ashes, tears rolling down her face.

Abram walked over to Fleck.

"Here's your rope. You don't owe me anything more."

Fleck greedily grabbed the rope.

Abram turned to comfort Sarai, but Sarai was already looking at Abram.

"Wait here," Sarai said.

Sarai turned and ran into the house. Puzzled, Abram waited for Sarai. Only a little later, Sarai ran out with a mace tied to her waist. Sarai addressed Abram.

"Let me come with you! Right now, you are the closest to family that I've got. My uncle was a paladin. He taught me the basics of fighting and field care. I won't hold you back."

Abram turned his head, not knowing what to do.

"You don't know where I am going, and I need to find my brother."

"Then I will help you find your brother. There's nothing more for me here."

"Don't think I am out of this yet," Fleck sneered. "You still owe me a hundred Jaja beans."

"I guess we have a party then," Abram acknowledged. "Let's head west to find my brother."

Chapter 6: Never Happily Ever After

"Do you know why I sent you, troll?" a dark and foreboding figure calmly stated.

"Jin, I can explain---"

"Do you know why I sent you?"

"Jin---"

"Because you are large and more than a match for an insignificant elf, a small girl, and a worm."

"They had magical weapons, Jin. They caught me off guard. My arm still has not grown back."

"Do you know the price of failure?"

"Wait! What is so important about this girl? I will find you another."

"Fool! I've seen into her future. Glimpses. Her line will raise nations. They will be nobles and kings, and if I can help it, they will be from my line!"

"I thought mages cannot have children."

"I will sire children! My line will continue! I will find a way!"

"Now, do you know the price of failure?" Jin said coolly.

The troll fell silent in fear.

A sinister smile crossed Jin's face.

"You will never have to worry about failing me again."

Jin snapped his fingers, and the troll burst into flames. The troll screamed, but even over the troll's cries of pain, Jin's sinister laugh rang.

Chapter 7: The Hunger Is Real

"I'm so hungry," Fleck moaned. "When will this adventure lead us to food?"

"How are we going to get food? We have no money," Abram reminded him.

"I see a village up ahead. Maybe we can get some work and buy food," Sarai suggested.

"That's a good idea. Why didn't I think of that?" Fleck said mockingly. "I think it's best we split up. I have my own way of making money."

"Alright then. Abram and I will go look for work while you do what you do," Sarai snapped.

Abram and Sarai went to the heart of the town while Fleck veered off to the outskirts.

"Where do you think we'll find work, Sarai?"

"I don't know, but the taverns bring all kinds of people. Maybe we'll find work there."

At that moment, a strange man walked up to Sarai and Abram.

"I couldn't help but overhear that you need work. I need a few hands picking in the candum fruit in my fields. You will be provided with a little money, supper, and all the candum fruit you can eat."

"I love candum fruit!" Sarai exclaimed.

Abram had never had candum fruit, but he could not help being taken in by Sarai's enthusiasm.

"You've got a deal, mister," Sarai agreed.

"Alright! I will show you the way," the farmer said.

The three walked out of the town going south. They came upon an expansive orchard with several people filling baskets already.

"Pick up a basket over there and start picking." The farmer said, pointing to the baskets.

"Yeah, candum fruit!" Sarai squealed.

"Now be careful; candum fruit bruises easily," the farmer warned.

Being a farmer, Abram had no worries about picking the fruit but was not sure if Sarai could calm down enough to pick the fruit gently.

"After you, Sarai," Abram bowed.

Sarai excitedly grabbed her bucket, and the two started picking.

It was the hottest part of the day when they started, but hunger motivated them to do a good job. Evening quickly came upon them, and most of the hands were leaving for the night.

"I guess it's time for us to go," Abram said.

A long, dark shadow came over the two. Abram paid little attention to it, thinking that it was the shadow of another worker.

"Look out!" Sarai yelled.

Heeding her warning, Abram just barely rolled out of the way of two fangs closing in on him.

"Giant spider!" Sarai shouted.

Abram could not believe it. Where did it come from, and how did it sneak up on him so fast? Abram pulled his blade, and the sword was glowing like day. Sarai pulled her mace and took a defensive position, ready to fight.

"Go for the legs. The spider will crumble under its weight if we take out a few!" Sarai yelled.

Sarai charged at the spider and bashed the front leg. The spider reared up in agony. It swiped at Sarai with its other front leg.

The bravery Sarai showed shocked Abram. He did not want to disappoint her, so Abram ran to the left side of the spider, slashing at one of its back legs.

Abram noticed sizzling as he severed the spider's leg.

The spider jumped back to get away from the two-pronged attack. The spider turned to Abram and leapt forward. Abram ducked down, avoiding being grappled by the spider. The spider flew over him. Abram stabbed upward as the spider flew over him, slicing the bottom of the spider, flipping it over him, and killing it on impact.

Abram watched as the spider collapsed on the ground and, from behind the spider, Abram made out a figure clapping.

Sarai's face turned pale.

"Jin…" Sarai gasped.

Sarai froze in fear.

"Just making a house call, dear," Jin said nonchalantly. "I will be back for you soon enough. I never let my precious treasures go."

The figure vanished in a puff of smoke. As soon as Jin disappeared, Abram's sword stopped glowing. He breathed a sigh of relief. As far as Abram was concerned, the threat had passed. But Sarai collapsed to her knees, mumbling over and over.

"He'll never let me go."

Chapter 8: Another Lover

A year earlier in Beterham

"You'd better stop daydreaming, Sarai. Jin doesn't like us standing around," Lesal, a mocha-haired server at The Walking Egg, said. "You need to take these drinks to the table over there and get focused."

Sarai walked forward, looking back at Lesal.

"I will…" Sarai stammered, but before she could get out all she wanted to say, she ran into a customer, spilling the ale all over him.

"I'm so sorry!" Sarai bleated.

"It's okay," the customer said calmly.

"Jin is going to kill me for wasting that ale."

Tears welled up in Sarai's eyes.

"Listen. I will pay for it. Don't worry."

"You will!" Sarai squeaked. "I can't thank you enough!"

"The only thing I ask is that you go with me for a walk."

"I don't know. Jin really doesn't like us talking to customers, and I really don't have time to walk until after work."

"Then it's settled. I will come after the Walking Egg is closed. We will walk to your hut. I'm Corvas, by the way."

"I'm Sarai," Sarai blushed.

Corvas was not an unattractive man. In fact, he was quite handsome. Sarai felt special because he took an interest in her. Other customers had grabbed and groped before. All those men seemed like pigs, but Corvas appeared to be different.

Sarai anxiously awaited the end of the day. Time crept by, but when the Walking Egg closed, Sarai ran out the door. Just as Corvas promised, he was waiting out front.

"They let you out late," Corvas smiled.

Sarai just blushed.

"So, how long have you lived in Beterham?" Corvas asked.

"Six months now," Sarai said bashfully.

"I must have left Beterham before you arrived. I joined Ares' army a while ago, but a friend invited me for a visit. My original plan was not to stay long, but I think I've found a reason to stay longer."

Sarai turned a brighter red.

"Do you have any family nearby?" Corvas asked.

"My family lives on a farm several miles away."

"Do you see them much?"

"Jin doesn't really give us time off. Here's my hut. I should go in. I have to wake up early to go to work."

"When can we do this again? Do you have a day off?"

"Jin does not give us days off."

"Well then, I will see you tomorrow after work."

Sarai walked into her hut thinking how lucky she was.

The next day, all Sarai could do was daydream about Corvas. Not even Lesal could snap her out of it. She knew she would be in trouble, but she did not care.

The end of the day came. As fast as she could, Sarai was out the door. However, Corvas was nowhere to be seen. Sarai waited for him until she was too tired to stand. Sarai walked back to her hut feeling rejected.

The next day, Sarai sagged from exhaustion. She wondered if she could just stay home. There would be hell to pay, but Sarai did not care. Her whole body hurt, and she felt crushed. Just when she thought she could not get any lower, a figure appeared at the door of her hut. It was Corvas.

"Corvas! I waited for you, but you didn't come!"

"I know. I'm sorry, but I must see you again after work. Meet me at The Sanctum Tree."

When Corvas was through speaking, he disappeared out the door. He seemed out of breath.

Sarai's mind was suddenly all aflutter. The Sanctum Tree was a holy place where lovers proposed their forever bond. That was where her father had proposed to her mother. Corvas did not live in Beterham. Sarai could finally get away from this town. More importantly, she could get away from Jin.

Sarai quickly made her way to work. She knew this was going to be her last day at The Walking Egg, and nothing was going to get her down. Night came, and Sarai sped through her closing duties, and went straight to The Sanctum Tree. When she got to the Sanctum Tree, something was wrong. Corvas was there, tied to the Sanctum Tree. A familiar voice filled the air---a cruel voice.

"Sarai, it seems like you caused a lot of trouble for this man."

Jin came out from behind the Sanctum Tree, and Sarai backed away.

"Whatever he says, do it!" Corvas pleaded.

"Now Sarai, you know I don't like you talking to other men. You have forced me to do something awful," Jin threatened.

"Please don't! I will go away and never come back!" Corvas insisted.

Sarai just watched, petrified, as Jin's hand became red hot.

"Now, I have to do this!"

Jin pressed his hand onto Corvas' face. The sound of searing skin filled Sarai's ears. She could see Corvas' skin boiling around Jin's hand. Cries of pain echoed through the night air.

"You can end his pain, Sarai. All you have to do is say you belong to me."

Sarai could not say a word. Jin pulled his hand off Corvas' face and dragged his hand across Corvas' chest.

"What will it be, Sarai?"

Sarai saw the muscles in Corvas' face. She heard Corvas's deafening cry. She saw his clothes catching on fire.

"Please stop! Please stop!" Sarai cried.

"What did you say, Sarai?" Jin asked.

"I belong to...you," Sarai said meekly.

"Louder!" Jin shouted.

"Please! I belong to you! Please stop hurting Corvas!" Sarai wept.

Jin turned to Corvas and the tree and called out.

"Ultimate Flame!"

A wall of fire burst from the ground, encompassing Corvas and the tree. To Sarai, the fire seemed to burn forever. When the flames finally stopped, Corvas was gone. The Sanctum Tree was gone. Everything was gone. The fire left only ashes. Jin walked calmly into the night, leaving behind Sarai with tears in her eyes.

Chapter 9: What Was He Like?

Abram helped Sarai to her feet. Before he could ask Sarai what Jin wanted, the farmer interrupted.

"You two are heroes! We would all have been eaten alive if it weren't for you two! You have more than earned your day's wage. I know it's not much, but I threw in a few extra copper coins. Take a basket of candum fruit."

"Thank you. You are too generous," Abram said, not really knowing what the copper coins could buy.

"I guess we should go find Fleck," Abram said, hoping it would snap Sarai out of her catatonic state.

"We should," was all Sarai could get out.

The two walked back into town. Abram looked at Sarai.

"We never picked a meeting place to find Fleck."

"I guess we didn't." Sarai stated flatly.

As if conjured by his name, a familiar voice rang out behind them.

"If it isn't the two hardest-working schmucks in town. I see you got a basket of fruit, and how many coins?"

"A handful of copper coins?" Abram said, as if questioning their merit.

Fleck laughed and pulled out a full pouch. Abram heard coins clinking within it.

"This town is full of money, and all you got was a handful of copper coins."

"How did you get so much money, Fleck?"

"Trade secret, Abram. But there is money lying around all over this town."

Fleck paused for a moment and looked at Sarai.

"What's up with Sarai?"

Abram's face grew grim. "We saw Jin, and I am pretty sure he sent a giant spider after us."

"Glad it wasn't me," retorted Fleck. "Spiders give me the willies. Why don't you two take this money and get the supplies we need? I will meet you on the outskirts of town on the west side. I think we should get out of this town and continue our adventure. After all, I am not getting my Jaja beans just standing around here."

"I am not sure if Sarai could take it. We should find a place to stay for the night."

"And I think we should really get on with our adventure," Fleck insisted.

"It's alright, Abram. I think putting some distance between us and Jin is a good idea," Sarai insisted.

"See, Abram. Sarai agrees," Fleck said with a fake smile.

"I guess we'll go," Abram capitulated.

Fleck parted ways with them and turned toward the outskirts of town, and Sarai and Abram went to the market area. When they met back up, Fleck was very interested in leaving town. So much so that soon Abram and Sarai quickly fell behind.

"So, you are looking for your brother, right?" Sarai asked, trying to start a conversation.

"Yes," Abram said shyly.

"How long has he been gone?"

Abram could not tell her the truth. "He's been gone a few years, but it feels like forever."

"How do you know where he is?"

"I don't know, to be honest. I don't want to tell Fleck, but I have a pendant that will lead me to him. When I find the end, he will be there."

"What if he is not there at the end of the trail? What if he has already moved on?"

"I just have a feeling that he will be there, and that he will be alright."

Sarai fell silent. Abram, sensing that the conversation would end there if he said nothing else, kept talking.

"How many brothers and sisters did you have?"

Abram kicked himself for bringing up her family again, but Sarai responded.

"I had one little brother and two younger sisters. I was the oldest."

"Why did you leave your home?"

"I wanted something other than farming. Meeting people who traveled from city to city seemed more exciting. Funny how much you miss the thing you were trying to get away from." Sarai looked to the distance and seemed to go deep in thought, but she came to.

She asked, "Why did your brother leave?"

"It's complicated, and I barely have a handle on it." Abram paused. "Our village may be in danger. It was hidden away from the rest of the world, but something threatened it. My brother was sent out to see if it was malicious and eliminate it. He never came back. Now all I know is that I must follow him and help him any way I can."

Sarai perceived the magnitude of his task and patted Abram on the shoulder, trying to comfort him. "We'll find your brother, Abram. What is his name? We can ask in the next town if people have seen him."

"His name is Levi."

"Funny, that was the name of my little brother. Finding him is like finding my brother. He was very shy, and whenever a family would come over, he would hide behind my mom."

Abram laughed. "That's nothing like my brother. He was part of the town council. There seemed to be nothing he couldn't do. He bested me in every challenge. Not only that, he bested everyone in town. He was so good-spirited. Everybody liked him. I am nothing like him."

Feeling tears welling up in his eyes, Abram tried to make a lighthearted joke.

"But he never had fruits and vegetables as good as mine."

Sarai saw the anguish in Abram's eyes.

"Maybe we should talk about something else."

Abram stopped for a moment. Then smiled and said, "I wish I could show you my village. I think you would like it."

Sarai smiled and responded, "Hopefully not too long from now, you can."

"That would be nice."

Fleck turned around.

"Are we finding your brother or not? With as slow you two are going, we will never reach him."

Abram agreed, "You're right. We should pick up the pace."

Abram and Sarai caught up to Fleck, and the three went on their way, following the pull of the pendant.

Chapter 10: Someone's Home

"Is it just me, or are those mountains getting closer?" Fleck went on. "First, they were teeny tiny in the distance. Then they grew and grew, and now we are almost upon them. Is your magical mouse leading you this way?"

Sarai looked at Abram confused.

"My brother was following a magical rat trail. Now I am following the same path to find him."

"That's a little unusual, but okay," Sarai admitted.

Still, Abram did not know if the trail would veer off when they got into the mountains. He could not actually see the rat's trail. He felt only the pull of the pendant.

"Yes, we are going into the mountains."

Fleck, exasperated, yelped, "So, we are going towards the frigid peaks where we will freeze to death."

Abram back stepped, "The trail is hard to see. It may veer when we get closer."

"Hard to see?" Fleck repeated. "And you said that you can get hundreds of these Jaja beans that will feed me for years?"

"Yes!"

"And…you'll throw in that sword when we are back at your village?"

Abram rubbed the back of his head, not knowing what to say.

"I guess…"

Pleased with his latest claim, Fleck exclaimed, "Well, let us sally forth."

Sarai whispered to Abram, "You're going to let him have your magical sword."

Abram shrugged his shoulders.

"Well, he already has the rope. What else can I give?"

Sarai responded unexpectedly, "Maybe we should cut him loose."

"I don't think we can."

Abram knew the two of them had no knowledge outside their small worlds. They needed someone who knew the lay of the land, and at that moment, it was Fleck.

"What are you two talking about?" Fleck questioned.

"Nothing." Abram cleared his throat. "We should probably pick up the pace."

To Fleck's displeasure, the mountains only got closer. As they moved forward, a cave appeared in the mountain, and Abram felt a pull toward the cave.

Fleck saw Abram veering closer to the cave.

"What is it, Abram? Do we freeze to death going over the mountain, or do we go into the cave and get eaten by who knows what? Where is your magical mouse taking us?"

Abram felt the pendant drawing him into the cave.

"I think we need to go into the cave."

Shouldn't Abram know where he was going, Fleck thought. Didn't he see the trail of the rat?

"Eaten it is," Fleck joked.

Into the cave, the three went. Not long into the cave, something caught Fleck's attention.

"Wait!" Fleck shouted

Abram and Sarai paused, expecting another calamity.

"Do you know what this is?" Fleck said excitedly.

Fleck pointed to what looked like scribbles on the wall. Neither Abram nor Sarai knew the significance. The confused looks on their faces prompted Fleck's reply.

"This is dwarven writing!" Fleck bubbled. "And where there are dwarves, there's treasure! Oh Abram, I knew staying with you would lead to big things, but this! I never imagined something like this! If we are lucky, they left this cave and didn't take their treasure. Come on! We must find this dwarven treasure!"

"I don't think we can go much further, Fleck. There's very little light. We should double back and find something to illuminate our path," Abram said disappointedly.

Abram regretted dropping the magical rod. Its flames could have lit their path.

"Why not pull that glowing sword of yours?" Fleck said, unconcerned.

Abram pulled the glowing sword, alarmed by it.

"We have to go forward to find my brother, but we need to be careful. The sword lights up when evil is near."

"Phooey on your sword. It's always lit," Fleck said dismissively.

"Still, I think we should move forward cautiously," Abram urged.

"Come on, Abram. We should get a move on. That treasure will not find itself."

Fleck pushed forward at a pace that worried Abram.

How can he be so calm with danger about? Abram thought.

Abram and Sarai matched Fleck's pace despite their reservations. Fleck was on a mission to find the dwarven treasure, and nothing was going to get in his way.

Abram, Fleck, and Sarai travelled deep into the cave. Abram did not know whether the cave had another opening. Maybe the rat doubled back. But the pendant pulled Abram forward. Sarai was done with the cave. She had not told Abram or Fleck that she had trouble with enclosed places, and this cave was too tight for her.

"Look! There's light straight ahead. Maybe we are almost out of the cave," Sarai said excitedly.

But Fleck did not share her enthusiasm, seeing that the light was moving towards them.

"Oh fluff. We have dwarves," Fleck said mournfully.

"How do you know, Fleck?" Abram asked.

"No creatures of the deep carry lights. They prefer to stalk their prey in the dark."

In a few moments, a party of squat, broad people were upon them. The oldest of them spoke. "Hello, strangers. I am Delfan, and you must be Levi's brother."

Abram was in shock.

"How do you know my brother?"

"Come, there is much to tell. We are having a feast in your brother's honor."

And with that, Delfan and the party of dwarves led the three deeper into the cave.

Chapter 11: What Your Brother Has Done

Not long, deeper in the cave, the cavern opened up, and before them was a giant city.

Delfan spread his arms as if he were embracing the city.

"Welcome to Thar!"

The city was amazing. The houses were meticulously carved from rock, all adorned with intricate details. Each house was different, but they looked as if the same mason had carved them all. Abram was in awe. But all Fleck could see was the gold that trimmed the houses.

The streets were teeming with activity. Trow had their harvest festival, but their festival had nothing on the dwarves' feast.

The street was full of dwarves dancing and drinking. Abram had never seen so many people.

"Did you invite another city to the feast, Delfan?" Abram asked.

"No. The main street is where most of the festivities are. You will find most of the side streets are quieter," Deflan laughed.

"And all this celebration is for us?"

"For you, Levi's family! We owe your brother an enormous debt, and we will gladly pay that debt in any way we can! Perhaps I should take you somewhere a little quieter to share your brother's story and how I know you are his family."

Abram, Sarai, Fleck, and the small group of dwarves made their way to the most ornate house.

"Welcome to my home. I am something of a chief, and with that comes certain benefits," Delfan said, gloating a little.

Delfan and his three guests made their way into the house while the other dwarves broke off to join the festivities.

Deflan led them to a common room and sat down.

Delfan began, "I have lived all my life in Thar. For three hundred years, I have seen Thar prosper. But we dwarves walk a delicate line. From above, we must trade for that which we cannot make here in Thar. From below, we must protect ourselves from the creatures of the deep. One black day, that line was tested.

Dwarves are sensitive to magic. So, we knew a mage was brewing from below. In the deep, there are beasts called Borak. Fiendish black beast with the strength of twenty dwarves and claws that can cut through the strongest armor. To fend one off, you need a small army. This new magical force had gathered them en masse and set them upon our city.

We took posts along our city wall. From the dark, the Borak erupted. We sent a volley of arrows. They had little effect, slowing down the Borak only a little. The Borak began climbing our city wall. We poured tar on the Borak and set them ablaze. That stopped a few, but more took their place. Soon, they were inside our walls. We were rag dolls to the Borak.

We normally trap them under a net and, with many dwarves holding the Borak down, we can strike at the head. This tactic was of no use. There were too many. For every Borak we took down, they took down thirty dwarves.

When everything was at its worst, we felt a presence. An aura so strong and like no other. We despaired, thinking it was the evil force that brought the Borak had come to trap us in from above, giving us nowhere to run and no quarter given to our women and children. We thought our city was through. Then came a bright light, startling the Borak. They were only used to the dark, and the flash of light angered them. The Borak ran towards the new threat, seeking to destroy it. But from that light came spears of ice, catching the heads of the Borak. The beasts that decimated us suddenly burst into flames, scattering the surviving hissing and wailing monsters.

The source of the magic made his presence known. He spoke.

"I will see to the end of your troubles."

He knew us not and had no reason to help us. He just knew good people were suffering at the hands of evil. Deeper into the cave, he put a protection spell to prevent future attacks from any evil forces. We have had very little to worry about from the deep and hardly have need to have a soldier to guard it. We owe your brother so much; that is why we hold this feast. The family of Levi is a family of ours, and we will greet them as such. I apologize; in all the excitement, I haven't even asked your names."

Fleck was the first to respond,

"The big guy is Abram. She's Sarai, and I'm Fleck."

"Fleck and Sarai, I was wondering if I could have a moment with Abram. If you would, join the festivities. This celebration is as much for you as for Abram."

Fleck quickly accepted the offer. There was dwarven treasure to be found. He would not find it in that room. Sarai graciously agreed. She was in a whole different world from what she knew. She had heard about dwarves, but had never thought to meet one.

Deflan escorted them out and shut the door. When he thought no one was within earshot; he spoke.

"You know your grandfather, Alucca, changed the fate of mages."

Abram was surprised to hear his grandfather's name. He was always Grandpa to him.

"What do you know of magic, Abram?"

Abram knew very little about magic, and his silence confirmed it to Deflan.

"Magic originates from another realm and comes here through the Rift. The Rift is everywhere and nowhere at the same time. Mages tap into the other realm through the Rift. But not every human can tap into it. Only a select few can use it, and at one point it took a God to open the Rift inside a mage. The effect was never the same from one user to the next. Some could control one element. Others could fly. Still, each has only one or two powers and one truth overall. They died only a few years later. But humans lined up to become a mage because mages were treated like kings.

This all changed with Alucca, your grandfather. His power preserved life. Not a few years, but indefinitely. Ares was the one who gave him his powers. For a time, Ares was pleased. His men now lived longer, and were at their physical peak. A God may only have a handful of mages at any one time, but Ares's mages did not die, and a handful became hundreds. Thus skewing his advantage over the other Gods. Ares was pleased until he wasn't.

Alucca led mages and soon found he could share his power with a few he led. There was a set within a set. Their new power frightened Ares. Then the mages discovered something else. A mage could open the Rift inside of another person who could yield its power. Until then, only Gods could open the Rift. This new ability struck fear into not only Ares, but all the Gods. For a time, the Gods found a common enemy in these special mages.

The Gods had many weapons to fight the mages. Dwarves were one of those, we were at one time used for finding mages and those aspiring to be mages. Our unique gift to sense magic and see the Rift bend around those with the magic potential made us ideal hunters of mages. The Gods used us until we were determined to be too soft. We had no quarrel with the mages and preferred dwelling underground.

What the Gods have in store for mages or, if they continue to have a quarrel with mages, is not known to me. We quickly lost track of the outside world and only came in contact with others through the occasional trade. But what I know is that your brother is a beacon. He either shares Alucca's power or is the perfect vessel for the Rift. The magnitude of his abilities is too incredible to fathom.

I do not wish to scare you. But if you are here, looking for your brother because he has not returned to your village, I dare say that you will share his fate if you continue your journey. Better to go back to your grandfather and hide away than chase your brother. If he found trouble he could not handle, you will stand no chance against it. You are strong in the Rift like your brother, but you have not been opened, and I must say that you do not have the potential of your brother."

Abram could not take the cold statements. Tears welled in his eyes. He could not accept the truth Deflan had shown him.

"I have to try…For my brother, I have to try."

"If that is how you feel, then the best we can do is to prepare you for the journey. Stay here a week and we will ready you."

With that, Deflan left Abram in the room with nothing to comfort him.

Chapter 12: We Have to Go Left

On the morning of the seventh day, a trumpet blast filled the air. The three travelers roused from their sleep in the house provided by the dwarves.

Fleck was the first to complain. "Can't they leave the dead to sleep?"

"Fleck, I think we should see what is going on," Abram countered.

"Okay, okay. I'm up. Let's go see what the dwarves are doing," Fleck said mockingly.

The three stepped outside, and an army unit of dwarves awaited them. Deflan stood at the ready with his battle guard.

Deflan spoke aloud.

"With our ability to see magic, we have learned to bend it to our will. We have become blacksmiths who can mold magical items. What you had until now mere trinkets. We have gathered every magical item in Thar and crafted items for you. First, we will clothe you in Wintergard. You will know no heat that makes you swelter or cold that frosts you. It will not chafe, nor burn, nor need mending.

Second, we have crafted armor. The Borak claws could not penetrate this armor, but it is practically weightless. The luster of the armor shimmers and will blind those who attempt to do you harm. It also increases your strength tenfold."

Next, we give you cloaks that no sound can be heard through their fabric. You will gain stealth that few can detect.

Fourth, helmets that will keep your mind clear even under enchantment.

Now we have the weapons we have crafted for you individually.

For you, Sarai, the mace of taunting. It will daze and disorient your opponent with every blow you make. Fleck, we have crafted for you an assortment of daggers. Each one has a unique ability that will be known to the user and cannot be used against you. For you, Abram, we have crafted a shield to go with your sword. A sound emanates from it that will deafen your enemy. It attracts and slows oncoming projectiles. A rock hoisted from a catapult will feel like nothing more than a pebble on the shield."

After Deflan handed over the weapons to Sarai, Fleck, and Abram, he pulled out what appeared to a plain red backpack and a circular object.

"Last but not least, the Bastion and this compass. No matter how many are in your party, the Bastion will create a camp for all. Mere minutes inside its tents will give a traveler sufficient sleep. You will not long for water to drink or food to eat, and the Bastion will warn you when anything approaches you with ill intent. All will be provided by the Bastion.

The compass. Give it a destination and it will point you the way there. You will never be lost again."

Deflan continued, "We will escort you to the edge of our territory, but we cannot leave with you. Our place is in our homes, protecting our people. Ready yourself for travel, for I fear the worst of your trip is yet to come. We will meet at the edge of the city."

With that, the military unit marched to the edge of the city.

Sarai and Fleck were jubilant about their new magical items. Abram wished he shared their enthusiasm. He faked a smile, so as to not dampen their spirits, but all Abram could think about was Deflan's words inside the house. If his brother did not stand a chance, what chance did they stand? Abram went through the motions, putting on his new armor and making his way to the edge of the city.

"Abram. Abram! You haven't said a word. We are finally on our way to find your brother. Aren't you excited?" Sarai asked.

"Yes, excited I am to find my brother!"

Sarai bought his lie. Abram was not excited. He was afraid. Abram could not do what his brother did. What help would he be to his brother?

Deflan saw the fear in Abram's eyes.

"Keep your wits about you, Abram. There is no doing this halfway."

Deflan then turned to his troops.

"Forward, march!"

And just like that, Abram started his journey out of Thar.

The group marched for a mile down the cave. Deflan raised his hand.

"Company, halt!"

Deflan turned to the three.

"This is as far as we take you. This is where your brother cast the protection spell. No evil can come from there to our city. You must go it alone from here. You will find a little farther, the cave forks. Stay to the right, and the path will lead you to the surface."

The dwarves turned and began their march back to Thar.

Fleck was glad to see them go and hurried forward, jingling the treasure he took from the dwarves. He only wished the pockets of the clothes the dwarves made for them were deeper. So many treasures he had to leave behind. In his haste, a jewel that he had stolen fell out of his pocket. Fleck turned and reached for the jewel, but he hit his head on something unseen and fell down. Sarai looked at him.

"You clumsy thief. Those dwarves took care of us, gave us so much, and you steal from them."

Sarai picked up the jewel and threw it at Fleck.

"Borrowed. Borrowed a jewel or two. What will we trade with when we are topside? They didn't give us any money."

"We are clothed, and the Bastion provides all our necessities. We are self-sufficient and in no need of dwarven jewels."

Fleck picked up the jewel.

"How do you know the food is any good? It may taste horrible. Then you are going to want something to barter with to get some decent food. That's when you'll come crawling to me."

Sarai knew Fleck still had the pouch of money he'd stolen previously.

"Never!" Sarai shouted.

"Fine! Live on your moral high ground!" Fleck snapped.

Abram, still unsteady, spoke. "We should probably push forward."

The three pressed on silently.

Abram was in no mood to talk. Fleck and Sarai refused to talk to each other. They would occasionally scowl at each other, but not a word was spoken.

Abram traveled in a daze. His feet moved forward, but his will did not. Before Abram knew it, he was at the fork. To the right was safety. Soon he would be out of the cave and above ground. But it was not safe.

His brother did not make it out there. What chance did he have? Abram's chest constricted. He could not breathe. Abram felt the pull of the pendant, and he slumped.

Then the impossible slipped from his lips.

"I think we have to go left."

Chapter 13: The Dissent

"What do you mean you think we have to go left?" Fleck questioned.

"I don't much like the sound of it either. Down there are the Borak and potentially an evil mage." Sarai chimed in.

Abram repeated, "I think we have to go left."

Fleck pressed Abram some more.

"You either do or do not know that we must go left. There is no thinking. Can't you see the path of the magical rat?"

Abram confessed, "I can't see the trail of the rat. I have a pendant that pulls me toward the rat's path."

Abram pulled the pendant out from under his shirt.

"Real-ly. A magical pendant and that is all it does? Pulls you onto the path of the rat?"

"That's not all it does, but what else it does…doesn't matter. All I know right now is the pendant is pulling me left."

"Alright. Let's go left." Fleck agreed.

"Is that all?" Abram stuttered, stunned by Fleck's agreement.

Sarai was in disbelief as well.

"Yes, I'm wearing armor that can withstand a Borak. We need to find Abram's brother, and when we get everyone to safety and stop whatever sent this magical rat, I am pawning off Abram's armor. Let's move along, shall we? Oh, Abram, you may want to pull out that magical sword of yours. These torches will not last much longer, and I feel we are in for a long trek."

Abram did not know if it was ignorance or bravery that made Fleck so bold, but at that moment he wished he had some of it as well. Abram gathered what little courage he had and moved on.

"My hands and face are getting cold down here. I am glad we have the magical clothes to keep us warm," Sarai stated.

Abram thought it was cold as well. He found it cool in Thar, but this was biting cold. Something was wrong.

A voice came from nowhere.

"Visitors! Visitors in the deep coming to see me. I haven't had visitors in so long. Come, come. I have little to offer, but I gladly give it."

The three moved forward uneasily towards the voice until they came to a small fire with a large rat roasting over it and a table with four chairs.

"Come, come! Join me! We feast tonight! The rat with the red eyes came today. Their meat is so tender. You must try."

Abram remembered the rat with the red eyes. His grandfather had smashed it, and the rat had caught on fire.

"What do you know of the rats with the red eyes?" Abram asked.

"They come often. Something draws them here. I let my pets catch them. They are quite tasty!"

Sarai saw the man and felt sorry for him. She spoke to him.

"How did you come here? Why are you all alone?"

"Chased out of my village, I was. They opened the Rift in me, and I made it cold. Crops died. They were hungry and had me to blame for their loss. But alone, I am not. I have the creatures of the deep to keep me company. They listen to me, and I hear them."

Sarai became alarmed.

"Are you the one who sent the Borak after the dwarves?"

"Worthless dwarves. They have so much, and I so little. I wanted to take what was mine."

Sarai casually excused the three.

"We must be leaving. We are trying to find his brother."

Sarai pointed to Abram, and the three slowly backed away.

"But you have eaten nothing. You must be hungry from your travels, and I can't let you go."

A sinister smile came over the man, and he let out a whistle. From all around them, creatures came out of the darkness.

"Are those Borak?" Fleck asked, losing his bravado.

"I don't know what they are, but we should run. We follow the path of the rat. It got in here. There must be a way out." Abram shouted.

Abram followed the pull of the pendant, dodging the creatures from the deep. The path started ascending.

Yes, this must be the way out, Abram thought.

Abram could see a little light ahead. He charged forward even faster. The turn ahead looked like the way out. However, Abram's heart sank when he saw what was at the bend. The light shone through a hole that was not even big enough for Fleck.

"We have no choice but to fight!" Abram shouted.

The three turned around and awaited the creatures of the deep.

Frightening beasts crept towards the three. Fleck let out a cry, and the monsters flooded in.

The three slashed and chopped through a seemingly endless horde, but no matter how much the creatures slashed and bit, they could not break the armor. Still, the three were growing weak from fatigue.

When they were the edge their breaking point. The beasts, sensing that it was a losing battle, went scattered.

Fleck was the first to speak.

"I'm pawning your armor and getting a thousand of those Jaja beans."

The three laughed. When they quieted, Abram pointed out their unfortunate circumstances.

"I think our only way out is through that hole. I feel we can't take much more of those creatures. If we go back, we may have to fight them again. We are going to have to dig to get out."

"Do I look like a dwarf to you? I don't dig," Fleck snapped.

So, Fleck kept watch as Sarai and Abram dug, both tired and sore from the fight. Despite that, Abram was in high spirits.

"Maybe I can help you after all, brother," he had begun to believe again. The fight had been hard, but Abram had gained confidence from their survival.

Chapter 14: Nowhere to Run

Abram, Sarai, and Fleck were exhausted, but they knew they could not sleep near the cave. They walked another mile before they stopped.

"Oh, Bastion, be everything Deflan promised," Fleck pleaded.

Abram placed the Bastion on the ground and opened it. From nowhere, three tents appeared, a small fire with a pot on top, and a trough of water materialized.

"Food! Water!" Fleck exclaimed. "I don't care what the food is. I'm so hungry."

Sarai sipped some water while Fleck made his way to the food. In the pot was a gray paste.

"What is this? It looks so unappetizing. Deflan duped us!" Fleck sneered.

Fleck grabbed a bowl and a ladle from beside the fire. As he approached the pot, his nostrils flared. The paste actually smelled superb. Fleck's mouth was watering. He pulled the spoon close to his face and slurped.

"Landian elk with all the spices."

"Let me try!" Sarai squealed.

Sarai filled up a bowl, and Abram did too.

"Candum fruit!" Sarai grinned. "So tasty!"

Abram took a bite.

"Cucumber!"

"Cucumber?" Fleck said in disbelief.

"I really like cucumbers." Abram shrugged.

"If the food is that good, I can't wait to get to bed."

Fleck stretched and let out a mighty yawn. Before long, all three were yawning and longing for bed.

"I'll see you two in the morning," Fleck said, going into his tent.

Abram and Sarai said good night and went to bed as well.

Sleep came quickly. Abram was the first to fall asleep and the first to know that he was dreaming. In his dream, he saw Fleck and Sarai.

"What are you doing in my dream?" Abram asked.

Sarai spoke up.

"I think we are in each other's dreams."

"How is this possible?" Fleck questioned.

A sinister laugh broke the eerie silence. Abram and Fleck wondered who it was, but Sarai knew the voice.

"Run! It's Jin!" Sarai shouted.

Sarai tried sprinting away from the sound, but it was everywhere. Fleck and Abram had trouble keeping up with Sarai. The ground shook, forcing them to stop running. The floor bubbled up, and rotting arms protruded from below. Before they knew it, a sea of undead surrounded them.

The laughing voice rang through the air.

"Sarai, you thought you could get away, but you can't. Now your friends will suffer, and you will go back to Beterham."

The undead horde shambled towards the three. There was nowhere to run. They had no weapons. Their doom was imminent. Sarai took Abram's hand.

"I am so sorry," Sarai cried.

The horde grabbed and clawed at them, pulling each one apart. The pain was excruciating.

Suddenly, Abram woke up in a sweat.

Abram felt his body. No tears or cuts. Physically he was fine, but mentally drained.

"Fleck! Sarai! Are you alright?"

Fleck responded, "I'm alright chief."

But there was no sound from Sarai. Abram rushed to her tent, throwing the flaps open. Sarai was on her knees sobbing.

"I'm sorry, Abram. I'm so sorry."

Abram wanted to comfort her but did not have the words. He decided to lie to her.

"Jin won't hurt you. We will be ready for him, and he will pay for what he has done."

Sarai cried harder, "Yes. We will be ready for him."

Abram did not know if what he said had comforted Sarai, but he could not think of anything else to say.

Fleck pushed his way in.

"If the two of you are done, we should push on. I don't want to wait around for whatever trap Jin has ready for us."

They readied their armor and weapons, closed the Bastion, and traveled forward into the unknown. Abram hoped the end was near but did not know how much longer they had to travel.

"Brother, please hold on."

Chapter 15: Hope Down the River

The three traveled forth over the open plain, and soon trees popped up in the distance.

"It looks like we are going to trek through some forest."

"Thank you for the obvious, Abram," Fleck joked.

The forest foliage was dense. They traveled for hours but made very little progress.

"Abram, next time you follow a magical rat, make sure it only goes over nice flat ground," Fleck mocked.

Abram laughed before pointing ahead.

"Look. You can see a little light ahead."

"Great! Thanks, Abram," Fleck jeered.

Abram laughed again and pushed his way to the edge of the forest. When he came out on the other side, he met a giant river.

"Please say the rat followed the shoreline," Fleck pleaded.

"No such luck, Fleck. We are going to have to find a way across," Abram sighed.

They started their path down the river, hoping it narrowed downstream. They walked for an hour, seeing no narrowing. In the distance, though, they saw a shack that had a boat attached to a rope that spanned the river. The three picked up the pace in excitement. When they got to the shack, they saw an imp had set up a business taking people across the river.

Fleck whispered to Abram, "Trust nothing he says. He's an imp."

Fleck opened up with a smile, "Hello, friend. We are trying to cross the river, and it appears you are our salvation. We would pay you three coppers to cross."

"Twenty coppers," the imp snapped.

"Twenty coppers? That's straight robbery!" Fleck replied.

"The river doesn't narrow for miles. Plus, there are statem fish. That boat is the safest place you can be."

Fleck became alarmed.

"You said Statem fish? And that boat is safe?"

"Yep," the imp replied.

"Twenty it is," Fleck responded.

"Did I say twenty? I meant twenty-five."

Fleck defeatedly reached into his money pouch and pulled out the extra five coppers.

The imp stored the money inside his shack and returned.

"Welcome aboard, travelers," the imp said, pointing to the boat.

Fleck walked stiffly onto the boat. He sat down, gripping the sides tightly. Abram did not understand Fleck's tension. He got into the boat casually then turned to Sarai and helped her into the boat with no trouble. The imp got in last and began pulling them across the river.

With every bump and rock, Fleck's face grew paler, and his grip grew stronger. Abram looked out onto the water and noticed something moving towards them. Fleck spotted it first.

Fleck shouted, "Tentacle! statem fish!"

The imp tried to hit the tentacle with an oar, but it was no use. The tentacle flipped the boat and the passengers inside.

Flecked popped up shouting, "Everyone for themselves! Make your way to shore!"

Fleck was already halfway to shore when the others popped out of the water. The imp was in the most trouble. He thrashed and splashed around because he didn't know how to swim.

The statem quickly pulled the imp under, and a burst of red bloomed in the water.

"Go to the shore, Sarai!" Abram yelled.

Sarai was closer to shore and quickly made her way the edge of the water. Abram was a few yards away from the imp.

Fleck shouted from the shore, "He ate the imp! He may not be hungry for you!"

Abram shouted back, "I feel something touching me!"

The statem fish tugged Abram under the raging water. Sarai and Fleck looked for him from the shore. They did not know if Abram was being thrashed and bitten by the fish, but it held Abram under the water for a long time.

Sarai cried, "He's been under too long! He'll never make it!"

Bubbles popped up, and another red cloud filled the water.

Fleck turned to Sarai.

"He's gone."

Sarai broke down. She had meant it when she said Abram and Fleck were the closest to family she had.

Suddenly, a light shone from the water, and a body splashed out from beneath.

Abram gasped, "A little…help."

Sarai was in disbelief.

"How are you alive? You were under for so long."

"We all have our secrets, and that is mine," Abram jested.

Fleck pulled out the magic rope.

"I'll throw out the rope and have it tie to you."

Fleck tossed the rope and it landed near Abram.

"Now, rope, tie to Abram!"

Nothing happened.

"Abram, you tricked me! That rope is no good. Pull yourself in."

Sarai took the rope from Fleck.

"Give me that," Sarai said indignantly.

Sarai pulled Abram in, and he flopped to the ground.

"Abram!" Fleck jeered. "You have another magical item. That's the only way you could have stayed under that long. The rope was no good. You have to give me that magical item to make up for the rope."

"What? You did not know I was my hometown's best swimmer. I can stay underwater longer than anyone in the village."

Abram was lying. He found it to be a useful tactic against Fleck. Fleck knew nothing about the rings that the Tangfu gave him.

"After that invigorating swim," Abram said sarcastically, "I think we should set up camp and catch some sleep."

"Maybe…with our helmets to prevent a repeat of last night?" Sarai interjected.

All agreed.

Chapter 16: Begin Again

Abram woke with a start. Something was different. Everything was silent. He could not hear the river. Something was wrong. Then he heard a cry.

"Our helmets are missing!" Sarai shouted. "What if Jin attacks again? What if he's the one who took the helmets?"

"I thought the Bastion would warn us if anyone tried to get into our camp? Is Jin powerful enough to slip by unnoticed?" Fleck interjected.

Unusually, all of this did not surprise Abram. Something bigger was brewing. Something bigger than missing helmets.

"The compass! It will point the way to our helmets," Sarai remembered.

Abram pulled the compass out of his pocket. Sarai snatched it away from him.

"Where are our helmets, compass?"

The compass pointed northeast.

"Let's pack up and head out," Sarai commanded. "The sooner we get our helmets back, the less chance we have of getting attacked by Jin."

Abram closed the Bastion, and the three set out.

Abram could not get over the feeling that this was all too familiar.

Abram noticed the grass was dense all around them except for the small path on which they were walking.

"Isn't it weird that the grass all around us is grown out, except on the path we are on?" Abram questioned.

"Must be a popular path," Fleck said dismissively.

Why haven't we seen anyone else? Abram thought.

"I welcome a pleasant path. Beats all the hiking that we did through the forest," Sarai said happily.

Why am I the only one concerned about all this? Abram thought.

Up ahead, Abram saw huts, but he knew they would find nothing. When they got close, Sarai spoke.

"Hello? Is there anybody here?"

The three checked some huts for anyone, but they were all empty.

The compass still pointed northeast, so they continued on.

Near the edge of the huts was a hunched-over old woman, waiting for something.

"Hello, ma'am. Are you here by yourself? Where are the rest of the villagers?" Sarai asked, concerned.

"A drought chased them away. I was too old to leave, and here I stayed. It is nice to see an occasional stranger. Would you do me a favor and have tea with me?"

Sarai put the compass in her pocket, and the three moved into the old woman's hut.

Four crude chairs surrounded a small table in the hut. As Abram sat, the pendant fell out of his shirt. The pendant caught the old woman's eye.

"I have seen that pendant before. Are you looking for Levi?"

"Yes, I'm looking for him! How do you know my brother, ma'am?"

"He spent some time with me long ago. He was a mage, and his powers were strong."

"Did my brother help you with his magic?"

The old woman laughed.

"No! An old woman can sense these things. We know more than you think."

Abram felt he would not get much information from her, but he did not know why.

"Here are your drinks. Some hot tea I brewed myself. Now drink up. Don't let it get cold."

The three drank. Almost immediately, Abram felt his eyelids getting heavy. He looked at the others, and they appeared drowsy as well.

The old woman smiled. "Yes. I think you should all take a nap now."

Abram woke up in the Bastion.

"My helmet! It's gone!" Sarai yelled.

Sarai got out of her tent and saw the other two did not have their helmets either.

"Jin could attack us at any time! We must find the helmet!"

"We can use the compass to find them. It should be in your pocket," Abram stated.

Sarai reached into her pocket.

"The compass. That's odd. I don't remember putting it in my pocket. How did you know it was there, Abram?"

"I don't know," Abram confessed.

"Compass, take us to our helmets."

The compass pointed northeast. The three walked a clear path to huts with no one in them and then to an old woman. All these things seemed familiar to Abram.

The old woman chortled, "Greetings, travelers. I don't get many visitors. Would you do an old woman a kindness and have a drink with me?"

Abram's hair stood up at the sight of the woman. His mind was telling him danger. However, no one else seemed concerned.

Sarai put the compass away, and Sarai and Fleck followed the old woman into the hut.

"You coming, Abram?" Fleck asked.

Abram said nothing, but he followed Fleck into the hut.

The old woman was pouring Sarai and Fleck's tea.

"Come now, young man. There is plenty for everyone," the old woman said, pointing to the empty seat.

The four sat down.

"Now drink up," the old woman urged.

Sarai and Fleck gleefully drank from their cups. Abram hesitated and noticed something.

"Why do you not have a cup?" Abram questioned.

"Because I am not thirsty, my dear. Now drink!" the old woman angrily insisted.

But Abram did not drink.

Abram saw the other two getting drowsy.

"What's in this drink?"

The old woman sneered.

"You are Levi's brother, aren't you?"

The old woman's comment left Abram stunned, and he had very little time to react to what happened next.

The old woman reared for a punch and hit Abram square in the chest. He flew straight out of the hut onto rocks far from the entrance.

"Do you know what I am?" the old woman said, charging outside after Abram.

Abram rolled out of the way of the old woman's path just in time.

"Do you know what your brother did to me?" The old woman seethed. "I am a Foregemenaut, and I controlled this village."

The old woman charged again, but Abram was on his feet and dodged her.

The old woman then began circling Abram.

"I live off the life energy of the people I ensnare in my village. With my magic, I confuse people so that they forget the day's events, or at least I could, before your brother came."

A mage's life force is particularly sweet, and I greedily invited your brother into my fold. His life energy was everything I could dream of and more. It appeared that he was another who had fallen into my trap, but he became restless. I quickly became the focus of his discontent. When he broke free from my magic, he vowed I would hurt no one again. With his power, he nearly severed my attachment to the Rift and made sure I could feed no more. I will starve to death because of him, and my magic can no longer fool a worm like you."

The old woman turned to stare down Abram.

"I feel we could do this all day, me charging you and you dodging. So, you are in for a rare treat. A Foregemenaut seldom takes on its true form. I assure you it's not because it's not formidable, but because it is not advantageous to our normal ruse. However, on an occasion like this, I can make an exception. I will reveal my true form to you and kill you. Then I shall continue to play with your friends until their death to spite you."

The old woman grew taller. Her hands curved into claws. Extra sets of legs burst from her stomach. Her skin turned green. Her eyes swelled in her head, and pincers sprang from her mouth. The old woman was now a behemoth the size of a tree.

The beast continued in a high-pitched trill.

"You will not find a sword that can penetrate a Foregemenaut's hard shell."

Abram pulled his sword. It glowed brightly.

"You have a magic sword. I see. No matter. I shall squash you just the same."

The Foregemenaut brought its foot over Abram and stomped. Abram rolled away and jumped back to his feet. The beast again tried to step on Abram, but Abram stood his ground and sliced his sword at the Foregemenaut's foot. Abram heard searing hiss as the blade cut through the monster's foot. The beast pulled back its foot in pain.

"That is a mistake you are going to pay for, whelp!" the monster raged.

The Foregemenaut launched a volley of slashes, fiercely slicing at Abram's body and sword, knocking him back.

"You are not the only one with strong armor, beast!" Abram scorned, but he still did not know how he was going to take down such a gigantic monster.

The Foregemenaut slashed Abram again with its right claw. Abram parried the attack, cleaving off the tip of its claw. The monster screamed and, in its rage, lunged its head towards Abram, attempting to swallow him whole. Abram leapt away from the face of the monster. Its head struck the ground.

Abram remembered how Sarai had slowed the spider by cutting off its legs. He ran to the Foregemenaut's left side, cutting off the beast's front leg. He then scurried to take the back leg. The beast no longer had a way to hold up the left side of its body and collapsed to the ground. Abram jumped onto the Foregemenaut's back and ran up its spine. As Abram approached the beast's head, he raised his sword and stabbed straight down into the creature's cranium.

Abram's heart raced out of his chest, and he gasped for air. The beast had fallen. The fight and the victory exhilarated Abram.

"Brother, I am coming for you!" Abram shouted.

He staggered back to the hut. Abram picked up the chair that was knocked to the floor after the Foregemenaut's first punched him. He sat waiting for his friends to wake up, catching his breath.

After his heart stopped thumping, Abram wondered how much more he could take. Would his travels ever lead to his brother?

"What have you left in your wake, brother?"

Looking around the hut, Abram spied a knocked-over chest. Among the contents that had spilled out were their helmets. Abram retrieved the helmets and put his on. He then placed the helmets on his friends.

"No nightmares. We sleep well tonight."

Abram closed his eyes and went to sleep.

Chapter 17: Prayers for Brother

"Abram! Abram, wake up!" Sarai shook Abram.

"I'm up…"

"What happened here?" Sarai questioned.

She pointed to the front of the hut as Fleck walked out.

"Is that a Foregemenaut! Abram, you killed a Foregemenaut alone!" Fleck exclaimed as he ran back into the hut.

"Kings would send entire armies to root out a Foregemenaut. They would have to kill the enchanted villagers one by one until they came upon it. Then it would take about the entire army to destroy it. Kings didn't much care about the loss of the soldiers or villagers. They would just have their villagers avoid the Foregemenaut's trap and done nothing if it was worthless, but the Foregemenaut is a delicacy known worldwide. Also, its hard shell makes excellent armor. If only we had something to pull this carcass, we would be wealthy beyond our dreams!"

Fleck paused for a moment.

"I'm taking its eyes. I need to find a large bag. And…you are in for a treat. Little did you know, I am an excellent cook. I'll grab the other eye, find some herbs in the huts, and cook it for us tonight. We are having Foregemenaut steak! We will feast like kings!"

Normally, Fleck got on Sarai's nerves, but even she could not help being pulled in by Fleck's enthusiasm. Still, she wondered how a Foregemenaut steak would compare to the Bastion's food. Sure, the steaks might look better, but could anything be better than candum fruit?

Soon enough it was time for lunch arrived, so Abram set up the Bastion. Fleck refused to eat anything unless it was the Foregemenaut steaks. By late afternoon, Fleck had assembled his ingredients, started a fire, and was cooking the Foregemenaut. For an hour, Fleck carefully turned it, paying special attention to flip-and sear the steaks properly.

"Abram. Sarai. Are your plates and stomachs ready for this?"

"Yes, Sir," the two chimed.

The three gathered in the old woman's hut.

"I give you, Foregemenaut steaks."

Abram took his first bite. The meat was tougher than expected, but the taste was heavenly. The more he chewed, the more he wanted. Abram saw the joy in Fleck's eyes as he and Sarai devoured the steaks.

"I made three for each of us. So, indulge!"

With that, Fleck took a bite of his Foregemenaut steak. It tasted better than he remembered. The Bastion could not imitate this delicacy. Before long, the steaks were all eaten.

"Well, I am going to call it an early night," Sarai insisted.

Fleck was tired too. Only Abram did not go to his tent. He took a walk, thinking about his brother. How many days had gone by without a moment of looking for his brother?

"Are you still out there, brother?" Abram asked the night.

Abram walked by Sarai's tent, and he heard muffled words. Who was Sarai talking to? He got close to Sarai's tent and opened the flap.

"Sarai, who are you talking to?"

"I am talking to the Gods. I am sending my prayers to Hades for my family."

"Gods?" Abram only knew what his Grandpa told him, and he made them sound bad.

"Yes. The Gods are the ones who look over us and protect us. I am sending my prayers to Hades to protect my family in the afterlife."

"Afterlife? No one in my village has died or spoken about an afterlife."

"Did they teach you anything in your village? After you die, Hades guides the good to the place of never-ending joy, but you can get lost along the way, forced to travel for eternity. Few who are lost make it to the land of never-ending joy. Hades finds the faithful and leaves the wicked behind. I pray Hades leads my family to safety.

You are searching for your brother. You should pray to Hermes for your travels to be a success. Unless you believe your brother is…" Sarai trailed off. "Here, let me teach you how to pray to Hermes for safe travel. My uncle taught me this."

> Though the road is long,
> May my feet never tire.
> To you, Hermes, I trust my way.
> With my heart's desire.
> Bless my path,
> And all I meet.
> Bring me safely home,
> And to you I give praise
> My one true protector.

"If that brought me to my brother, I would pray it all day," Abram confessed.

"Put your faith in the Gods, Abram. They will guide you," Sarai encouraged.

Abram's eyes grew heavy, and he excused himself. But before he went to sleep, he prayed to Hermes and Hades.

Chapter 18: A Proposition

"Abram… Hello Abram."

Abram stood alone in a black haze.

"I must be dreaming. Who's there? Who's calling my name?"

From the darkness emerged a figure he had only seen in the distance.

"Jin! How are you in my dream?"

Abram looked at Jin. He wore red, scaly armor. He had blonde hair and a charismatic face. Abram could see why people might trust Jin at first. But Abram knew that there was darkness behind that carefree smile.

"Don't worry, Abram. Your little helmet is doing its thing. I am not trying to seduce you. I'm only visiting in your dream."

"What do you want, Jin?"

"Your brother, I know you are looking for him. I have peered into your mind."

"If you have done anything to my brother, I swear I will kill you."

"I cannot do anything to your brother… for he is already dead."

"Liar!!!"

"How long have you searched for him and still not found him? Alucca should have told you from the very start. He can speak to the dead as well."

Abram's face fell.

"Surprised, I know your granddaddy. We were part of The Twenty. The first twenty mages to share their power. Awful name. Three others joined, but we didn't become The Twenty-Three. Doesn't roll off the tongue, I guess. Unfortunately, there are only six of us now. Wait, I killed four of them. So, it looks like it's only me and Granddaddy left. Don't worry, I have no intention of killing your grandfather. I could not take any more power ripping through my veins, at least not right now."

"If you are so powerful with magic, how can you hide it?"

"You think your granddaddy was the only one to find the Tangfu? Maybe it's not as glitzy as hiding a village, the way I use them. But it gets the job done."

"Face it, Abram. Your brother is dead. I have seen him and spoken to him on the other side. There is nothing more you can do for him…but there is something I can do for him… and you."

"What are you getting at, Jin?"

"I can raise the dead to varying degrees. For instance, your brother, I could make him whole again. The life of the party when he was alive…or…"

"Or what, Jin?"

"I could add another half-dead slave to do my bidding."

"You're a monster, Jin!"

"Abram, I want to bring your brother back, happy and healthy like he was. I just need a small favor."

"What do you want, Jin?"

"Put this necklace on Sarai."

"What will happen if I do?"

"Nothing or…something."

"Stop with the games. What will happen?"

"If you put it on her, nothing will happen. She will go about her day like nothing has transpired… What I need you to do is have her accept it."

"What's the difference?"

"See, Abram, by accepting this necklace, she is accepting my control. She doesn't have to know it is from me. But she must accept it and put it on herself."

"I'll never do it for you."

"Well, Abram, have fun searching for an eternity for your brother."

"Even if I wanted to do it, how would you give me the necklace without Sarai knowing it?"

Jin walked close to Abram and put his face up against Abram's ear. Placed the necklace in Abram's right hand.

"You just have to wake up."

Abram snapped awake, panting.

Then he felt something in his right hand. A necklace. A bright red necklace.

Chapter 19: Anything

Levi and Abram were enjoying a warm day by the creek in Trow.

"Have you been practicing the sword training Grandpa taught us?" Levi asked.

"A little," Abram responded.

"Well, let's see what you've got."

Levi picked up a stick and hopped onto a log that bridged the creek. He waved to Abram to come over. Abram picked up a stick of his own and took a position on the opposite end of the log.

"Come at me!" Levi urged.

Abram let out a yell and tried striking Levi with an overhead chop. Levi parried and smacked Abram in the stomach.

Abram tried lunging at Levi. Levi deflected and smacked him in the back.

When Abram put his guard up again, Levi lunged. He pressed himself against Abram. Levi's eyes met Abram's eyes.

"You are going to lose," Levi laughed.

Levi kicked, sweeping Abram off his feet, knocking him into the creek.

Levi laughed, but Abram did not.

"Come on, Abram. It is just some friendly teasing."

"You think I'm a big joke," Abram scowled.

"Abram, you're not a joke to me. I may rattle you with a friendly scuffle, but I would do anything for you and Aleese."

"Anything?" Abram questioned.

Levi put out his hand to pull Abram up. "Anything," Levi said earnestly.

Abram took Levi's hand and pulled him into the creek. Levi sat in the creek laughing.

"I'd do anything for you too, Levi."

Chapter 20: Temptation in a New World

The day after Jin's encounter, Abram could not help feeling distracted. Could he betray Sarai like that? He was so agitated that he almost walked into a wall right in front of him.

"Did you almost run into that wall!?!" Fleck gasped. "It's huge. Must be over ten times your height, Abram, but you were about to stroll right into it. Look. It's all metal! I've never seen this much ore, and there is no visible door to get in."

"We should find the entrance and see if they know about your brother," Sarai chimed in.

"It's worth a try," Fleck agreed.

The wall seemed to go on forever in either direction.

"We can use the compass to find the entrance." Fleck said, pleased with his idea.

The compass pointed north, and the three began walking along the side of the wall looking for an entrance. They walked for what seemed like miles until a bend in the wall appeared. Around the corner was the entrance to the city.

"Hello! Is there anyone here?" Fleck shouted.

A guard peered over the entrance.

"I'm sorry, friends, we do not take outsiders unless they are here for business," the guard interjected.

"I'm sorry, sir. We are looking for someone. Maybe he came this way. His name is Levi."

The guard looked stunned and disappeared behind the wall. He came back with another, larger guard.

"How do you know Levi, strangers?" the additional guard questioned.

"He is my brother, and I fear something bad has happened to him."

"We'll let you in, but you will have to leave your weapons at the entrance," the large guard insisted.

The gate opened, and the three made their way in. The guards were waiting for them inside.

"Tell me your name," the large guard insisted.

"I'm Abram. This is Sarai and Fleck."

"An elf? Is he to be trusted?"

"You can trust me as much as I can trust you," Fleck quipped.

"I can vouch for him. He has been with me since I left my village," Abram acknowledged.

"I'm touched, Abram, that you feel so highly of me," Fleck joked.

"If you are truly who you say you are, what is the name of your village and your sister?" The guard questioned.

"Trow and Aleese."

"That settles it. Normally, we don't allow outsiders into the inner circle of the city. Most merchants don't go any further than this, but I feel we can make an exception for Levi's brother. I'm Sault."

The four began their walk to the inner circle. It was a tight path that could only fit a small wagon. The path weaved its way through the thick forest. As they neared the end of the forest, Sault quickened his step to get in front of the small party. He turned around and swung out his arms.

"Welcome to Aulmad!"

What the three saw shocked them. Buildings as tall as the wall. Roads covered in something black. The paths were not just dirt. Posts lined the road with white globes on top. And there was something else.

"Abram!" Sarai shouted, "That cart is moving by itself."

The cart shocked Abram as much as Sarai.

What did we step into? Abram thought.

"This is the market street," Sault added. "The houses are farther into the circle, and our city center is in the middle. But here is where I am going to leave you. The information that your brother is missing is grave news, and we must plan our path forward. I will return with how the committee will respond."

Sarai rushed to the vendors. Fleck did his normal disappearing act. Abram followed Sarai.

"Look at all these fruits and vegetables. picini fruit, stafor berry, and muten plant. There's even cucumber, Abram," Sarai giggled. "There is so much here."

Sarai pressed on to a vendor selling clothes. Abram turned across the road to look at a vendor selling jewelry. It reminded him of the necklace. He clenched the necklace. It was like a cancer he wanted no part of. The necklace felt hot, making Abram's hand sweaty. Could he go through with this?

Abram turned to meet up with Sarai, who was still looking for clothes.

"Abram, look at this dress! Look at how fancy it is, and it is my favorite color, red!" Sarai bubbled.

"You know I saw a necklace that might go with this dress." Abram said flatly.

"That's incredible! Let's go look at it!" Sarai said excitedly.

Abram paused for a moment that felt like forever to him.

Could he go through with Jin's plan? Abram could feel the intense beating of his chest. A cold sweat came over him. He felt his lungs getting tight.

"You know…" Abram stammered, "It's not even the right color. Let's look at some more dresses."

"Okay!" Sarai replied, pleased with the idea.

Abram could not help but feel sick. Had he betrayed his brother? Did he betray Sarai?

Abram could feel the beat of his heart. Thump! Thump! Thump!

Luckily, there was something to distract him.

"Looky what I got! A brand-new satchel, and I got a great deal on it. The vendor was practically giving it away," Fleck gloated.

"That is so incredible, Fleck!" Sarai exclaimed. "Would you happen to have enough for a dress?"

"I think I might have that, but you would owe me," Fleck contended.

"Whoo-hoo!" Sarai gushed. "It's the red one over there!"

Fleck paid the vendor, and Sarai grabbed the dress and began dancing with it.

Abram felt sicker.

"You don't look so good, chief. You doing alright?" Fleck said somewhat concerned.

"I'm fine. I just want to get back to finding my brother." Abram said wanly.

Fleck moved over to Abram and patted him on the back and said, "If you say so, chief."

Abram looked away from Fleck and saw Sault coming back.

Chapter 20: The Way Forward

"We have come to a consensus. Abram and Sarai can come with me. The elf stays," Sault stated.

"You know a way to find my brother?" Abram inquired.

"There is much to tell. Follow me,"

Sault led Sarai and Abram to the center of town to a statue of two men pointing forward, and Abram could not believe what he was seeing.

"As you may have guessed, this is no ordinary town, and we have these two men to thank for it. Alm and your brother," Sault explained.

"This city has an interesting past. It was founded by Alm. He built here because of an unusual tree. He called it The Tree of Knowledge. Him and a friend, Taran, were lost in the woods, weak from hunger. They came across the tree and began eating its fruit. The two began having visions of the future. Alm saw endless possibilities, but Taran saw this as forbidden knowledge. Taran wanted to do away with the tree, but Alm convinced him otherwise. Alm went about making a town around the tree.

He gathered like minds and they also ate from the tree. With these visions, they made drawings and crude contraptions, but something was missing. With all their knowledge, they still could not create a power source to move them forward. All that knowledge sat dormant on paper, and then misfortune hit them.

Taran, who returned to condemn their actions, finally did the unimaginable. He poisoned his friend, Alm, and burned down the tree. Despair filled the town. The dream of Alm's was disappearing. The townsfolk tried planting a new Tree of Knowledge with the seeds of the fruit, but it would not grow. That is where your brother came in.

A stroke of good luck came with your brother. He came across our town, and even though he was a stranger to us, he was friendly and offered his help. The townsfolk explained their troubles and that a solution was not readily available. However, a villager who was thought to have disappeared, returned. He had been mining in a cave a little ways away. He returned with a bevy of metals. With the new ore and your brother's magic, we were able to make something we could not make before. We made a power source. With the power source, the town exploded with new devices to perpetuate the town's growth, but that was not all.

Your brother examined the seeds and used his magic to bring forth a sprout. We had a new Tree of Knowledge growing. We built the wall to keep Taran from discovering the new Tree of Knowledge.

Your brother had done so much to push this town forward. He assured us he would return to see the town. We made a promise to him---he would be the first to eat the fruit from the new tree. It bore its first fruit last year, and no one has eaten it. However, we are making an exception.

We want you, Abram, to have the first fruit. Your brother has not been back for twenty years. We are worried about what happened to him. The tree will give you glimpses of the future. Perhaps you will see where your brother is."

"I will eat it for my brother. I must know what happened to him," Abram said, full of hope.

"Follow me," Sault requested.

Sault took them around the city center to a glass house. Sault opened the door and pointed to the tree.

"Abram, take a piece of fruit and eat it," Sault stated.

Abram went to the tree and plucked a piece of fruit. He examined it and then took a bite.

"What do you see?" Sault asked.

"There are glimpses of so many things. I see Jin with three people behind him. I see Levi. I see two tall women; one of them is sick. The sick one is hoarding some kind of jewels. I see… a God! She is beautiful. I see myself holding a stone. My brother again this time leading a faceless army. I see multitudes climbing a mountain. Everything else is moving too fast to see."

With that, the vision stopped. Abram became elated. His brother was alive. Then he remembered Jin and what he was going to do to Sarai. Abram was ashamed and angry. He would make Jin pay for this.

"I am relieved to hear your brother is still alive," Sault admitted. "Will you be staying much longer, or will you go out soon to find your brother?"

"There is still daylight. I think we should go."

Sarai and Abram walked back to the market to find Fleck.

"What did they tell you?" Fleck asked.

"My brother is alive. We must continue our search, and we are going now while there is still daylight."

Abram thought he could finally throw out the necklace Jin gave him, but when he checked his pocket, it was not there. Abram was upset that he could not dispose of it himself but was glad that it was gone.

Chapter 21: What Have You Done

The three had little time to travel. They made it only a few miles before darkness started to fall.

"I think we should stop here," Abram decided.

Abram opened up the Bastion. Out popped the tents, fire, and food.

"None too soon if I say so myself," Fleck conceded.

Fleck threw down his new satchel, and something new fell out. Abram did not notice it, but Sarai did.

"That is a pretty necklace. Did you get from Aulmad?"

"Actually, I... found it on the ground."

"Can I have it?" Sarai asked.

"Sure! Why not?"

Abram turned and saw the necklace. It was the red necklace Jin gave him! Abram dropped his food and dove for Sarai, snatching the necklace just before she put it on.

Abram threw the necklace into the fire, causing it to crack and bellowed black smoke.

"Why did you lunge at me, and why did the necklace create all this black smoke?" Sarai questioned.

"The necklace was from Jin. He wanted me to give it to you. He said it would put you under his control. I couldn't do it."

An eerie silence fell between them.

"Was that the necklace you were trying to give me in Aulmad?"

"I couldn't go through with it, Sarai," Abram stammered.

"That wasn't the question, Abram. Was that the necklace you offered me in Aulmad?"

Abram hesitated and then shamefully answered. "Yes."

"Abram, I promised you I would help find your brother, and I will. But I can't trust you anymore."

Sarai ran to her tent, tears streaking down her face.

Chapter 22: I'm Coming

"Abram. Aaaaaabram. Are you enjoying your slumber?"

"Who said that?" Abram said, half awake. "Jin! Why did the Bastion not warn us!"

"Magic, Abram. I have more power than your toy tent," Jin gloated. "Abram, Abram, Abram. What am I going to do about you? I gave you a simple task. Give the girl the necklace, and you destroy the necklace."

"You lied to me, Jin. My brother is alive!"

"Abram. It was just a little white lie. I think we should focus on what is important. Giving Sarai over to me."

"Why would I help you now?"

"You are going to help me, Abram. Deliver Sarai to me, or I will kill you slowly. Save your life. I am in the city of Tarton, ten miles to the north. Deliver the girl there, or I will come at you full force. Oh, you can wake up now."

Abram woke in a cold sweat and jumped out of his tent.

"Fleck! Sarai! We have to go! Jin is on our trail!"

Fleck and Sarai came out of their tents, rubbing the sleep out of their eyes.

"Go where, Abram?" Sarai asked.

"Jin said he was in Tarton. Ten miles north of here. We should go as far away from there as possible."

"Tarton?" Fleck replied, "I may know a place we can go, but I don't know how inviting they will be."

"We don't have many options right now. Where do you want to take us?" Abram asked.

"We can go to the homeland of the elves, KeeRi. It is a two-day journey from Tarton. But I did not leave on good terms. So, I am not sure how much they will help us."

"Let's pack up and head out," Abram asserted.

Chapter 23: Not the Stomach for It

In the town of Uperville, two boys played Sincot.

"Kick the ball over here, Fleck!" said Kile excitedly.

"Coming your way!" Fleck replied.

"Ardan! Stop playing and come over here at once."

"Yes, mother," Fleck said defeated.

Fleck walked to his mother with his head hung low. Once they were out of earshot, Fleck's mother scolded him.

"You should not play with the minister's son, and you need to drop this childhood nickname of yours. Fleck is not a proper name."

"Yes," Fleck sniffled.

"We are the right hand of the Hessin. We must act properly. Playing childish games with the minister's son makes us look bad."

"I know," Fleck responded.

"Then why do you continue to disobey?" his mother said exasperated. "The Hessin has given us new orders. I will discuss them with you when we are home. You wait in your room until I come to tell you them."

Fleck's mother walked off, leaving him to his sad walk home.

Fleck waited in his room until evening. His mother came in.

"Fleck, we have new orders from the Hessin. The minister has forgotten his place and has cut the tithing to him. He wishes to send a message. He wants us to kill the minister and leave no one to avenge him. That's why Kile will have to die as well."

Tears welled up in Fleck's eyes as his mother continued.

"The Hessin believes it is your time to prove your worth. He wants you to kill the son tonight. I know this is hard, but the will and the word of the Hessin is law for the elves. I know you have never been to KeeRi and have never seen him. So, you may not understand why his will is law. Know that one day you will see him and understand."

His mother left the room.

Fleck had been a long-time friend of Kile. Fleck decided to sneak out to warn him.

Fleck snuck out to the minister's home and climbed the wall to Kile's room. Kile was sleeping. Fleck put his hand over Kile's mouth and tapped on his shoulder. Kile screamed but Fleck's hand muffled the sound.

"Shhh." Fleck voiced. "We must leave this place tonight. We have no time to warn anyone else."

Fleck and Kile heard screams from around the minister's house.

"What do you mean we have to leave tonight? Do you know why people are screaming?" Kile questioned.

"Your father stopped giving tithes to the Hessin. Now he wants to kill all who aided the minister, and all he loves, including you."

Tears fell down Fleck's face. He pulled Kile towards the window, but it was too late. Fleck's mother came into the room and knocked Fleck aside, then grabbed Kile.

"I thought you would try something like this. I will teach you your place, Ardan. Stand up."

Fleck stood but did not look at his mother.

"Now grab your dagger."

Fleck did nothing.

"I said. Grab your dagger!"

Fleck pulled his dagger.

"Now put it against Kile's neck."

"Don't do it, Fleck!" Kile pleaded.

Fleck's mother put her hand over Kile's mouth.

Fleck put his dagger against Kile's neck. His mother removed her hand from Kile's mouth and grabbed Fleck's hand. While Kile screamed for his life, she pulled Fleck's dagger across Kile's throat.

Blood spurted out of Kile's throat, splashing Fleck. Fleck's eyes widened. Time stopped as he watched Kile die.

His mother smiled.

"You are no longer a child. You are now a tool of the Hessin," Fleck's mother coolly stated.

"NO!" Fleck shouted, looking at Kile. "No! I will not be a tool of the Hessin, or you, or anybody. I don't need the Hessin, I don't need Kile, and I especially don't need you. I will make my own way, and I will need nobody."

Fleck ran to the window and fled into the darkness.

Chapter 24: Welcome Home

Abram, Sarai, and Fleck trekked their way to KeeRi with as few stops as possible. With the need for sleep being only a few minutes in the Bastion, they could travel day and night, stopping only for rest and food.

After a full day and night of traveling, they arrived at KeeRi. Guards paced around the perimeter. When one saw Abram and Sarai, they spoke up.

"No one but elves can enter the city of KeeRi."

Fleck moved in front of Abram and Sarai.

"The humans are with me. We wish to see the Hessin."

The guard rebuked, "No one can bring humans into KeeRi."

"I am not just a no one," Fleck sneered.

Fleck pulled back his sleeve and revealed a red dagger tattooed on his forearm. The guards whispered among themselves until one spoke up.

"We will take you to the Hessin, but I don't think he will be pleased."

The guard grabbed Fleck tightly. The other guards did the same with Sarai and Abram. They pulled the three towards the Hessin's palace.

In front of the palace was a line of elves, all waiting to see the Hessin.

A guard explained, "We will wait in line to see the Hessin."

The day rolled on. Everyone who went in seemed to come out unhappy.

The three guards and captives finally reached the front of the line and were waved in to see the Hessin.

He sat on his throne. Even though he was sitting, Abram could tell he was large for an elf in both physique and height. The Hessin wore vibrant red clothing and a necklace with a large black gem on it. The guards surrounding him wore pure black garb that shone in the light.

One of the guards leading the three walked up to the Hessin and whispered in his ear. The Hessin spoke agitated.

"I understand that you bear the insignia of the Alhar, the right hand of my will. Do you know that imitating the Alhar is a crime punishable by death? I know all in the Alhar, and you I do not recognize."

"My name is Ardan, son of Kip and Katanna. We seek aid from the elves."

"Ardan! Now that is a name I have not heard in a long time. If I remember correctly, you defied my will trying to save a boy. Brought shame to your family. But now, here you are requesting my aid. However, you will find me very forgiving. You must simply prove your loyalty to me. Kill your human friends, and then I will give you all the aid you require."

Fleck spoke up, "The aid I need is to protect myself and them. Without them, there is no need for aid."

The Hessin's nostrils flared, and an eerie purple light emanated from the gem on his necklace.

"I SAID KILL THEM!!!" he commanded.

Fleck did not budge.

"I do not know how you defy my will, but I have nothing for a traitor. Take their weapons and send them to the dungeon. They can rot there."

The guards seized all their weapons and pushed them towards the dungeon.

Chapter 25: A Promise Is a Promise

Fleck, Abram, and Sarai waited in a cell in the dungeon of KeeRi.

"So, we are captured, but still safe from Jin," Fleck mused.

"What are they going to do to us?" Sarai asked.

"More than likely, they are going to let us starve. But I have been in worse circumstances and still came out on top," Fleck gloated.

A loud bell reverberated through the city.

"What is with all the banging, Fleck?" Abram asked.

"I don't know. This is my first time in the city as well. Could be anything," Fleck admitted.

The three were looking out the window and did not notice the figure opening their cell door.

"How did you do it?" the figure asked.

Fleck turned.

"Mother."

"There is talk all around the city about your defiance of the Hessin. How did you do it?"

"Is it so strange? An elf defying the Hessin?" Fleck questioned.

"The gem on the Hessin gives him control over all elves. There should be no way that you can resist him. But that doesn't matter now. The city is under attack from a sea of trolls coming up from the south. You must head north and get out of the city."

More elves came into the cell with weapons. Fleck recognized them as his cousins.

He could not understand what they were doing.

"Why are you doing this for me, Mother? Why are you defying the Hessin? I left you so many years ago."

"With the Hessin, I have seen the elf nation grow stronger in the dark. You defied the Hessin. Maybe with your strength we can grow stronger in the light. Now go!"

The three gathered their belongings and raced out of the dungeon. Outside, they ran aimlessly through the streets, not knowing where to go. They made their way to the edge of the city through a back alley. But, as if someone knew exactly where they would be, a band of trolls came out of the woods as they approached.

There was no time to run. The trolls were moments away. Abram pulled his sword and shield and charged the largest troll, hoping to disband the other trolls in fear of his wrath. Abram ran his sword through the troll's belly. His momentum pushed the large troll onto the ground.

But the other trolls did not flee in fear. In fact, the attack sent them into a blind rage. The trolls surrounded Abram, and mercilessly banged on him. Abram's sword and shield flew away. Another troll smacked Abram on the head, knocking off his helmet and sending him tumbling to the ground. Sarai did not waste a moment. She flailed her mace at the trolls. Three Elven guards came out of the alleyway, brandishing flaming arrows in their bows.

"We have to pull Abram to safety, Fleck! Grab one of his arms and I will grab the other!" Sarai yelled to Fleck.

Fleck looked at Abram. Then he looked at Abram's sword. There were no trolls around it. They were all busy with the guards. Fleck picked up the sword, pulled his invisibility cloak over himself, and ran into the forest.

Fleck ran until the shouts were silent echoes. He pulled off his cloak and eyed the sword. He had wanted the sword from day one. A magical sword shining bright! The mint he would make from selling it.

Then Fleck thought about Abram. Abram had vouched for Fleck. Abram tried to save him from the ogres when they first met. He stopped a Foregemenaut and saved all of them. Abram was good, and as Fleck thought about him, the sword flickered. Once Fleck knew what he had to do, the sword went dark.

"Well, I'll be damned," Fleck snapped.

He ran as fast as he could back towards the city. Fleck could only hope that he was not too late.

As he came out of the woods, the sword flared up with its bright light. Fleck saw several trolls lying on the ground, smoldering. He also saw the three guards dead on the ground. Then finally, he saw Sarai defending what appeared to be Abram's dead body with three trolls closing in on her. The trolls did not see Fleck. He mustered up his courage and charged towards the middle troll. Silently, he jumped onto the troll's back, stabbing it. He flipped off and sliced the legs of the troll to his right. The sword cut through the leg as if nothing were there to block it. Fleck lunged at the last troll, stabbing it in the chest. As Fleck pulled the sword from the troll's body, the sword flamed with a blue fire.

"Is he alive?" Fleck said, concerned.

"I don't know," Sarai responded.

Fleck rushed to Abram's side.

"Come on, buddy, this is no time to take a nap."

Fleck smacked Abram's cheeks and noticed that Abram was still breathing.

Abram opened his eyes.

"You saved me, Fleck," Abram said, half in a daze.

"Yep. You're not getting out of owing me those Jaja beans, and I am sure they won't let me collect them if you are dead. But there is no time to talk. We need to get out of here."

Fleck and Sarai helped Abram up. They moved as fast as they could away from KeeRi, but before they knew it, a small troop of black-armored elves found them.

"Hessin, the two humans and the Alhar traitor have escaped from their cell," a guard shouted.

The three heard a voice of pure rage.

"Seize them. I want them alive!" The Hessin screamed.

The escapees were soon surrounded, and The Hessin burst through the guards.

"You have brought this danger to us! You have destroyed the great city of elves! I will have my revenge!!! Grab the humans! I challenge you, Ardan, to holy combat. I call upon the rite of Taknu-ra!"

The Hessin removed his necklace and shirt.

"Are you familiar with Taknu-ra, Ardan? We each receive a dagger dipped in poison. A single scratch of the blade means death. The poison takes hours to kill and causes excruciating pain. I have killed hundreds in my climb to Hessin, and I will kill hundreds more after you. Remove your armor and fight me."

The Hessin grabbed two daggers from his belt and threw one before Fleck. Fleck removed his helmet and armor and grabbed the dagger.

The Hessin cried out, beginning his assault. He was fast, and Fleck was totally unprepared for his speed. The Hessin swung a mighty fist, catching Fleck in the head, knocking him to the ground.

He mocked Fleck.

"Is that the best you have? If I had used my blade, you would already be dead. But I do not give such mercy to my adversaries. I tear my opponent apart piece by piece, then I prick them with my blade and watch them writhe in pain as the poison slowly kills them. Your death will be no different. Now get up!"

Fleck got back up on his feet and waited for The Hessin's next move. The Hessin lunged at Fleck, grabbing the forearm of Fleck's dagger hand throwing him forward. As Fleck fell, the Hessin kicked his back. Fleck tried to get up but fell down limp onto his stomach.

"Is this all you have, 'Fleck'?" The Hessin mocked. "Do you fall so easily?"

The Hessin walked over and reached down to scratch Fleck's back. Fleck burst back to life, twisting and slashing him knocking The Hessin's dagger away from him.

The Hessin noticed a warm sensation on his forehead. He put his hand to it and then looked at his hand. The Hessin began to laugh.

"You have destroyed my city, and now you have destroyed me. You outsmarted me, Fleck, but I will not be the only one to die tonight."

The Hessin picked up his dagger and raised it over his head and once again lunged at Fleck. Fleck threw his dagger, catching the Hessin in the stomach. The Hessin stopped, shocked by the dagger strike. His own dagger fell from his hand, and then The Hessin collapsed dead on the ground.

Fleck got up expecting to be impaled by the guards, but one of them came up to him. The guard grabbed Fleck's arm and yelled, "All hail the new Hessin!"

All the other guards chanted. Another guard brought The Hessin's necklace to Fleck. For a moment, Fleck considered it. What it would mean for him. The power that he would have from the moment he killed The Hessin.

"Now is not the time for a new Hessin. Now is the time all elves decide their own fate."

Fleck grabbed the enchanted gem and smashed it on a rock.

The guards were stunned.

"What will we do without the Hessin? Who will lead us?"

"The Alhar have been the right hand of The Hessin and now they will rule in his stead," Fleck answered. Then he walked over to Abram and Sarai.

"What are we going to do now, guys? It's obvious Jin will come at us no matter what," Fleck bemoaned.

"We should find my brother and hope that he can help us," Abram stated in grief.

So, the three continued their journey.

Chapter 26: The End?

Three days passed with no sign of Jin.

"I think we are at the source of the magic. The pull on the pendant is so strong here," Abram declared.

In front of them, they saw an enormous castle.

"I've never seen a castle that big," Fleck gasped.

The three got closer and closer, and the pendant's pull became stronger and stronger.

They stood in front of the castle, mouths agape at the sheer size.

Then a familiar voice came from behind them.

"You want something done right, you do it yourself!"

Abram looked back to see a large ball of fire moving towards him. Abram evaded the worst of it, but Fleck was not as lucky. The fireball erupted, blasting him into the air. Fleck slammed headfirst into the castle, knocking him unconscious.

Sarai was out of the blast radius but stood frozen, powerless.

Abram rolled out and quickly jumped to his feet, drawing his sword and shield.

Jin blasted a volley of fireballs. Abram's shield did as the dwarves said. Jin's blast veered towards the shield. Though Abram did not fear fire burning him, the explosions on his shield forced him to take a defensive position with his face behind it.

Jin, enraged by the ineffectiveness of his blasts, began creeping towards Abram. Abram was unaware of Jin's movement. He could do little other than protect his face from the blast.

When Jin was only a few steps away from Abram, Jin spoke.

"May I offer you some advice, Abram?" Jin paused and then shouted, "Never take your eye off your enemy!"

Jin ripped the shield away from Abram's arm and rasped, "Ultimate flame!!!"

Fire erupted from the ground, swallowing Abram whole.

A tear fell from Sarai's eye as she watched Abram being engulfed by the same fire that killed Corvas.

Suddenly, a blue light cut through the flame and into Jin's armor.

Jin shouted enraged, "You fool!!! You ruined my armor. Its Tangfu skin hid my magical presence from the Gods! You'll pay for this, Abram!"

A voice from beside Jin caught him by surprise.

"Jin! This is over!"

A mace slammed down on Jin's head. The sound of Jin's skull cracking could be heard far and wide.

A triumphant Sarai stood over Jin.

"You want something done right, you do it yourself," Sarai mockingly declared.

Sarai ran over to Abram and threw her arms around him.

"I thought I lost you, Abram. A thought that I found unbearable. I don't blame you for trying to give me the necklace. You were doing it for your brother. I never want to be apart from you anymore."

Abram felt peace in that moment. However, the feeling was short-lived. A shrill voice echoed from the top of the castle.

"Where is the mage? I felt his presence, then it vanished."

At the top of the castle, Abram saw a woman with bat-like wings.

Abram ran and picked up his shield and then ran over to Fleck to protect him.

The woman flew from the top of the castle to the ground below, eyeing the battlefield as she came down.

"You have killed him, worms! I could have feasted off his magical energy for years."

The beast looked directly at Abram.

"But wait." The woman screeched, pointing at Abram, "I have seen an aura like yours before, but yours is not as immense, and you are not full of magic like the one before."

The woman squealed with excitement.

"I can take you to my master and have him open a hole in the Rift, and you will fill with magic like the other one. I fed off him for so long."

"You know my brother Levi? What have you done to him? Where has he gone?"

"Levi? Is that his name? He tricked me and got away; I care not where he went. I'll kill your friends, then take you to my master!"

The woman spread her wings and shot up into the sky. With great fury, she swooped down, knocking Fleck from his place next to Abram.

The beast spoke as she hovered in the sky, "This is going to be so easy."

The beast grabbed Abram's shield from his hands. She held the shield in front of her. The beast's chest opened, and the shield glowed. Its aura drained into the heart of the beast. As the aura dissipated, the shield crumbled.

"What a nice snack!" the beast tweeted.

The monster prepared for its next strike but stopped midair. She thrashed wildly. Despite the beast's best efforts, she could not move. The beast grabbed at her throat and gagged as if an unseen force was choking her. She tried pulling away from the invisible hands. Her face turned red, and she gasped futilely. Her eyes bulged out of her head as she went limp. Sarai had to look away from the grotesque scene.

A voice came from the horizon.

"I never liked her."

Abram strained his eyes trying to see who it was, but the sun shielded the owner's identity. All Abram could make out was the silhouette of a man in scarlet armor.

"Levi...? Is that you?"

The figure came out of the sunlight.

"Yes."

Abram ran to embrace his brother, hardly taking a moment to look at him. When he did, Abram immediately noticed something was different.

"Levi. You have grown older."

"And you look like you have not aged a day. Life outside Trow had been hard on me, but worry not. I am still your brother."

Abram smiled.

"The beast threatening Trow is dead, and we have found you, Levi! Grandpa will be so pleased."

"He will. Will he not."

Levi spoke in an icy voice that Abram found a bit unsettling.

"What was that creature? It said it fed off you, but you escaped. How did you get away?"

"That was a succubus. She does not always have that vicious form. She came to me as a young woman. Offered me a kiss for my help, and that was how she ensnared me. I was trapped by her for years. She fed off my magical energy, which also caused my life essence to be drained. I knew all she wanted was magic. She ignored everything else but the source. I began storing my excess magical energy in my pendant. Through much meditation, I sealed my cut in the Rift. That is when I got her with my ruse. I said the true source of my power was in the pendant. She fell for the trick and threw me out."

"But you killed her with magic. How did you get your magic back?"

"Well, Abram, I found a group of like-minded individuals, and they opened the Rift in me again. But that is a story for another time. I am eager to get home. I think we should take care of your friends and then find our way home."

Abram breathed a sigh of relief. Jin and the rest of the journey were behind him. Now, he could relax and tend to his hurt friend. Levi and Abram were going to be home soon.

Part II:

For Trow

Chapter 1: Almost Home

Abram's excitement was boundless. He was just a few steps from Trow's forest. Victory was in his eyes when his brother made a strange request.

"Stop here for a moment," Levi insisted.

Abram stopped, and Levi walked ahead. Abram did not know why Levi wanted him to wait outside of Trow. The misadventure was over. The threat to Trow was gone. Everything Abram did to bring back his brother was done.

Levi stepped just in front of the forest and turned with a dark look on his face.

"Abram, what did Alucca give you to defend yourself?"

Abram wondered why Levi referred to Grandpa so coldly?

"Grandpa gave me nothing. He said he had nothing left to give me. The Tangfu were the ones who gave me my weapons. Grandpa did cast one spell on me."

"Alucca gave me so much power, but he had one catch. If I were tainted by the Gods, I could not find Trow."

"Grandpa cast that spell on me too. But what does that matter now? We are home, and we can go back to our old lives."

"Did you know I suffered for years under that succubus? With all the magic Alucca gave me, I was a fattened calf to her. When I finally got away from her, my memory of Trow was gone. I tried to help a creature who I thought was an innocent woman, and the penalty was never going home again. Then, when I saw you without magic, I realized something. I was the bait. I was there suffering so this succubus would not think of going to Trow again. She had everything she needed, and Alucca knew you would kill her. Still, there is one thing Alucca did not expect. I survived, and I grew stronger. Ares found me and nursed me back to health. Now, I am going to destroy this village and everything Alucca holds dear."

"Levi, you are talking madness. What of Aleese? You destroy the village, you kill her too."

"Everything Alucca holds dear will bur…"

Before Levi finished his sentence, he was struck in the back. Levi looked down at a spear protruding from his chest. He coughed blood and collapsed to the ground. The Tangfu Chieftain stood at the edge of the forest, his eyes locked onto Abram.

Abram was in shock.

"How did you do that? Why did you do that? I could have talked to him. He could have seen reason… I could have stopped him! He did not need to die!"

Abram looked at Levi's crumpled lifeless body. Unmoved by the sight, the Chieftain addressed Abram.

"Your adventure is not done. I cannot be sure whether your brother has contacted Ares. If he has, then Trow is not safe. You must seek help. The only thing that can save us from a God is a more powerful God. Seek Aphrodite. She and Ares have always been at odds. We may use their hatred of each other. But we will have to prepare you. The Gods do not lend their power to those they find weak, and you can no longer trust just magical items. You must pull on the same primal energy that feeds the Gods. We must open the Rift within you. We have a relic that can do so."

"But if I accept this power, will I not die faster? Will I no longer be able to have children? How will I stop myself from being tainted like my brother?" pleaded Abram.

"None of that will matter if we wait for Ares to come and kill us. You are destined for greater things. Now sleep."

The Chieftain blew a powder at Abram, and he fell to the ground asleep.

Chapter 2: While You Were Sleeping

Abram woke up in agonizing pain. He was on a bed with the Chieftain standing over him.

"What have you done to me?" Abram demanded.

The Chieftain lit a bundle of herbs. The aroma of the herbs calmed Abram but did little for the pain.

"We had to put you to sleep. The pain from opening the Rift in you would have been too much for you to take. You would have passed out from the pain or worse. Your spirit could have left your body during the process. We put you to sleep for your safety."

"The Rift is open in me…? Does that mean I am a mage? But what of the curse on mages?"

"We had no choice but to force this upon you. The threat is too great. The only way that you can face your new foe is with magic."

"But will I age faster? Will I not be able to have a child?"

"The pendant will make the speed of your aging negligible, and the needs of Trow outweigh your own."

Abram stood up.

"The needs of Trow…" Abram paused.

Abram felt pushed into a fate that he had no choice but to accept.

How could they do this to me? Abram thought.

"Come now, Abram. We must see how the power of the Rift manifested in you."

The Chieftain led Abram to a clearing in the forest. Fleck and Sarai were waiting there. Targets were at the opposite end of the field. Abram clearly saw that the Tangfu used this space as a range.

"Good to see you made it," Fleck said, winking at Abram.

"They let us see the opening of the Rift. Your body quivered violently. I was worried you would not live through it," Sarai confessed. "But you are alive!"

The Chieftain turned to Abram.

"Abram, I need you to concentrate on the target at the other end. You will feel energy flowing through you. Do not block it. Imagine it going through you to your hands."

Abram looked at the target and put one hand towards it. At first, Abram felt nothing, but as he concentrated, he felt a force flowing from his stomach to his hand.

Abram called out, "Phantom light!"

Abram's hand began to glow, and shortly after, a ball of white light traveled from Abram's hand to the target.

Abram's spirit perked up. He felt he could forget the tribulations of being a mage and embrace his new life. Abram looked to the Chieftain for approval, but the Chieftain looked grave.

"Phantom light has manifested in you. The seed will always hit your target but will do little damage. The power fires rapidly and can distract another target, but the light will give away your position if you are careless."

The Chieftain looked towards the targets.

"Abram, I want you to well the energy in your stomach, then release it through both your hands at all six targets."

Abram lifted both of his hands towards the targets. He felt the energy in his stomach. He let the power sit and grow, then pushed it to his hands, calling out, "Phantom light. Phantom cover."

Abram's hands grew white, and seven balls of light erupted from his hands, striking the middle target twice and all the others once. But something else strange happened.

Abram disappeared. Fleck and Sarai hooted wildly, but the expression of the Chieftain did not change.

"Why aren't you happy? He fired multiple shots and look! He disappeared as well." Sarai pleaded.

The Chieftain answered, "The damage he can inflict is still little. His disappearance is only of his physical form, which will make him invisible to normal eyes. However, any creature that can see magical energy will still see him. He could get past them only if they were not paying attention. We must continue testing your skills. You must have manifested a power that could increase your chances of success."

Abram continued testing his powers, but no new magic came from it. Abram fell into a deep depression.

Chapter 3: The Road Ahead

Abram woke up the next day before the sun came up. He had a sinking feeling. His brother was dead. He now had magical powers, a curse he had never asked for, and now he had a more dangerous task than finding his brother.

The Chieftain told Abram he would fill him in on the plan today. Abram slowly made his way to the Chieftain's hut. Fleck and Sarai were already there. The Chieftain spoke.

"Ares has made his presence known. The body of your brother's body has gone missing. We believe Ares will arrive in force soon. We have no choice but to seek the aid of another God." The Chieftain elaborated, "We must seek the aid of a greater God, one that may listen to us. The Tangfu have a long history of shielding the magic city of Eglasia for Aphrodite. She may now listen to our pleas and choose to aid us. She could provide us with more mages and the Dunwi, magical beasts that protect Eglasia. They would be more than enough to quell any forces that Ares sends. We pray Ares does not come to aid the fight."

"I need to go tell my mother about Levi. I need to see my family!"

"There is no time, and you have only been missing in Trow for a short while. I am sure Alucca has already fabricated a reason for your absence. We will update him on our current situation. For Trow, you must go now. Eglasia is a flying city. We know the city is close, but we cannot be sure of the exact location. We can give you Greymeer wolves to quickly close the distance between our two cities. Their fast speed will be invaluable to you. However, when you meet Aphrodite, you must say nothing of Alucca. The Gods know of Alucca. He represents a threat to all of them, and they may not help you if they know of his involvement."

The Chieftain beckoned them to follow him outside. Weights filled the Abram's feet felt weighed down by dread. He was the last one to leave the Chieftain's hut.

"The Greymeer wolves will be a great asset to you. They can travel three times faster than any horse. We can tell you that Eglasia is to the south, and we can give you this gem. The gem grows brighter when it is close to Eglasia. It will also give you the ability to blink into Eglasia. Don't lose this gem or you will have to find an alternate way to get into Eglasia, and you have no time for that."

Sarai and Fleck felt confident in their mission. They had a secret that would let them find Eglasia faster. They had the compass from the dwarves. The only worry for the two was the turmoil Abram felt. They could tell Abram was being torn apart from the inside.

"Abram, I know you lost your brother, but we are here for you. We are like family. We will save your village," Sarai assured.

Abram faked a smile. He had nothing left to give.

The three mounted their Greymeer wolves, and Sarai asked Fleck to get the compass ready. The compass gave a heading, and with that, the three were off to save Trow. Abram looked back once again. Homesick and downtrodden, he longed to be home.

Chapter 4: Trouble in the Woods

The Greymeer wolves were everything the Chieftain said. Their speed was incredible. The three travelers had to hold tight and stay low on the back of the wolves. In a short time, the gem glowed. The three stopped a moment to get the heading from the compass.

"We can't be far from Eglasia. Look how bright the gem glows," Sarai noted.

"The compass has not changed its heading. Eglasia should be straight ahead," Fleck added.

From behind the party, there was a loud snap. The wolves growled, and suddenly, from all directions came ogres, goblins, and other creatures of the night. A lone human appeared in front of the party carrying a strange artifact.

"Allow me to introduce myself. I am Lamund, second in command next to Jin. You may not know me, but I know you well. I shared a link to Jin. I could see all that Jin saw. He was interested in you, and I saw you in his last moments. I applaud your efforts. I too plotted his death in my mind, but had no way to execute it, because he saw what I did as well. Jin could see everything all his three lieutenants were doing. But in his death, I have flourished. There is a grab for power, and I am mostly on top. I know that when I kill the three who killed Jin, I will cement my place as the leader of his fallen empire.

I see you are curious about how I ambushed you? That's my little secret. Also, don't think the magic weapons or whatever powers you have will save you. This Tanton I have nullifies any magic. Your end is certain."

Abram pulled his sword, but it did not glow. The outcome looked bleak. The three dismounted their wolves and went back-to-back, readying themselves for the fight.

"Whatever you have is not enough to take us down!" Fleck jeered.

"We will see. Attack them!" Lamund commanded.

The beasts charged in. An ogre was the first to strike. It raised his sword and attacked Sarai. Sarai did the unexpected. She charged the ogre. Stabbed her mace like a sword at the ogre's face, Sarai smashed it with the tip of her mace. The beastly creature lost its footing and dropped its sword.

Sarai took this as an opportunity to slam down her mace on the ogre's head. Then she fell back into their circle.

All the creatures were stunned by her vicious attack and hesitated, waiting for another of their party to attack. But none did. Lamund was furious.

"There are only three of them. Attack!" Lamund cried.

The creatures then came en masse. Six ogres charged the party. Three on Sarai, two on Abram and one on Fleck. Fleck darted around the ogre coming after him and stabbed it in the back. With great quickness, he went to aid Sarai. Sarai unleashed a heavy swing at one ogre, catching it by surprise. Sending it spinning into one of the other ogres, knocking them to the ground. The third froze in fear. Sarai smacked her hand with her mace, which sent the shell-shocked ogre running. The two ogres on Abram simply ran away at the sight of the heroes' deadly power.

Once again, the monsters hesitated, but this time they began howling and barking. From the crowd of monster, came eight trolls, pushing their way to the three humans.

"This doesn't look good. Trolls don't go down without a little fire or a magical weapon, of which we have none," Fleck interjected.

At Fleck's last word, an immense object flew towards Lamund, striking and shattering the Tanton. Abram's sword erupted into a low blue flame.

"Now's our chance!" Sarai shouted.

The three widened the circumference of their circle, slashing at the trolls before them. Only one troll dared stay. It grabbed for Abram, who swung his sword in a circle, slicing off both of the troll's arms.

Lamund quickly joined the ranks of the retreating monsters.

"This isn't over. We will succeed where Jin failed!" Lamund taunted.

Fleck pulled a dagger from his belt and smoothly threw it at Lamund. The dagger landed in his back. He stumbled and fell.

The three cautiously walked to Lamund. Before they reached the body, they could tell that the throw was fatal. Lamund laid on his stomach gasping for air. Sarai flipped him onto his back. Lamund winced as he rolled over, cursing them as the dagger was pushed deeper into his back.

"This changes nothing…." Lamund wheezed, "You were dead… the moment you killed Jin. You are just prolonging the inevitable…"

Lamund shut his eyes, convulsed, and then died.

"Down one lieutenant, two to go," Sarai chirped confidently.

Abram did not share her optimism. This journey was getting harder and harder. This fight resolved nothing. His brother's body was missing, now he had Jin's followers to worry about, and he still had to convince Aphrodite to protect his village without mentioning his Grandpa. All before Ares destroyed his home.

How could this get worse? Abram thought.

"Giants!" Fleck shrieked.

When Abram looked back, he saw two female giants moving into the clearing from behind some trees. One of them spoke.

"Please believe me. We come in peace. We saw your predicament and came to your aid."

"What is your purpose here, GIANTS!?!! How do we know you are not one of Jin's lackeys looking to make a name for yourself?" cried Fleck.

"We know not Jin!" the larger giant spouted.

"Calm down for a moment, everybody," Sarai soothed. "Tell us why you are here."

"We are here because of our father's dying wish. An evil shaman cursed the giants. We now shrink with every new generation. The shaman wanted us to attack a settlement. Our clan had found peace with the humans there and wanted nothing to do with the shaman's request. For our opposition, the shaman cursed us. In only three generations, our mighty clan is now smaller than the trees."

Our father took us, his two daughters, to search for answers in the east. He feared for our safety and left us with monks who kindly offered to care for us and train us in combat. Our father continued his journey. Several years went by with no word from him. The better part of four years had passed when we received a letter from our mother. Father had made it home but was mad with fever. Mother could make little of what he was saying. The only thing she could say for sure is that he had found a cure. Aphrodite's tears can clear any curse. Now we know what we have to do. We must find Aphrodite and beseech her to lift our curse.

The monks had little to give us. They gave us rations and a lucky talisman. They said to trust in ourselves and the talisman and we would be successful. We traveled for a few months with little to go on, but we were down by the river praying for a sign when we overheard you talking about finding Aphrodite. The two of us have been following you ever since. We knew this was our chance. The talisman had led us where we needed to be. We must join your party and make the trip to Aphrodite together."

The giant gasped, "We have given you our story, but we haven't even introduced ourselves. I am Layla and this is Kya, of clan Alistar."

"Wait a minute!" Fleck interrupted, "You want us to believe that you are full-grown giants that have made peace with humans, lived with monks, and don't want to eat every creature in sight? What kind of trick are you pulling? You are probably going to lead us to a trap!"

"Fleck! They seem to want to follow us, not to lead us to a trap. If you ask me, we could use the extra muscle," Sarai said glibly.

"Don't tell me you are falling for this too, Abram?" Fleck deflected.

"I don't think we're in a position to turn down any help." Abram conceded.

"Maybe we should ask those nice trolls if they want to join our party as well," Fleck mocked, "Be ready for an 'I told you so' when they try to eat us in our sleep."

Fleck kicked some rocks and grabbed his Greymeer wolf by the reins.

"The compass's heading has not changed. Eglasia should be a straight shot from here," Fleck snapped. "Did the Chieftain explain how the gem works?"

Abram walked over to Sarai and grabbed the gem.

"He said the gem was a one-way trip. To activate it, you simply hold the gem over your head like this and say intrare…"

Before Abram could say another word, fire engulfed him and left nothing but smoke where he stood.

"I'm not touching that!" Fleck quipped.

"Come on, Fleck, we can't leave Abram by himself," Sarai retorted.

Sarai picked up the gem and spoke intrare, and she disappeared into smoke as well.

The two giants were next to grab the gem. The Greymeer wolves and Fleck were the only ones left. Fleck looked at the Greymeer wolves.

"You think they would mind if I stayed here and watched you?"

The wolves gave Fleck a puzzled look.

"Ah! The things I do for these so-and-sos. Intrare!"

Chapter 5: Are we there yet?

Abram stood up, disoriented and stiff.

"Sarai, Fleck, Layla Kya."

"My sister and I are here, but I know not of your friends."

"Where are we?" Abram questioned.

"It appears we are in a back alley in Eglasia. I assume."

"We should make our way towards the city center and locate Aphrodite," Abram observed.

The three made their way out of the alley. What Abram saw amazed him.

"I've never seen so many beautiful people."

Abram bumped into a citizen of Eglasia and received a strange welcome.

"Get a mask, trash!"

The citizen spat on the ground in front of Abram.

"What a weird greeting." Abram observed, "We need to find Fleck and Sarai. Maybe somebody has seen them. We should ask around."

Abram and the giants began asking citizens of Eglasia if they had seen an elf and a red-haired woman. No one would talk to them. The people yelled slurs. For a good five minutes, they tried to get the attention of an Eglasian citizen. It was not long before a citizen walked up to Abram with three masks.

"Your appearance is dreadful. Put these on."

"Please, sir. Have you seen an elf and a red-haired woman?"

"It looks like they are being taken to the Hall of Aphrodite."

Abram looked behind him and saw Fleck and Sarai being carried off by a throng of people.

"Why are they parading them? Where are they taking them?" Abram inquired.

"Probably taking them to the hall of Aphrodite to be sacrificed," the man responded nonchalantly.

Abram turned to Layla and Kya.

"We need to follow that parade."

"You'll never make it to her. Lower enders are not to be anywhere near the hall of Aphrodite," the man responded.

"What are lower enders?" Abram asked.

"The dreadfully ugly citizens that have to wear plain masks, like you," the man added and walked off.

"What are we going to do? We have to save Fleck and Sarai, but we are not allowed near them."

Layla put her hand in her pocket and pulled out a bird's leg marked by inscriptions.

"We must trust the talisman." Layla stated.

"I don't think that leg was lucky for the bird, and I don't see how it will be lucky for us," Abram barked.

A man approached Abram.

"Did I overhear you need to go to Aphrodite's Hall? You can not get near with lower ender's masks."

Abram was dumbfounded. Did the talisman work? He thought.

"Yes, we need to get to the Hall," Layla confessed.

"Follow me," the man insisted.

The man led them back to the alley.

"I have masks in my possession that are only worn by the gentry of Eglasia. I will trade it with you."

"What do you want in trade?" Abram asked.

"That helmet of yours. It's dwarven?"

"Yes."

"Is it magical?"

"It protects the mind of the wielder from magic."

"Give me the helmet, and I will give you these masks."

Abram did not trust the man. Abram cracked his sword from its hilt and saw just what he suspected. Even with only a sliver visible, Abram saw the blue hue of his glowing sword.

"What guarantee do we have that these helmets will get us into the hall of Aphrodite? Where did you get them from?"

"You'll be amazed what people trade in desperation, and I see a fruitful association with you."

Abram weighed his options. He had to get to Sarai and Fleck, but had no other option other than these masks. Abram had to take the chance.

"I see no option right now," Abram agreed.

Abram took off his helmet, gave it to the man and in return, the man gave Abram three masks.

Abram took the lead and ran into the crowd with Layla and Kya following him. Abram could barely push through the crowd.

"We will never make it in time at this rate," Abram despaired.

"Maybe we should take the lead," Layla added.

The two giants stepped in front of Abram.

"Excuse us!" Layla shouted as she parted the people like blades of grass.

The pushing aggravated the people, but when they turned to see the eleven-foot-tall giants; they fell silent. In a short while, Fleck and Sarai were in view, chained to two crosses.

Abram saw Sarai struggling against the chains as Fleck tried to talk his way out of the predicament. A priest was preparing a knife. Abram was only a few yards away, and Fleck and Sarai were only moments away from being sacrificed.

"We have to move faster," Abram shouted.

"Kya and I have an idea," Layla yelled back.

Kya bent low and jumped forward. She landed on top of the priest, knocking him unconscious. Kya pulled off the chains that restrained Fleck and Sarai.

Abram made his way to his companions. He looked back and forth for a way out, but there were people everywhere in front of them.

"There!" Abram pointed. "We will go through those doors and blockade them behind us. We can only hope no one is inside. We can come up with a plan from there."

The five made their way to the door. Inside there were two heavy statues on either side of the door. Kya and Layla pushed them over, blocking the door.

"That should hold them off for a while," Layla said, dusting her hands off.

"Where are we?" Sarai asked.

Behind them, a voice rang out.

"The throne room of Aphrodite."

The five looked behind them, and there stood the most beautiful woman any of them had ever seen.

"Aphrodite is my name. I do not know how you deceived your way into my hall with such ridiculous masks, but you have not deceived me."

Abram slipped his sword from its sheath. The sword glowed bright blue. Abram could not believe their bad luck.

"Aphrodite, we came here to ask for your help," Sarai pleaded. Sarai pointed to Abram.

"Abram's village is under threat from Ares. We are not sure if his people can defend themselves against him."

Aphrodite looked shrewdly at Abram, then laughed.

"This woman speaks for you, Abram. I can tell you are fond of her, but so is the elf."

Abram could feel his will being twisted, and jealousy filled him. He slowly turned around and looked at Fleck.

"Yes, Abram," Aphrodite laughed, "Make her yours and yours alone."

Abram charged with his sword in hand towards Fleck, attacking him with a sweeping strike that nearly took off hiss head.

"What are you doing, Abram? We are on the same team."

Fleck dodged a volley of Abram's blows.

"Abram what…?" Sarai tried to speak, but suddenly could not. Aphrodite smiled.

"You wear my sigil, girl. There is nothing you can do that I do not allow."

Sarai watched the fight, frozen. Fleck tried to talk sense into Abram, but nothing slowed his fury. Abram was in a pure rage.

"Come on, Abram! Don't make me do something I will regret!" Fleck urged.

Sarai struggled to say something. As she struggled, her sigil burned. The skin of her sigil boiled until the sigil was gone.

"Abram, I love you! Not Fleck! I want to always be with you!"

The spectacle amazed Aphrodite.

"You…love…me?" Abram stuttered.

Abram stopped fighting Fleck and turned to Sarai. Sarai ran and threw her arms around Abram.

"I love you. I love you so much," Sarai said, teary-eyed.

A calm fell over Abram. For a moment, he forgot his troubles and looked forward to the future.

"You dare defy a God!" Aphrodite shouted.

The group prepared for the worst, brandishing their weapons, but then a smile came over Aphrodite's face.

"Maybe there is a way you can be of use to me. You have proven yourself to be quite tenacious. We may have a common enemy. As of late, Ares and Hades have been seen together often. I fear what the two have planned. Their cooperation could mean trouble for me. I wish to level the playing field and strike first. Hades has a precious stone that gives him power over the souls of the dead, the Neccrum. I wish for you to steal it. This will not be easy. No one knows where Hades hides the Neccrum. Whatever magic you used to find my city may be useless, because it is believed to be outside this realm. Seek Hades's head mage, Ren. You must force the information out of him."

Layla then spoke up.

"Aphrodite, we also beseech you."

"Are you with them?" Aphrodite asked.

"We have come to their aid," Layla responded.

"Help them find the Neccrum and I will help you as well," Aphrodite quipped.

Aphrodite waved her hand, and a black orb surrounded the party. The black orb dissipated, and they were back where they had left the Greymeer wolves.

"Now what?" Fleck questioned.

"I guess we look for Ren," Sarai responded.

"And what about the giants? We have only three Greymeers. Not that they are small enough to ride one. Not that I trust them," Fleck stated.

"We can run, and we mean no harm," Layla assured.

"Well then, I guess it's settled. Fleck, ask the compass where to go," Sarai chimed.

"I don't like this, but what am I to do?" Fleck admitted.

Chapter 6: A Sad Realization

Day one of the trip was uneventful. Night came upon the party, and everyone retired to their tents.

"Abram?"

A soft voice whispered from outside Abram's tent.

"Sarai? What is it?" Abram inquired.

"I was lying in my tent alone, and I realized I don't want to be alone anymore. Can I sleep in your tent?"

Her question made Abram overjoyed. He had always wanted to get closer to Sarai.

"Yes," Abram responded, hoping not to sound too excited.

Sarai pulled the covers over her and got close to Abram.

"Comfortable?" Abram said bashfully.

"Yes," Sarai replied.

Abram set his head on his pillow, and the two lay quietly, but Sarai had a burning question and broke the silence.

"Abram. Have you ever wanted a family?"

Once again, Abram bubbled over with joy at her inquiries. Then a realization hit him, and Abram sobbed.

"I can't have a family," Abram replied.

"Why not?" Sarai questioned.

"Mages cannot have children." Abram said tearfully.

"Sh," Sarai responded, "All I want is you."

The two lay in silence for a minute.

"Marry me," Abram said

"Do you mean it?"

"Marry me," Abram replied once more.

Sarai did not answer. Abram did not know if she really did not want to marry him, or if she was purposefully putting him in agony.

Sarai smiled and practically shouted, "Yes!"

Abram kissed Sarai, and she smiled even more.

"We don't have to be alone anymore," Sarai assured.

A voice from outside came to break the moment.

Fleck shouted, "Are the two of you done? Can we get some sleep now?"

Abram and Sarai turned bright red.

"How long were they listening?" Sarai belted.

"No! It's beautiful. Let them talk."

"Is that you, Kya? You talk?" Fleck said in disbelief.

Stark silence met Fleck's attempt to pry words from Kya. The happy moment passed, and soon the party went to sleep.

Chapter 7: Boom Town

The next few days passed uneventfully.

"Sarai! Abram! Hold up for a moment!"

The party came to a stop, and Sarai and Abram looked towards Fleck.

"What is it, Fleck?" Sarai asked.

Fleck appeared to be very excited.

"I know where we are! We are only a little way from Boom Town! We have to go!" Fleck assured.

"Fleck, I don't know. We don't have time to go out of our way," Abram replied.

"No. We can't be more than a forty minutes' walk, even faster on these Greymeers. Look. Boom Town is a magical town. A building marvel that has never been seen anywhere else. Beds softer than down feathers, and the city is surrounded by an impenetrable wall. I know the Bastion warns us of danger, but wouldn't you like to sleep where you are totally safe? Plus, you could get married there!" Fleck pleaded.

"And they have a good bit of gambling," Fleck muttered under his breath.

"I am tired of sleeping on the floor," Sarai agreed. "The sooner we get married, the better!"

"I guess it is decided. We go to Boom Town," Abram conceded.

"I can't wait until you see this town!" Fleck happily spouted as they approached Boom Town.

"It's just..." Fleck stopped as he looked at Boom Town.

Something decimated Boom Town. There were no buildings left. Everything was rubble and burnt ash.

The party began ride through the rubble.

Women, children, animals--- no one was spared the wrath of this unseen force.

"What happened here?" Sarai questioned as tears flooded her eyes.

"I don't know," Fleck responded in disbelief. "This was supposed to be the safest city anywhere."

Up ahead, they saw a lone man going through the rubble.

"Sir, what happened here?" Abram asked.

The man was crying.

"They came. An entire army unlike anything I have ever seen. A man in red armor led the army. They came up to the wall. We readied the army at the front gate. No one thought they stood a chance of breaking the wall. But the man in red armor raised his hands, and out came a wave of energy that smashed down the wall. I was there on the wall when it happened. The blast pushed me a hundred yards and knocked me unconscious. When I came to, rubble had buried me. I don't know how I survived. I woke to ash and destruction, and I wanted to leave, but I don't know where is safe. Now, I've been rummaging through the ash for food and warning everyone who comes about the army. Nowhere is safe now."

"Could that man have been your brother, Abram?" Sarai asked.

Abram was still shocked by the story. A man who could be Levi was leading an unstoppable army. How could his brother be alive? What could do this much devastation? What chance did he have of stopping this army from destroying Trow? More questions. More uncertainties. More problems on his mind.

"Abram, are you going to be alright?" Fleck added after a long moment.

"Yes."

That was all Abram could say. He did not know whether he was going to be alright.

"Here."

Abram retrieved a pack from the saddlebag on his Greymeer wolf and handed it to the man.

"These are Jaja beans. They will feed you for a while."

Abram turned away.

"We should go," Abram said morosely.

No safe bed, no impenetrable wall, no buzzing city, and another day not married to the one he loved. The only thing Abram could do was move ahead of the others, so they did not see his tears.

Chapter 8: Dead End

The party rode away from Boom Town for three days with no sign of Ren. They knew Ren was on the move because the heading on the compass changed.

On day four, the party saw fire coming from the outskirts of a forest. The compass trajectory did not change. They had found Ren, but they were not sure of what else they would find.

Abram looked towards the giants.

"You and your sister stay here. We will scout ahead," Abram insisted.

Fleck, Sarai, and Abram moved to the edge of the forest. They saw thousands of men all adorned with Hades' sigil.

"This must be the group that attacked Boom Town. We must make them pay," Fleck sneered.

"We are not here to avenge Boom Town. We need to find Ren and find out where the Neccrum is. There is nothing we can do about Boom Town. We may still save Trow. We will have to sneak in during the night and find Ren," Abram expressed.

The three dropped back and rallied with the giants.

"I am afraid you are going to have to sit this one out, ladies," Sarai reported.

"We cannot fight off the horde of men there. We are going to have to sneak in, grab Ren, and take him to a place where we can interrogate him." Abram observed.

"Then you agree we do not come?" Layla inquired.

"Yes. You backstabbing giants will have to find another way to kill us," Fleck scowled.

"Fleck! They already saved us twice," Sarai interjected.

Layla and Kya exchanged a look but did not respond.

Later that night, Abram, Sarai, and Fleck crept to the edge of the forest. They could barely see anything. The stars provided just enough to make out the silhouettes of tents. But no one appeared to be near them.

"So, this is the plan?" Fleck asked.

Neither Abram nor Sarai said anything.

"That's what I was afraid of," Fleck said forlornly.

Abram slipped his sword out of its sheath to confirm his suspicions. The sword glowed.

"Here, Abram. Bring that a little closer so I can see the compass."

Fleck got their heading, and they tiptoed into the camp.

The three were several minutes in when Fleck stopped Sarai and Abram.

"No lights. No guards. What's their deal? Do they know something we don't? We are deep in the camp. Should we be thinking of Plan B?" Fleck whispered.

Abram and Sarai shook their heads uneasily.

"I don't have a different plan," Abram whispered back.

So, the three continued on until they came to a large tent far into the camp.

Fleck put his head into the tent.

"The tent is pitch black. Abram, when we are in, pull your sword. Sarai and I will have to locate and gag Ren before he can call for help."

Abram nodded his head, and they stepped into the tent, being sure to close and secure the tent flap behind them.

Abram pulled his sword, and light poured onto Ren. The sight of his condition staggered them. He stood in a meditative trance. Fleck stepped over to Ren and waved his hand in front of Ren's face.

"He's out of it," Fleck confirmed. "Abram, get your rope and tie him up."

A sinister smile came over Ren.

"Good evening, visitors. You have foolishly wandered into the Red Army of Hades. For what I do not know, but you will not be leaving this camp," Ren mocked.

"No. We are getting out of this camp, and we are taking you with us or turning you into a pincushion," Fleck affirmed.

Ren roared with laughter.

"You threaten a disciple of Hades with death. We look forward to our death. It is at the end of this life and the beginning of our true life with Hades."

The three looked at each other nervously.

"Tie him up, Abram," Fleck spouted in a panic.

Abram knocked Ren down and threw the rope over him.

"Tie," Abram commanded, and the rope twisted around Ren.

"More people are coming! We need a distraction." Fleck anxiously whispered while looking around.

He spotted a pan of oil.

"Perfect," Fleck said with intent.

Fleck threw the oil pan at the back of the tent and quickly lit it.

"Fire! Fire! Fire!" Fleck shouted.

"Let's get out of here," Abram piped.

The three ran from the tent, trying to stay out of the fire's light. The night was their shield, and as long as they stuck to the darkness, they were certain they could make it. But they had run directly onto a main thruway. Soldiers carrying torches were rallying around them. They saw no way out as the soldiers continued to surround them.

Just then, a loud cry echoed in front of them. Torches flew into the air. Men screamed as the silhouettes of two giants appeared in the distance.

The three kidnappers did not waste this opportunity. They ran towards the giants.

"How did you know where to find us?" Abram asked.

"We followed the lucky talisman!" Layla exclaimed.

Kya ran over to Abram and Sarai, who were struggling to carry Ren. Kya grabbed Ren and threw him over her back.

Arrows whizzed by them.

"We need to get to the Greymeers! That's our only chance to outrun them!"

The group raced towards the Greymeers. The arrows continued to whiz by, and sorcerers joined the fight, throwing magic at the party. Lightning and fire filled the night sky. But the trio got to their Greymeer wolves and raced away through the night.

Fleck laughed and hollered.

"We made it!" he shouted. "Now we just need to pick Ren's brain."

When the group arrived at a safe location, they stopped. Layla walked over to Kya to look at Ren.

"It looks like we were too late," Layla said angered "Ren's head has already been picked."

Kya put Ren on the ground, and everyone saw an arrow through Ren's eye.

"Do you think they did that on purpose?" Sarai asked.

"They aren't taking down any more big cities with him gone. That means Trow as well," Fleck said, trying to console everyone.

Abram did not have any words. They had stopped Ren, but what was stopping Hades from finding another mage? They could do the same to Trow as they did to Boom Town. He felt he was no closer to saving Trow. He had to find the Neccrum!

"Abram, are you still with us? You are staring out into the distance. Look, we will find the Neccrum. Aphrodite will protect Trow."

Fleck appeared to be certain and sincere, but Abram was not sure if it would be that easy. Finding the Neccrum and giving it to Aphrodite seemed impossible and dangerous. The sword glowed in the presence of Aphrodite. She might take the Neccrum and kill them all. She might discover the truth about Alucca and destroy the city herself. Nothing was easy. Nothing was straightforward. Abram had to deceive a God about Alucca's existence. He did not even know if that was possible.

"Abram, we are probably asking the compass the wrong questions. Let's just ask it where the Neccrum is," Fleck suggested.

Fleck picked up the compass. "Where is the Neccrum?" he asked.

The compass needle spun around wildly.

"Where is Hades?" Fleck continued.

The needle continued to spin wildly.

"Where is the path to the Neccrum?"

The needle stopped for a moment and shot straight north.

"What did I say, Abram? You've just got to ask it the right question. The frozen North, here we come!" Fleck cheered.

Abram still did not feel like rejoicing, but he faked a smile just the same.

Chapter 9: The Walls Have Eyes

"Hermes! Son! What news have you for me?"

"Mighty Zeus…"

"Please call me Father. You are always so formal."

"Yes, father. A small band, including two giants, has left Eglasia in search of the Neccrum. Aphrodite instructed them to bring it to her."

"The Neccrum! The source of Hades's power and the device that gives him control of the souls of the dead. To what end?"

"Aphrodite's intentions are unknown, but she would gain enormous power with it and may challenge your rule."

"I don't think Aphrodite would be so bold, but if that artifact should go to anyone, it should be me. You said they had two giants in their party. Giants are loyal to me. Perhaps if they should get the Neccrum, I can convince the giants to give it to me."

"Father, if the giants gave the Neccrum to you, can you imagine the power you would have? You would have total supremacy. With the energy of the faithful and the Neccrum's forces, you would have powers greater than Ares when he had the twenty as his mages."

"That was a waste of strength. So much power for a god who had no vision. But I have heard that Ares is up to something. He has been seen with Hades. What do you know of that?"

"The business between Ares and Hades is still a mystery, but their visits have become more frequent."

"What these two are doing and why Aphrodite wants the Neccrum are of the utmost importance. Keep your eye on all of them."

"Yes, Father."

Chapter 10: The Forest That Never Sleeps

"Hold up, everybody!" Fleck shouted.

The party was on the edge of a dark forest that not even the noon sun could brighten. Its eerie silence put the party on edge.

"I know this forest. This is no normal forest. It is The Forest that Never Sleeps. Creatures haunt it night and day. They say that if you go into this forest, tiny creatures whisper in your ear until you go mad," Fleck warned. "Here. Put this cotton into your ears."

"We ride into this carefully." Abram said, troubled. "We don't know what we are going to see. Best to be on our guard."

The party entered the woods. Abram and the others kept their heads on a swivel, but in the darkness, they saw very little.

A loud crack broke the silence. An unseen force knocked Fleck off his Greymeer, throwing him into a tree.

A sinister voice spoke in the darkness.

"You were unwise to come here, but I am glad you did. You do not know me, but I know you well. Lamund told you a little about me because I am one of Jin's lieutenants. I know you killed him, but I will not be so easy to kill, especially in this forest. For you see, the mystical creatures of the forest listen to me. I can have them kill you and never show myself. Though you will not live long to speak it, my name is Showlar. Now, creatures of the forest, attack!"

Upon Showlar's command, unseen creatures scratched and pulled at the party's faces and armor. Abram and the others swung their weapons wildly at the invisible attackers to no avail. The creatures knocked Abram and Sarai off their Greymeers, and all the wolves reared up and ran away. Abram reached for his sword, but a creature pinned his arm to the ground.

"Everyone close your eyes," Abram shouted. He raised his free arm and commanded his magic, "Blinding light!!!"

White light beamed from his hand, blinding all the creatures surrounding them. He heard them falling to the ground. Abram jumped to his feet.

"Phantom light!"

Abram watched the ball of light heading further into the forest. Abram followed. In the distance, he saw a woman. Abram rushed at the woman, stabbing at her belly.

Blood spurted from the woman's mouth. She chuckled.

"You are getting good at killing, Abram. I guess I stood no more chance than Lamund. Maybe with the third it will be different. Goodbye, Abram."

Showlar fell backwards as Abram's sword slipped from her stomach.

Abram paled and felt himself go cold. He did not consider himself a killer, but death had seemed to follow him since he had left Trow. Abram was not sure he liked what he had become.

"Abram! Are you hurt!?!" Sarai said, concerned for her future husband.

Abram felt hurt in his heart.

"No," Abram said, holding back tears.

"That light. How did you know you could do that?"

"I didn't."

Sarai bit her lip.

"Did anybody see which way the Greymeers went? Are we hoofing it now? That's going to make our trip longer and more dangerous," Fleck worried.

"We should hurry. The sooner we are out of this forest, the better," Fleck said.

Chapter 11: Further into the Forest

Without the Greymeers, the party was forced to walk. In the thick forest, traveling on the wolves was slow, but walking on foot was even slower.

Layla felt their low morale, but she was confident.

"We have nothing to fear. We put our faith in the talisman, and we will be good."

"Well, it worked in the Red Army camp. Maybe it will work here." Fleck chuckled.

Everyone but Layla realized Fleck was joking. However, the group had a laugh, and the gesture still did what she wanted.

But unbeknownst to them, a chilling wind blew from behind the party that hid a small unseen creature, the mind eater.

The creature tugged out the cotton in Kya's ear and whispered to her, "They are against you."

Kya abruptly stopped and twisted her body as if she was being stabbed throughout.

"Kya, are you okay?" Layla said, worried for her sister.

Layla put her hand on Kya. Kya threw a two-handed swing at Layla, roaring as she rolled.

She then charged Abram. In one powerful movement, she tossed him into a tree.

"Kya must be under the spell of a forest creature." Fleck realized. "The only way we can stop her rage is to kill the creature attacking her mind. Abram, use your Phantom Light."

No words met Fleck's request. Abram was unconscious. Fleck smacked Abram in the face.

"Come on, buddy. Wakey, wakey."

Abram stayed unconscious.

"Anybody have an idea of how to kill an invisible creature!?!" Fleck said emphatically.

"I have an idea!" Layla shouted, "Sarai! Distract Kya!"

Sarai took off in a sprint towards Kya, smacking Kya in the back. The enraged Kya turned to Sarai, barely batting an eye.

"Oh, shoot!" Sarai exclaimed. "Now would be the best time for your plan, Layla."

Layla looked at the talisman and began grabbing at the air.

"There is no way…" Fleck was abruptly stopped by a crunch.

Fleck saw a liquid oozing down Layla's arm.

Layla threw the now-visible creature to the ground and flicked the goo off her arm.

"How is that even possible?" Fleck said, astonished.

"I put my faith in the lucky talisman," Layla responded, happy with herself.

"That's amazing!" Sarai beamed.

Fleck was still stunned, but turned his attention towards Abram, who was still unconscious.

Fleck propped Abram up against a tree and smacked him again.

Abram opened his eyes, groggy.

"What happened?"

"You had a little nap while we fought a giant," Fleck said, smiling.

"Is Kya alright now?" Abram asked.

"Kya, are you okay!?!" Fleck shouted.

There was no response.

"Yeah. She is just fine," Fleck chuckled. "Let's get some more cotton in those ears before we get another tantrum. I'm not sure how much longer we can spend in this forest. If only we had the Greymeers again…"

Like magic, the wolves appeared from the dark forest.

Fleck looked at Layla and opened his mouth.

"Lucky Talisman?" Fleck said, puzzled.

Layla did not answer. She just smiled.

"Lucky Talisman," Fleck said in disbelief.

Chapter 12: Training

Several months prior, in Maling, Layla and Kya went to their master to inform him of their plans. They found him meditating in the temple.

"Master Sho, we have word from our mother. Our father is dead, but his last wish is for us to find Aphrodite and lift the curse from us giants." Layla uttered.

"If you must leave, let this be my last lesson to you," Sho replied. "Through your training, you have proven to be powerful fighters, but you rely on your size for the advantage. You must find strengths that are greater than your size to ensure your victory. Now attack me!!!"

"But, Master, you are one man, and we have an advantage with our staves." Layla interjected.

"I said attack me!" Sho insisted.

Kya and Layla readied themselves. Kya took the first shot with a forward chop at Sho. He jumped onto Kya's staff, flipped backwards from on top of it, and kicked Kya in the face as he flew through the air. Kya stumbled back.

Layla could not believe what she was seeing and was determined to do better. She steadied herself for her attack. Layla stepped forward and swung her staff at Sho. Sho squatted down below the swing and before Layla could catch her balance, Sho kicked the back of her knee, bringing her to the ground. Sho sent her rolling with a push to her side.

"See. I am no match for your size, but you are no match for my cunning. Learn from this lesson."

The two giants got up and bowed. "Yes, Master. We will take this lesson with us."

"One more thing. Before you leave, I have a gift for you. It is a talisman that came to this temple many years ago. The talisman has brought great fortune to our temple. I now give it to you. May it bring you luck on your journey."

"Thank you, Master. We will cherish it."

The two giants bowed to their master one final time.

Chapter 13: More Destruction in the Wake

The group was grateful when they had finally put several miles between themselves and the dark forest.

Up ahead, they saw smoke from a fire.

"We have a settlement!" Fleck exclaimed. "Maybe we can get some chewable food. No offense to the Bastion, but I want real food that is not paste."

"Real food!" Sarai squealed, snapping the reins of her Greymeer. The wolf took off in a sprint.

Abram and Fleck hastened their pace as well. The giants even picked up speed, passing Sarai and getting far ahead.

The two giants came to a sudden stop. Fleck and Abram pulled up to Layla.

"Why did you stop?" Abram asked.

"That's not the fire from kitchens. That's a village burning."

"We should go see what happened," Abram insisted.

As they walked through the tiny village, all they saw was death and destruction. Livestock slaughtered. Houses burned. The dead of both humans and livestock.

"This is recent. Could the Red Army have done this? Did they come this way following us? Did we cause this?" Fleck questioned.

Abram shook his head, stunned. "I don't know."

"We have to do something," Sarai asserted. "What do we do?"

"We bury the bodies, giving the dead a final resting place," Layla answered.

Abram felt the pinch of time. His village could be the next to burn like this, but Abram wanted to do something. There was nothing he could do for Boom Town, but Abram could do something here.

"Yes, let's put these people to rest," Abram agreed.

When the bodies were buried, Fleck spoke up.

"What do we do now?"

Layla replied, "My people would say a prayer."

Though their time has come, we move on.
Though they sleep in darkness, we move on.
Though their words may never touch our ears again, we move on.
We move on until one day we meet again in the heavens.

Sarai sobbed, her face in her hands. Abram put his arms around her. He did his best to ground himself, but Abram felt more helpless than ever.

Who will save us from this? Abram thought.

Another question unanswered.

Chapter 14: Taken

The next day, Fleck, Abram, and Sarai were late getting up.

"Are Layla and Kya still sleeping?" Fleck asked in disbelief.

"Kya, Layla! Wakey, wakey!" Sarai chimed.

Sarai pushed back the flap on Layla's tent, but no one was there. Abram then pushed back the flap on Kya's tent, but she was gone as well.

"Look over there! That's Layla's staff! Somebody took them," Fleck pointed out.

The three walked closer to the staff.

"Look. There are wagon tracks leading west. We have to follow them and save Kya and Layla!" Sarai exclaimed.

Abram was not sure what to do. He wanted to save Layla and Kya, but he needed to keep moving to save his village.

"Let's get on our Greymeers and find them!" Fleck shouted.

Fleck and Sarai ran to their wolves. Abram hesitated.

"Abram! You coming?" Fleck hollered.

"I just have to get the Bastion."

Abram collected the Bastion and got on his Greymeer with a heavy heart. This was the farthest from what he wanted to do.

There is no time. Abram thought. But what could he do now?

"We should catch up with them fast!" Fleck cried.

The group rode for an hour, and before long they saw a wagon in the distance. Fleck quickened his pace, and Sarai followed. Abram hung back. Fleck and Sarai pulled in close. He heard Sarai yell something at the wagon rider, and the wagon stopped. The driver stood up, turned around, and made a gesture. Then something strange happened. The Greymeers collapsed to the ground, and Fleck and Sarai fell off their wolves.

"Sarai!" Abram screamed.

Abram whipped the reins of his Greymeer.

The driver of the wagon gestured at Abram to come closer. He waited until Abram was within earshot.

"You are Levi's brother?" The wagon driver shouted.

"How do you know that name and what did you do to them?" Abram probed.

"Don't worry. I just used a sleeping powder on them. They will have a few bumps from the fall, but they should be alright. The better question is, what do you want to do with these mangy giants? The only thing they are good for is slaves. I'm going to sell them in the next city."

"Layla and Kya are part of our group. You should let them go."

"Wait. Aren't you Levi's brother? He could tell you that there are no good giants. He fought with us to save our village from the giants. Without their size, they have been relying on deception. They act good but turn on you when the moment arises."

"I cannot speak for all giants, but Layla and Kya saved us from death. Hades's Red Army almost captured us. They fought many of their soldiers to get us to safety. Maybe some giants are bad, but Layla and Kya are not."

The wagon driver quickly reached for his bag of sleeping powder, but Abram was quicker. He fired a bolt of Phantom Light. The bolt knocked the driver off the wagon. Abram dismounted his wolf to check on the wagon driver. He showed no sign of severe injury, but sleeping powder covered him.

Abram went over to Sarai. He pulled her onto his lap. Sarai was in a deep sleep. He wondered what she was dreaming. He hoped it was a better place than this.

Chapter 15: A Request

Abram sat in silence until he heard a rustling behind him. Abram moved to the wagon. Layla and Kya were chained with a third giant inside the wagon. Abram went to the driver and carefully searched him for the key.

After Abram found the key, he freed the three from their chains. The third giant bowed.

"I am eternally in your debt, stranger. My name is Valadameer, and I am one of many of my people who have been sold as slaves."

Valadameer was a few feet taller than Kya. Abram could only wonder how big full-size giants were.

"I know you saved me, and I am in no position to be asking for anything, but I must. My village was ransacked by these humans, who decided they could sell my people for profit. I must save them, but I can't do it alone. Can you help me?"

Abram wanted to say no, but once again, someone else decided for him.

"My sister Kya and I are at your side. These three are good people. I know they will help you as well."

Abram wanted to shout, there is no time, but held his tongue.

Why must everything come before my home? Why must everything come before Trow!?! Abram thought.

Abram did not notice Fleck and Sarai waking up.

"Why does my head feel like it is going to explode, and who is this tall, dark stranger?" Fleck jested.

"Sleeping power knocked you out. This is Valadameer. He needs our help to free his people," Layla insisted.

"Do we know what we are up against? If they are taking down giants, I don't see how the three of us will stand up against them."

"Our people were peaceful and put up no resistance to their captors. However, I know that if we rise against them, the evildoers do not stand a chance."

"Boss man, I think this is your call?" Fleck said, turning to Abram.

Abram wondered how so much ended up in his hands. Did Levi have the same trouble, knowing full well that one more day out here might be the last day of Trow? Abram doubted himself. Levi had so much power, and he became a monster bent on destroying Trow and everything in it. What chance did he have?

Abram did not want the same thing happening to him. He would take what came to him day by day. He had to clear what was in front of him in order to push forward.

"We will help you, Valadameer. The three of us will go to the next city. You, Layla, and Kya stay here and wait for me to come get you. I don't want to get any unwanted attention," Abram directed.

Chapter 16: Town with an Evil Past

Abram, Sarai, and Fleck traveled two or three miles down the path before they saw a town with a giant white tower appearing in the distance.

"I know where we are. The tower is a dead giveaway. This is Millet. Taking slaves is only the tip of the depraved things their townsfolk do. They also are not big on elves. So, I think I will cloak myself and stick with you in the shadows," Fleck asserted.

"Is it really that bad?" Sarai asked.

"Imagine a city of Jins and then you have Millet," Fleck said flatly.

"I guess we go cautiously then," Sarai said solemnly.

When they got into town, there was no one around. Not a man, woman, child or even a dog. The three made their way to the center of town, where they found a well-dressed man. The man waved to them.

"Well, I'll be. I know every person who goes through this city, and I believe I have never seen either of you. The name is Emmit. What brings you here?"

Abram cleared his throat.

"We are farmers looking for hands to help us with our harvest."

"Mighty odd time to have a harvest," Emmit pointed out.

Emmit's comment caught Abram off guard. He knew it was true. Sarai jumped in to help him.

"Where are all the people, Emmit? We've heard some colorful things about Millet and wonder if they are true."

Neither Abram nor Sarai was good on their feet, and Emmit knew it.

"Now, I know Millet has had a sordid past. I will be the first to admit that, but this town has changed so much. In fact, all the townsfolk are at the afternoon service. Why, yes. A preacher of Zeus came into this town and turned it right around. You will not find a holier bunch than the people of this town. We have even renamed the tower the Spear of Zeus. But, if workers are what you need, I think you will find what you need four miles to the west."

"Thank you," Sarai replied.

The three turned to the west and began walking.

When they thought Emmit was far enough to not hear them, Fleck spoke up, "I don't know what Emmit is selling, but I'm not buying it."

"We will continue to the west. Fleck, you check out the town and be careful." Abram rejoined.

With that, Fleck slipped away from Abram and Sarai.

"I don't like this, Abram. There is something that Emmit is not telling us," Sarai replied.

"I don't like it either, but we have to find of where Valadameer's people are."

Sarai shook her head, and the two continued their journey.

Chapter 17: Into the Deep

Fleck wasted no time in getting to the temple. As he approached, he did not hear a preacher, a congregation, or anyone for that matter. Fleck slowly opened the door to the temple and walked inside. There was no one there. It looked like at one time it had been a temple to Zeus, but everything of value had been removed.

"The people had to go somewhere," Fleck thought.

Fleck slipped through town and noticed a well-traveled path heading north. He followed it to the edge of town. A few hundred yards out of town, the path abruptly stopped at the forest. Fleck stared at it, puzzled. The people could not have returned without making tracks circling around.

Fleck went to the edge of the tracks and stepped forward. There was a flash of light, and Fleck realized that the forest was an illusion.

In front of Fleck, there was a massive chasm, and inside the chasm were giants, elves, and the townsfolk. They were mining something that Fleck could not see well. Around the slaves, bandits kept them in line.

Fleck wanted a closer look. He crept down the path into the chasm. He saw the slaves were mining Mercrite, a powerful stone that amplifies magic.

Fleck did not know what to do. He could go about freeing the slaves. However, if the bandits had strong mages with Mercrite, they could kill everyone in the chasm in a heartbeat. Fleck had to even the odds.

Fleck saw five guards, but he thought that could not be enough to keep these slaves from revolting. He knew that there must be something else keeping the slaves scared. Fleck noticed an anomaly. Something invisible bent the light from the sun. Fleck thought it was a flying, invisible sentry. The question, though, was Fleck strong enough to destroy these sentries? Fleck saw the chasm twist out of sight of the guards and a lone sentry travel through it. This was his chance to find out what these sentries could do.

Fleck followed the path down the chasm to the bend and climbed up to the height of the sentry and waited. He could see the light bending near him. Now was his chance.

Fleck leapt onto the sentry. It immediately became visible. Fleck noticed a gem on it lit up. He smashed the gem, and the sentry fell to the ground.

Fleck realized several things. The sentries could not attack without becoming visible. If he smashed the gem on the sentry before it attacked, the sentries were easy to take down. No other sentry came when he destroyed this one, so the sentries were not in communication with each other. However, it would only be a matter of time before they searched for this sentry. Fleck had to make his next move.

The sentries did not alert each other, but the five guards would scream for help if he made an abrupt move. Fleck had to take the guards out quietly.

Fleck pulled off his invisibility cloak and waved down a nearby giant. The giant saw Fleck, and the destroyed sentry. The giant quickly made his way to Fleck.

"What have you done? The bandits will notice this sentry missing, and they will send for Sagar the sorcerer."

"I won't let that happen," Fleck assured. "The sentries do not communicate with each other. We can destroy them easily with no one noticing. The only problem is the five guards. I can kill them before they alert anyone else. I need you to prepare the other giants to destroy the sentries. They cannot attack unless they are visible, which will give you a short time to smash their gems. If you can obscure the vantage point between each guard and the sentries, we stand a better chance of not being noticed by the other guards and the sentries as I take out the guards."

"I don't like this plan," the giant admitted, "but I don't see us having much of a choice in the matter."

Fleck put his invisibility cloak back on. The giant knew he could not just whisper the plan to each giant. The giant picked up a large boulder and placed it in front of the guard closest to him. He directed his fellow giants to dig in places that blocked the sentries' view.

Fleck took no time in dispatching the guard behind the boulder. Fleck placed his hand over the guard's mouth and sliced his throat.

One down, four to go. Fleck thought.

Fleck saw the next two guards were blocked, so he quickly took care of them. The other slaves saw the dead guards. Some seemed relieved by their deaths. Others fretted over Fleck's actions. They stayed quiet just the same.

There were only two guards left, but they would be harder to get, and they were on the path out of the chasm. All the giants knew there would be trouble if they came close to the path. The giant aiding Fleck took a deep breath, walked up the path between the two guards, and began digging. The guard farthest up the path yelled at him.

"Don't dig here. We need this path to get in and out, you stupid giant."

Fleck snuck up on the guard behind the giant. Fleck tried to take the guard out like the others. However, at the moment he was going to strike, the guard moved. Fleck stabbed the guard, but not before the guard cried out in pain. The guard in front of the giant heard the scream and became irate.

"What are you doing? What is happening?"

Before the guard could get any louder, the giant raised his fist and brought it down on the guard before him. Until the death of the last two guards, Fleck avoided being spotted by the sentries, but there was no hiding the death of the last two guards. All the sentries became visible. However, not one fired on the slaves. All the giants in the chasm went into action, smashing the sentries from the sky. The giant helping Fleck shouted.

"NOW'S OUR CHANCE! FLEE!"

The slaves of the chasm ran towards the path out. Not one of them wanted to see what would happen next. However, what the prisoners feared the most came to fruition. A voice that the slaves knew all too well rang out.

"So, you cretins have killed my guards and destroyed my sentries. I never thought you could do this, but I assure you no one here will escape."

The giant who aided Fleck yelled to him, "That's Sagar!"

Sagar raised his hand with a giant piece of Mercrite in it. The clouds became dark. Lightning struck the Mercrite, and Sagar redirected it towards the slaves below.

Fleck knew he had to do something, and fast, before more people got hurt.

"Throw me!" Fleck commanded the giant.

"What are you talking about? Are you crazy? We should flee while we can!"

"Throw me at Sagar!"

The giant looked at Sagar and the damage he was creating. The giant picked up Fleck and threw him towards Sagar.

Fleck flailed in the air. Sagar saw the elf flying towards him. He redirected his lightning towards Fleck, grazing him with a bolt, but it was too late for Sagar. Fleck smashed into him, laying him out on the ground. Sagar was no more, but Fleck was also injured and blacked out.

Chapter 18: The Other Way

Sarai and Abram walked at a steady pace. Neither of them wanted to spend any more time looking for the giants than they had to. Abram's quest was to save his people. Sarai wanted to help Abram fulfill his quest.

As Sarai and Abram approached the two-mile mark, they saw several small shacks with armed bandits coming out of them.

An unarmed man shouted, "Hello, puppets! I see Emmit has sent us some more tasty treats. You can surrender now, and we will just hurt you a little. Then put you to work as a slave. Or you can resist. Then we will put a lot of hurt on you, and you will still become a slave."

Sarai readied her weapon.

"This isn't going to happen like you imagine. You can tell us where the giants are, or we can make you tell us."

"Listen, puppet, those who resist me end up feeling the burn."

The unarmed bandit's hands glowed red.

"Get behind me, Sarai!" Abram hollered.

Sarai dropped back behind Abram just as flames exploded from the bandit's hands.

Abram put up his hands, and a shield of red light materialized in front of him, completely blocking the flame.

"You are full of surprises, Abram," Sarai jested.

"It's the ring the Tangfu gave me. They said the ring's power would grow stronger as my will increases. I wouldn't let these bandits hurt a hair on you and I think the ring knows it."

Sarai blushed. She knew Abram loved her, and this was proof.

The flames from the bandit abated. The bandit was breathing heavily. He was a weak mage, and casting tired him.

"Now it's our turn!" Sarai cried, shooting forward from behind Abram.

Sarai swung her mace in a powerful uppercut to the bandit's head. He was too tired to put up any resistance and fell to her swing.

With their mage down, the bandits rallied.

They cried out, "Berserkers!"

Five large ogres came out of a hut. The ogres growled. With a loud roar, they charged Sarai and Abram with nothing more than wooden clubs. Sarai closed the space to the closet ogre and swung her mace. The ogre did not protect himself from Sarai's blow. The swing hit the ogre in the chest, but the blow had little effect. Barely fazed, the ogre unleashed a flurry of swings at Sarai. She tried to dodge them as best as she could, but the ogre's attacks knocked her onto the ground.

Abram charged in to protect Sarai. He thought he could slow down the ogre's fury by destroying their clubs. Abram dodged the ogres' swings and slashed at their clubs. He broke each of the ogres' clubs, but his efforts only enraged the ogres. They threw their clubs aside and attacked Abram with their bare hands.

Abram swung his sword at the ogres, but his sword barely scratched their hides. Their skin was too thick and strong for even Abram's blade. Abram did not know what to do.

Abram's sword tingled. A calming energy emanating from his sword fell over Abram. Then, as if the sword knew what trouble Abram was in, it erupted with a large blue flame.

Abram sliced at one ogre. The swing of the sword cut off the ogre's arm. Abram now had the edge. With his sword superpowered, the ogres fell prey to Abram's attacks.

The bandits fled with disbelief on their faces. Abram grabbed one of the bandits, catching him before he ran off. He brought his sword to the bandit's neck.

"Tell us where the giants are, or I will end you right here!" Abram commanded.

The gesture was a bluff, but the bandit was taking no chances.

"They are north of the village. They have them digging for Mercrite. That's all I know."

Abram pushed the bandit away.

"Abram, that means Fleck might be in danger. We have to go back for him!"

"We need to speak to Emmit. I am sure he knows more than he led us to believe. Maybe he can tell us where Fleck is," Abram said intently.

Sarai and Abram hurried back to Millet and rushed to the north side of town. When they got there, all they saw was the illusion of the forest.

"Do you think the bandit lied to us?" Sarai questioned.

"I don't know, but we should find Emmit," Abram said, hoping they were not too late to help Fleck.

When the two reached the center of town, Emmit was gone.

"Emmit is nowhere in sight, and the town is empty. We should go to the temple and see if Emmit was lying about everyone being there," Abram asserted.

But before they could go to the temple, they heard a weak voice behind them.

"I found the giants," coughed a familiar voice.

Abram and Sarai turned around to see Fleck limping his way to them. Sarai ran to Fleck and wrapped her arms around him.

"We thought we lost you forever!" Sarai exclaimed.

"Thank for the sentiment, but this hurts a little," Fleck responded. "Also, I found this."

Fleck threw a piece of Mercrite at Abram.

"That is Mercrite. It increases a mage's power. You should hold on to that. I also found this."

Fleck pulled out a piece of cloth with a symbol stitched onto it.

"It is the Red Army symbol. That must be how they obliterated Boom Town. There is a whole mine north of here. There is no telling how much Mercrite the red army has," Fleck emphasized. "We should get out of here though before the Red Army returns and sees what happened to their mining operation."

The three made their way back to Valadameer, Kya and Layla. Valadameer was pacing.

"Have you found my people?" Valadameer asked.

"They should be walking their way back to your village," Abram said joyfully.

"Thank you!" Valadameer said exuberantly.

"You should go back to your village and get ready to move your people. The Red Army is the group that orchestrated this, and there is no telling what they will do when they find out you all have escaped."

"Thank you again. Take this as a symbol of my appreciation," Valadameer said, handing Abram a large golden coin with a symbol etched on it.

Abram did not know the significance of the golden coin, but Layla did, and the gesture astonished her.

"That golden coin is the Hienick, and the leaders of the giants receive those. All good giants swear to follow anyone who holds that coin."

Finally, something to help us protect Trow. Abram thought.

"We should get back on the path to the Neccrum," Abram said.

Having saved the giants, the party was back on track to find the Neccrum again.

Chapter 19: Joy in Massis

Abram and the party traveled for another two days. Late evening on the second day, they reached a town. None of the party knew the name of the town, but soon they crossed paths with one of the townsfolk.

"Excuse me. What is the name of this town?" Abram questioned.

"This is the town of Massis, strangers. The town is small, and we don't get many visitors, but you will find most people are welcoming."

"Thanks, old timer," Fleck interjected. "By the way, do you have a priest? We have a couple here that want to tie the knot."

"Is that so!? You will find Father Tomen at the temple of Athena. He should be finishing up his evening Mass."

The news overjoyed Sarai. This was a moment she had waited her entire life for. Abram was the kindhearted man she always wanted.

Abram shared some of Sarai's sentiment. He had become infatuated with Sarai the moment he saw her, but the fate of Trow still weighed heavily on him. He could not be happy in the moment, so he faked a smile for Sarai.

Massis's Temple of Athena was the most ornate building in town. The temple had stained-glass windows and a tall steeple.

"I can't believe this is happening!" Sarai said excitedly.

Sarai's exhilaration eased some of Abram's worries. He was glad that Sarai was happy.

The group went into the temple as Father Tomen was finishing his sermon.

"Though you grow weary, remember Athena provides to those who believe in her. She cuddles the weak. She empowers the strong. I know you question Athena's power in light of the recent tales of cities crumbling with no one left alive. Keep the faith. Athena will protect us in our time of need. Give your hearts to Athena. Now, my flock, go and give praise to Athena."

The congregation stood to leave the temple. Father Tomen remained at the front of the temple.

His sermon had Abram worried. If the news of destroyed villages had reached this small town, the devastation had to be great.

The party walked up to Father Tomen. Abram was the first to speak.

"Father Tomen, is it true that cities are crumbling with no one left?"

Abram's words hurt Sarai. She thought the only concern was their marriage. But even right now, Abram was more concerned about Trow's fate.

This should be a day of celebration for us! She thought.

"Tales of terror only get larger as they go along. I have no doubt that these are merely travelers' exaggerations. Just the same, we have Athena protecting our village. I see no reason for concern. I take it you didn't come here to talk about tales. Something else, I am sure, has brought you here."

"Yes. We wish to be married," Sarai asserted.

Sarai would not let the concerns of Abram ruin this day. She had anxiously waited for their wedding, and now it was going to happen. Sarai was going to be happy despite their circumstances.

"A joyful day this is. I will have our Grand Mother Niesee come get you, young lady. You, sir, will come with me. The two-day ceremony will start tomorrow. The first day will be the vigil of the soul in Athena's name. On the morning of the second day, you will be married, and the celebration can begin."

Two days! Abram thought. Abram felt he did not have two hours, let alone two days.

"Father Totem, we are on a mission of grave importance. Can't the ceremony happen a little sooner?"

"Nonsense. A moment like this is not to be rushed, and this town will welcome the chance to celebrate your unification. It is a welcome change from the gloom we are hearing from travelers."

Sarai, once again, felt hurt by Abram's response, and Abram noticed. Sarai's reaction only increased Abram's stress. Two days was a short duration for Sarai, but it seemed like an eternity to Abram.

Why is this happening to me? The two thought.

"You stay here, my dear, and I will go get Mother. You, my boy, come with me. We must prepare your soul for this unification."

Father Tomen led Abram away.

Two days passed and, according to the town's tradition, Abram did not see Sarai in that time. The day of the ceremony, Father Tomen led Abram to the temple of Athena.

"You have come so far in your two days. If you have any reservations now, it is better to walk away."

"I'm ready for this, Father Tomen. I was ready the day I saw Sarai."

"Excellent!" Father Tomen exclaimed.

Father Tomen led Abram to the front of the temple. It was full of villagers who were excited to celebrate a wedding, even a wedding of strangers.

Fleck was at the front of the temple. He winked at Abram as he passed by.

Abram and Father Tomen stopped at the altar.

"Abram. You may turn around and see your bride."

Abram turned around as Sarai walked through the doors of the temple. Abram thought Sarai was more stunning than he had ever seen her. Sarai wore a flowing white dress, a wreath of flowers, and held a bouquet of chrysanthemums. She positively glowed.

Sarai and Abram could not believe this was happening. So much seemed to be in their way, but finally their moment was here.

When Sarai reached the altar, Abram spoke.

"You look… incredible," Abram said meekly, barely able to get a word out.

"You don't look so bad yourself," Sarai said, smiling.

"We have gathered here today in love, a love between Abram and Sarai. A unification made possible by the love of Athena. Athena has made a match between every couple so that they should be stronger together. A sum of parts that equals something greater than anything they could imagine with anyone else or alone. I ask Athena to bless this marriage. Let it last for eternity, in Athena's name. With this, I dub you husband and wife."

Abram and Sarai embraced each other.

"I am so happy!" Sarai exclaimed with tears in her eyes.

Abram forgot about his troubles for a moment and felt the grandeur of the event. But that peace would soon fade.

Chapter 20: Something Different

The party left Massis the next day. Sarai, Abram, and Fleck mounted their Greymeer wolves and rushed of town.

The party traveled for a week. One day they noticed smoke in the distance. Sarai pulled her wolf to a stop.

"Look! Smoke!" Sarai said.

"That's a lot of smoke for a town," Fleck threw in.

"Maybe they need help," Layla said, concerned.

The group agreed and quickened their pace towards the town.

On the outskirts of town, Abram saw a man in armor that masked his face, setting huts on fire.

"We have to hurry. There is a soldier setting fire to the town."

Abram pulled in close to the soldier and jumped from his wolf onto him, knocking the soldier to the ground. He pulled his sword, and to his surprise, the sword did not light up. The act baffled Abram. How could one do something this sinister and not be evil?

"I'm sorry, sir. There must be a misunderstanding. I thought you were destroying homes. Perhaps we can talk about what is really going on here."

The soldier did not say a word. Instead, he stood and pulled his sword. He slashed quickly with no concern for himself. Abram could barely block the attacks.

"Sir, I beseech you to stop. If you do not, I will have to strike back."

The soldier showed no sign of acknowledgement. Abram jumped back and stabbed towards the soldier. The soldier did not block, but swung his sword downward at Abram. There was no time for Abram to dodge. He was committed to his action and could not change his trajectory.

Just before the soldier could finish his attack. One of Fleck's daggers flew into the soldier's neck. On impact, the soldier evaporated, and the armor fell to the ground, empty.

What transpired shocked Abram. How a person could just disappear baffled Abram.

"What kind of magic was that?" Fleck said aghast.

"I don't know," was all Abram could say.

But the attack gathered the attention of more masked soldiers.

"We must protect this village!" Layla screamed and charged towards the soldiers.

Kya quickly followed Layla.

"Wait!" Abram yelled. "We do not know what the soldiers are capable of!"

It was too late. Layla and Kya had already engaged the soldiers, and the only thing the others could do was join the fight.

Layla and Kya fought fiercely. Their blows knocked the soldiers back and onto the ground, but no matter how hard they hit the soldiers, they would not stay down.

"We put dents in their armor, and they do not stay down." Layla fretted.

"I do not think these are people," Fleck responded. "I think we need to hit a soft spot with a magical weapon like the dagger I threw."

"We have no magical weapons," Layla said, distressed.

"If you can knock off their helmets, I think we can do the rest," Abram shouted.

"We can!" Layla agreed.

She pulled a wild upward swing at the closest soldier. The soldier's helmet flew off, revealing a human visage. But the head was translucent.

Abram charged the unmasked soldier, stabbing at its face. As his sword pierced the face of the soldier, it disappeared and the armor fell to the ground.

With their new knowledge, the party quickly defeated the other soldiers.

"We are lucky there were not more of those soldiers. They would have overcome us by sheer numbers," Fleck admitted.

"They could have sent an entire army. We would have overcome them," Layla said boastfully.

"Just the same, take this."

Fleck handed Layla and Kya a dagger each.

"Those are some of my magic daggers. You won't be so helpless if those soldiers get in our way again."

"We need to go check if anyone is still alive in these huts," Sarai stated.

"You're right," Abram agreed.

The five companions spread out, checking huts.

"They're dead. They're all dead. We were too late," Sarai cried.

"Do you think these things took down the other cities? Are there more of these men?" Fleck asked. "Do you think they are part of the Red Army helping Hades?"

"I don't think so, Fleck," Sarai remarked. "Inside the armor is the mark of Ares. I am worried. Ares does nothing on a small scale. This was probably just a small group from the full army."

"Didn't Aphrodite say Ares and Hades were seen together? Could this be both their work?" Layla asked.

"It's hard to say with what we know now," Abram commented.

Abram felt his heart sink. Abram knew Alucca had been in Ares's army and that Ares had tried killing the Twenty. If Ares still held a grudge, he could attack Trow at any time.

Abram did not know what other power Ares had.

Were these soldiers just the tip of the sword? Does Ares have a greater evil force? What else can Ares and Hades throw at us? Abram thought.

"You okay, Abram? You have a million-mile stare," Fleck said, worried.

"Yeah. I'm fine," Abram responded after a long pause. It did not fill Fleck with confidence.

After another long silence, Abram spoke.

"There is nothing we can do now. We should get going."

Abram did not know what was in store for their group, and he really did not like that.

Chapter 21: The Killer Inside

Not long after their run-in with the unusual soldiers, the party made camp.

Abram was mentally exhausted. Death seemed to follow him, and he was unsure how much more he could take. Plus, Abram felt no closer to saving Trow.

What more can I do? How much more can I take? Abram contemplated.

Sleep did not come easily for Abram. He tossed and turned, but finally succumbed to exhaustion.

Suddenly, Abram heard chanting and did not know where it came from. Abram opened his eyes, and the world around him was black.

What's happening? Abram wondered.

From the darkness, Abram saw people moving towards him from a distance.

Abram looked all around and saw they came from all sides. The people surrounded him. As the people got closer, the chanting became clearer.

"Killer, killer!" they said.

Abram heard the chanting all around him, and as the people drew nearer, Abram saw they were the strange soldiers he had fought the previous night.

Unusually, Abram did not feel fear. The chanting angered him.

Abram pulled his sword, but once again, it did not light up.

They're not evil! Abram thought. Why are they coming after me?

Abram saw the soldiers were preparing for an attack. They pulled their swords and charged forward towards Abram.

He thought he had no choice. Abram had to fight them.

He heard the soldiers chant even louder as he closed the gap between them. The chant resonated around him.

When Abram was right on top of them, he made a wide sweep with his sword, slicing a group of soldiers. The soldiers did not block his attack. Those that were hit by the swing merely fell to the ground. The soldiers swung their swords at Abram. Their moves were predictable, and he could easily knock them down. However, as a soldier would fall, the other soldiers would chant louder, wearing on Abram's psyche.

"Killer, killer!"

The chant was louder than ever, and it made Abram seethe with rage.

"I was protecting myself!" Abram shouted back.

But the chant continued.

One by one, the soldiers fell to the ground, and Abram noticed something. The soldiers did not disappear as they did in the village. Their bodies lay lifeless on the ground.

Abram did not care. He stepped over the bodies as he attacked.

Many soldiers lay dead on the ground, and the soldiers attacking him became fewer and fewer. But the chanting did not stop.

"Killer, killer!!!"

Abram had dispatched all the soldiers but one. He was bubbling over with anger. The last soldier charged Abram. He voraciously tore through the last soldier. With the soldier's death, silence. The chanting stopped.

However, the silence did not last long. Laughter replaced the chanting. Abram saw a figure in the distance. Abram knew it was Ares.

Abram turned white and felt compelled to pull the helmets off the soldiers. He frantically ripped the helmets off them. The face he saw under the helmet was all too familiar---his own brother, Levi. Abram became outraged and charged towards the figure in the distance, screaming as he went.

As Abram charged towards the figure, a voice pierced the laughter.

"Abram! Are you okay, Abram!?!"

Abram awoke, infuriated. He did not know if Ares had caused his dream, but he knew Ares would pay for what he had done to his brother.

"Abram. You had me scared. You were screaming in your sleep, so angrily. Are you alright?" Sarai shared.

"It was nothing," Abram said shortly.

"It was not…nothing. I've never heard you so furious. I am your wife. You can trust me with anything," Sarai pleaded.

Abram did not know what to say. The rage that the dream invoked made him feel ashamed. This was not the first time his brother had shown up in his dreams to be killed by him. He still did not know what to say.

"I'll tell you later. We should sleep now. I'm sorry for worrying you."

Sarai did not say a word and lay down uneasily. Abram laid down again with his back to Sarai. Neither of them slept anymore that night.

Chapter 22: Bonds Tested

The next morning, Sarai was tired and on edge. Abram had promised to tell her about his dream, but Abram had hardly said a word to her.

None of the party members had said anything about the late-night screaming. They seemed okay. They just went through their morning routine.

The others must not have heard Abram scream last night. Sarai thought.

Sarai pulled in close to Abram so nobody else would hear.

"Abram, you promised you would tell me about the dream today," Sarai insisted.

Abram cringed. He did not know how to respond. His dream would only worry Sarai more. He decided not to tell her the entire dream.

"Ares appeared in my dream," Abram said quickly.

"And...?" Sarai asked.

"And nothing. He was in my dream laughing at me."

Sarai knew Abram hated Ares for what he did to his brother, but Sarai suspected there was more. Abram was not telling her something. Still, she did not want to push the issue.

"Okay, but if you need to talk more, I am your wife. I am here for you through thick and thin."

The words comforted Abram, but he kept his feelings about the attack away from Sarai, hoping to ease her mind.

He had a secret, and he was not ready to share it.

"Oh, you two sharing secrets over there like two lovebirds," Fleck teased.

"Something like that," Abram quipped.

"Eh, if you do not want to kiss and tell, I totally understand," Fleck deflected.

Abram knew the problem was his own and felt bad for replying to Fleck's joke with such a harsh response.

"The day is getting away from us. We should get going," Layla said, trying to lighten the mood.

Everyone seemed uneasy now. The party took off after the Neccrum, following the compass, uncertain of where it was taking them and what danger it would bring.

Chapter 23: A Helpful Hand?

The party traveled for several weeks, and the dream and the fight became distant memories. The party found themselves in a tavern in the river town of Hartly. Fleck raised his cup to his companions.

"You know what I like most about a tavern other than the obvious, ale? The food. Here's to not eating the Bastion's slop."

"Elves don't know how to hold their ale," Layla joked.

"I'll tell you, Layla. I could drink you under the table. The both of you. In fact, I am getting another round to show you how much I can take."

As Fleck stood up, a robed man put his hand on Fleck's shoulder.

"I think you have had enough."

Fleck fell back into his chair.

"Who do you think you are?" Fleck demanded.

The robed man did not pay Fleck much mind. He sat in a chair next to the party's table, keeping his face covered as he spoke to them.

"You will not find what you are looking for with that trinket in your pocket. It will take you to where you need to be but will be of no use in the maze."

Fleck snidely addressed the stranger, "I do not know what trinket you are referring to. But we…"

Before Fleck could finish, the man waved his hand, and Fleck could not open his mouth.

"Where was I? The compass does point you to the desired location, but it will put you no closer to your end. You will come across a maze. You must travel west for three days and find a jewel: the Winds Landing. When in the maze, if you are going in the right direction, you will feel the wind upon your back. Go too far in the wrong direction, and it will take you back to where you began. Also, I must warn you, the maze will test you. Ready yourselves."

The mysterious man stood up and quickly exited the tavern. When the stranger left, Fleck regained the use of his mouth again.

"Forget that! We aren't taking the word of that crazy man!" Fleck shouted out.

"I think we should do as the man said," Sarai shared. "He knew about the compass and our destination. I don't like the situation, but we have no other leads."

Abram agreed with Sarai and was about to speak, but Layla voiced her opinion first.

"We do what the old man said then!" Layla blurted.

"Then I guess it is settled." Abram remarked.

Chapter 23: Greetings from Beyond

The party travelled for three days west. Rain followed them all the way.

"Achoo," Fleck sneezed. "This weather is making me miserable. When are we going to get some sunlight?"

Abram stayed quiet. He thought this journey was cursed. Nothing seemed to work out pleasantly on their trail. Every turn seemed to bring something worse than what they had seen before.

"The rain will break. The sun always comes out," Layla added.

Abram wished he shared her optimism.

On the third day, the party saw something in the distance. As it came closer, the party could tell it was a castle surrounded by an impressive city wall.

"Do you think that is where the old man was leading us?" Sarai inquired.

"There is only one way to find out," Layla insisted as she picked up her pace towards the castle.

At the gate of the city wall, there was something eerie. A metal gate blocked their way, and on the other side, a pile of bones.

"There are no bones outside the gate. Something trapped those people in the castle," Fleck observed. "Do we really want to go in? I'm thinking we take our chances within the maze."

"We've gone this far. We must get the Neccrum or Aphrodite will not help us," Layla emphasized.

"Well, that gate is blocking us from getting in, there is no way in," Fleck asserted.

"We'll take care of that," Layla stated confidently.

The two giants each took a side of the metal gate, grabbed it with their powerful hands, and lifted the gate above their heads.

"Glad you are on our side, Layla and Kya. I would hate to be your enemy," Sarai interjected.

"Right this way, my tiny friends!" laughed Layla.

The party quickly ran under the gate. Layla and Kya stepped under and let the gate drop with a loud crash.

"You're going to wake the dead making all that noise," Fleck scolded.

The two giants chuckled.

"Don't worry, Fleck. We'll protect you," Layla jested.

In the city, everything was quiet, and piles of bones lay about everywhere they went.

The party moved closer and closer to the castle in the center of the city. Fleck felt an icy chill as they approached its door. Abram tried to push the door open, but it was jammed.

"Maybe we should leave this castle behind and skip finding out what evil lies behind the scary doors," Fleck said.

The two giants pushed Fleck aside and started pushing on the door with Abram. In a few moments, the mighty door cracked.

"We just have to push a little harder," Layla grunted.

The two giants stepped back and rammed their shoulders against the door, snapping the plank holding the door shut.

Upon opening, a horrible musty odor wafted out of the castle. The smell was putrid. All the party felt sick to their stomachs.

Layla peered inside and saw a round banquet table. Surrounding the table were knights and a kingly figure at the head, in his royal robes now in shambles.

"Cowards! They hid in this castle while their people were dying. I hope their death was painful," Layla sneered.

Abram looked in and noticed a large jewel on the king's chest.

"I think we found the Winds Landing," Abram said as he pointed towards the king's body.

"Well, you go get it, cause I'm not going anywhere near those bodies," Fleck insisted.

"I have it," Layla boasted.

As Layla moved around the banquet table to the king, Abram got a bad feeling. Abram cracked his sword out of its sheath. Its blue light clearly radiated out.

Layla reached for the jewel.

"Layla! Wait…" Abram screamed.

The corpses sprang to life. The king grabbed Layla's wrist and slammed her onto the table.

"Wights!" Fleck yelled, "We need to get Layla away from the king! Wights steal your spirit!"

The king pinned Layla to the table, his head pulled in close to hers. A white mist puffed from Layla's mouth. She quickly aged as the wight took her spirit.

The wights outnumbered the small party, and they attacked viciously with nothing more than their bare hands.

"Does anyone have a plan? We are a few more of them than us, and Layla isn't looking good," Fleck shouted.

Kya saw her sister's life force fading. She roared and pushed away the two wights that were on her. She fought her way to Layla's side and grabbed the king. The king screeched, and the other wights stopped their attacks on Sarai, Abram and Fleck and charged Kya. It was not long before the wights had pinned Kya down.

"Cover your eyes!" Abram hollered. "Blinding Light!"

The king covered his face and hissed. The other wights covered their eyes and cringed with the king's pain.

Abram grabbed his sword like a javelin and threw it towards the king. The sword pierced the king's chest and pinned him to his throne. The wight king flailed. His jaw fell open, and from his mouth poured all the souls the king had stolen. When the last soul escaped, the king's body fell limp and turned to dust. All the knights crumbled as well.

Kya jumped back to her feet and ran towards Layla. Kya grabbed her sister.

"She's cold and pale," cried Kya.

"That's because she is not out of the woods yet," Fleck added. "She survived the wight trying to take her soul, but the touch of the wight is fatal. If we do not get her to a healer, she'll become a wight as well."

Kya pulled Layla to her and sobbed.

"You must do something, Abram," Kya cried.

Abram was wracked with indecision. He felt he had no time for this. Trow was on the brink of destruction, and here was another hurdle put in front of him. Abram felt as if a piece of himself was dying.

"Okay, Fleck. Ask the compass where we can find the nearest healer," Abram said morosely.

Chapter 24: A Prayer Unanswered

The party made a crude stretcher out of wood and tapestry from the castle and hung it between two of the Greymeers. The party's pace was hindered.

"We must go faster," Kya insisted.

"Kya, you know we can't. If we move too fast, we are going to break the stretcher. We will have nothing with which to fix it. We must just hope we have the time to save Layla. A full Moon cycle has to pass before the wight's touch is fatal," Sarai insisted.

Kya grimaced, and Abram lamented. They both felt they did not have time for any of this. Kya feared for her sister's life and Abram suffered knowing he was helping a giant he barely knew at the risk of losing Trow and everyone who lived there.

Both Abram and Kya could think of almost nothing else, but the sound of a woman loudly sobbing broke their train of thought.

"Where is the crying coming from?" Sarai questioned.

"It sounds like it is up ahead a little," Fleck stated.

The party moved forward and found a woman pressed up against a tree. She barely noticed the group in front of her, but when she did, she sprang forward to Sarai with her child.

"You must help me. Everything I have is gone. The only thing left is my child, but she is not safe. She must go with you. I can't protect her, but you can."

"Ma'am, we will help you if we can. But what has happened?" Sarai asked.

"I come from Melt. Hundreds of masked soldiers came trampling through our fields, burning everything as they walked forward. We ran from our homes. We had no way to fight these soldiers. They chased us relentlessly, hunting us down. I was with a small group and fell. The others did not see that I tripped and continued. I rolled into the forest. The soldiers must not have seen me and continued to follow the group I was with. I held my child close to my chest so the men would not hear her crying. I waited until nightfall. The soldiers were still scouring the woods, searching for survivors. I eluded them, and I have not stopped trying to get away for two days. I try to rest, but the soldiers haunt me in my dreams. Please take my child. I cannot rest until I know my child is safe."

Sarai took the child in her arms.

"We have to take the child." Sarai insisted.

Abram pulled in close to Sarai.

"We can't take the child. We have Layla to worry about."

"But the woman is in no condition to take this child," Sarai persisted.

"Give back the child. We have no time for this," Kya commanded.

Trying to keep everyone calm, Abram proposed a compromise.

"We will open up the Bastion and let her get some rest, and then we will talk about our next move."

The party let the woman rest in the Bastion as they talked about the child's fate. The woman did not make any noise. Total exhaustion made the woman ready for sleep.

She woke from her sleep and pushed open the tent. Outside, she found a teary-eyed Sarai waiting for her with a pouch.

"Here is some food from the Bastion. You will not need any other food or water. Here is a dagger. It's magical, and the soldiers cannot take a hit to the skin from it. The nearest town is to the south. We can't take your child. I'm sorry."

Chapter 25: A Little Luck Dashed

The party came upon a village with strange crystals surrounding it. Sarai got excited.

"This is the legendary town of Chant. My uncle told me about it. The crystal around the town keeps the villagers young and healthy, but it also protects the town. My uncle said if anyone of ill will comes into town, they will burst into flames."

Fleck then spoke up.

"I don't know about you guys, but I think I am going to sit this out. Catching on fire would ruin my day. I'll open the Bastion and make my camp here."

Sarai grabbed the compass from Fleck. Abram, Sarai, Kya and Layla continued into the village. The group found many villagers meditating, oblivious to the world around them. The rest of the villagers were gracious and welcoming.

The group reached a hut that looked better than all the others.

"This is our stop," Sarai assured.

The four stepped into the hut and were immediately greeted with a friendly welcome.

"Come in, friends! Welcome to my humble abode. I am Norum. What brings you to Chant? I'm afraid we have little to offer. Most of our villagers spend their time in quiet meditation. The crystals sustain us, and we need little else."

Sarai said, "We need a healer. A wight has touched one of our party and she has fallen ill. We are desperate for a cure."

Norum responded, "This is a grave situation. A cure takes two days to put together, and there is not much time today to gather the items for the cure."

Kya interrupted, "Layla does not have two days. Tomorrow is the last day of her cycle."

"Then we must do what we must. We shall split the gathering of the cure's elements," Norum continued. "There is only one thing I need you to get. The venom of a nest spider. This is the most difficult item to gather. The spider's venom is deadly, and you must take it from a living spider. It is not potent enough if you take it from a dead or dying nest spider. The venom will be difficult to obtain. However, the nest spiders become docile when a light is cast upon them, making the extraction of the venom possible, but be careful; a torch may stop one or two nest spiders in front of you. They will try to attack you from behind if you are not paying attention. The deadliness of their venom is second only to their cunning. Take this jar. Make the Spider bite the top and squeeze its head to get the venom out. I will collect the herbs and spices necessary for the ritual. That compass you have should point you to a hive."

Sarai was astonished, "How do you know of the compass?"

Norum answered, "You will see I know much. The crystals have a unique bond to me. I know everything about a person when they step into my village, and it is of the utmost importance that I know. I am not only the healer here, but I am its protector as well, and anyone that I find a threat to the village, I ensure cannot hurt the village. Let us not dally any longer. We have little time."

Norum hastily walked out of the hut.

"I guess we have little choice. Compass take us to the hive of the nest spider," Sarai requested.

Chapter 27: Silence

Abram, Sarai, and Kya walked to Fleck.

Near the camp, Abram shouted, "Fleck, we are on a timetable. Help us put Layla in the Bastion and get on your Greymeer."

Fleck did not know what was going on, but he quickly did as Abram commanded.

"Where to now?" Fleck asked, mounting his Greymeer.

"We are going northeast. We need the venom of a Nest Spider," Sarai replied.

"The venom of a Nest Spider! Are you crazy? We will get eaten for sure!" Fleck retorted.

"It's the only way to save my sister! We must go!" Kya cried.

"I guess this is not the first time we've risked our lives. What could go wrong?" Fleck said sarcastically.

Sarai, Fleck and Abram mounted their Greymeers and charged forward with Kya running behind.

Before long, Kya ran past the rest of the party.

Sarai shouted to Kya, "You cannot go to the Nest Spider's nest alone. Stay with us."

"No! You make your Greymeers run faster!" Kya jeered.

Kya picked up her pace and pulled even farther ahead of the party. The others flicked the reins of their Greymeers to get them to go faster.

"I don't know how long we can keep this up," Sarai said, concerned for the Greymeers.

Up ahead, a forest came into view, but something was different about it. As they drew closer, they saw white silk that completely covered the trees.

The party saw a hole ripped in the white silk.

"The Nest Spider has an incredibly sticky web. Kya must be much stronger than we knew," Fleck said, amazed.

"Well, at least we have a way in," Abram observed.

The three made their way to the hole Kya tore through the web. As they stepped into the nest, their boots stuck to the silk on the ground, hampering their movement.

"This is going to take forever," Sarai said, struggling to move her feet.

A little way into the nest, the party came across Kya moving in a blind rage. Spiderwebs covered Kya. Her anger was the only thing moving her. Behind and above Kya, the Nest Spiders crept around her.

Sarai looked around and noticed the spiders were pulling in close to them as well. The spiders surrounded them.

"Abram! We have to do something. Abram!!" Sarai yelled.

Abram felt his magic welling inside him. Abram raised his hand and shouted, "Holy Light!"

The Spiders stopped in their tracks and turned to see the light.

The party was relieved with the docile state the spiders took, but something was wrong.

"The light! It's killing the nest," Sarai observed.

The spiders and the nest began to droop and smoke. All the spiders caught in the light were dead.

"Everyone, grab a branch with the web on it and pull in close to me!" Abram shouted.

Sarai, Fleck, and Abram grabbed a branch and brought it close. Abram pulled his hand down and focused the light on the web-covered branches. The web on the branches began to smoke and catch on fire.

"Form a circle and hold the branches high," Abram ordered. "We have to stop Kya from raging."

Sarai pleaded with Kya, "Kya! Remember your sister! We have the venom!"

What Sarai said was a lie, but she did not know what else to say. Kya turned around.

"Layla! We must get the venom to the healer!" Kya stuttered.

The party worked their way out of the nest with Fleck leading them. The party was only a short distance from the edge of the nest.

Fleck yelled, "We made…"

A nest spider crashed down on Fleck. The spider reared back its head. Abram jumped in with the jar in hand. The spider slammed down into the jar.

Fleck threw his hands around the spider's head and pushed it, smashing its head and releasing the venom.

"Kya? Think you can help us up? We're kind of stuck to the floor."

Kya stepped over Abram and grabbed the jar and walked past Fleck.

"You lied to me. Find your own way out," Kya scorned.

Sarai grabbed Abram's back and helped him up. Then the two helped Fleck.

"Well, I think our giant-helping days are behind us," Fleck said coldly.

"No, they still need our help. They need the Neccrum as much as we do," Sarai pleaded.

Abram wanted to say no, but something stopped him.

Fleck laughed, "If we must, we must. I guess. Layla still has the luck charm. We could use a little luck right now."

The three mounted their wolves and began their trip back to Chant.

Chapter 28: Confrontation

Sarai, Abram, and Fleck made their way as quickly as possible to the healer's hut. As they pulled near, they saw Kya waiting outside.

Sarai approached Kya.

"Kya…"

Kya did not give Sarai a chance to talk.

"What are you traitors doing here?"

Sarai started over.

"Kya, we are here because of our concern for your sister."

Kya reputed, "Is that why you lied about having the venom? You have no concern for my sister!"

Abram kept his feelings out of it. He wanted to continue his journey to save Trow. He had no concern about Layla. But he did not have to show his feelings because Sarai still made her case.

"Kya, we only told you that because you were in a rage. If the Nest Spiders killed you, we never would have gotten the venom."

"What do you know of my actions? You are the reason she is in this predicament! If you had told her sooner about the danger she was facing, The wight would not have grabbed her! She would not need the healer! We could be on our way to the Neccrum! We could be giving the stone to Aphrodite right now!!"

"Kya, Abram warned Layla as soon as he could. The action we took will save your sister."

"It is your fault, because if it isn't your fault then it is my fault. I failed my sister. I let her get touched by the wight. I am the reason we almost did not get the venom. I let my sister down."

Kya collapsed in tears. Sarai put her hand on Kya's arm.

"Kya, you did not let your sister get touched by the wight. If it were not for you, we would never have found our way to the center of the nest. You tried everything you could to help your sister."

Kya kept her eyes down.

"The healer does not know if he can heal Layla. He is not sure whether there is enough time to complete the ritual. He sent me out to give his complete attention to Layla. If he cannot heal her, I have failed…"

Sarai realized there were no words that could comfort Kya at this moment, but she tried anyway.

The healer walked out of the hut.

"Is Layla alright? Did the ritual work?" Kya pleaded.

"I have finished the ritual, but there is no way to know if it worked. We will move her to an empty hut and check on her in the morning. If she is well, you are free to take her, but you will still need the stretcher. She will be in no shape to move. But if she succumbs to the wight's touch, I will have to end her life. You are welcome to stay with me and see through what is soon to come."

Kya's eyes welled with tears.

Fleck walked over to Kya and put his hand on her shoulder.

"Kya, you did everything you could."

Fleck's words meant nothing to Kya. She still felt Layla's fate was her burden to bear.

Chapter 29: Friends Forever

"Here's your baby sister."

Layla's mother leaned forward with the swaddled Kya in her arms, so Layla could see. Layla doted on her sister.

"She is so cute!" Layla said excitedly. "Can I hold her?"

"She is still a little too young to hold. Once you and her are a little older, you can."

"I am going to hold her all the time when she is older."

Two giant years passed.

A joyful Layla came running to her mother.

"She's walking. I can't believe she is already walking!"

"Let me see."

Layla went over to Kya and propped her up on her feet. Little Kya took four steps, then fell down.

"See mom! She's walking."

Layla's mother could not help being caught up in Layla's enthusiasm.

"She did walk, and you helped!"

"I know, and I will help her walk more. I am going to be the best older sister!"

Three giant years later.

A bully was harassing Kya.

"Look how tiny you are. You're nothing but a baby."

The bully was an older eighth-generation giant and towered over Kya.

Kya teared up and began to cry. Layla overheard her sobbing, and she came running to Kya's side.

"What are you doing to my sister, jerk? She's done nothing to you!"

The bully turned his attention to Layla.

"I can do whatever I want to you, runts. I am bigger than you ninth-generation whiny babies."

The bully's comments did not deter Layla. She pulled back her leg and kicked the bully in the shin. Then she punched him in the stomach. The bully ran away crying.

"Don't worry, Kya. That bully will not hurt you when I am around."

Kya looked up at her big sister, smiling. Layla patted Kya on the head.

"We are going to be best friends, Kya. For always."

Chapter 30: Morning's Trial

The tension within the party was high, and though it was difficult, sleep fell over them all.

That morning, Sarai was the first to wake and notice that Kya was missing.

"Kya! She is gone! We need to check on Layla!"

Fleck and Abram quickly wiped the sleep from their eyes and made their way to Layla's hut.

Sarai was already in Layla's hut and came out to address Fleck and Abram.

"Layla is gone! Do you think the healer had to take her life?" Sarai questioned. "Do you think Kya took her?"

All the commotion brought Norum over to the hut. Sarai spoke up.

"Where are Kya and Layla? Did you have to kill Layla?"

"I did not kill her, and I do not know the giants' current location. The crystals have told me they left to the east."

The party quickly mounted their Greymeers and shot off to the east. The three did not have far to travel before they found Kya and Layla. Kya was in a clearing, sobbing over Layla. She did not notice the others as they approached.

"No, no, no. I cannot let them kill you. You must wake up. You have to wake up."

Sarai tried to ease Kya's mind.

"Kya, this is not only your burden to bear. Let's take Layla back. Maybe Norum can still help her."

Kya turned crying.

"I can't let him kill her. If she must die, let it be by my hands. Her life or death is mine. And if I take her life, I will take my own!"

Sarai once more pleaded with Kya.

"Please don't say such things. Your sister will make it. I know it."

As if Sarai's words held their own power. Layla's eyes slowly opened.

"What happened…? Where are we…? Did we get the jewel?"

Kya embraced Layla with tears running down her face.

"You're alive, Layla! You're alive! I thought the wight corrupted you. But Norum's ceremony saved you!"

Kya's behavior dumbfounded by Layla, not knowing what had passed.

"What are you talking about, Kya?"

"What I am talking about matters not. We will take you back to Chant, and the healer will help you become strong again. Then we will make our way to the Neccrum and lift the curse on our people!"

Kya lifted the tired body of Layla and started leading her toward Chant.

Chapter 31: What's to Come

The next day, something strange happened. Layla was up and walking with no sign of ailment. However, the healing concerned Norum. He confronted Layla in front of the group.

"You walk as if you had no contact with the wight. The crystals speak to me and tell me you are stronger than you ever have been. How is that so?"

Layla pulled the talisman out of her pocket, and staring at it, answered.

"I do not know how I know this, but the talisman has fueled my body and fixed my broken spirit."

Norum did not believe Layla.

"The crystals tell me of any magical presence, and the crystals say that is a mere trinket not capable of any such miracles. However, the crystals do tell me that your healing is dark in nature. I must ask all of you to leave, or I will be forced to make you leave."

His words shocked the group. Hearing the change in the healer's personality was unsettling. The healing of Layla was nothing short of miraculous to them. They did not share Norum's fears. Sarai was the first to refute Norum's judgement.

"Layla is kind and courageous. I see her taking no part in something heinous."

"I know only what the crystals show me, and they say her healing will only lead to something more foreboding if left unchecked. Heed my words. Seek to purge the evil that becomes her or suffer an ill fate. Now leave!"

Chapter 32: The New Holder

Abram was mentally exhausted, but nervous energy kept him moving. The Bastion's magic did little for Abram's mind. His nights were restless. It was apparent to Abram that the power of the Bastion cured his aches but did not heal the hole in Abram's heart. He was all too ready to get back on the path of the Neccrum and relieved that Layla kept pace with the Greymeers. However, he was unsure that the Greymeers could keep pace with Layla.

"We are moving too slow! We must pick up our speed. Too much time was lost because of the curse of the wight." Layla commanded.

"I think we are already pushing the Greymeers to their limit. If we abuse them, they will not be able to take us anywhere," Sarai pleaded.

"You are too soft!" exclaimed Layla as she slowed her running.

Fortunately for Abram and Layla, their detour did not take them far from their destination, and soon they reached the mouth of the maze.

"This cave looks like the mouth of the maze," Fleck said. "I guess we bring out the Winds Landing and make our way through. Boss man, do you want to pull out the jewel?"

Abram reached inside his satchel for the jewel, but it was not there. Abram became frantic.

I did not travel so far to be stopped so close to my goal. Abram thought, but then he saw Layla tossing up an item in her hand.

"I was going to find the way to the Neccrum with or without you," Layla said glibly.

Abram took no comfort from the jewel not being lost, but was instead upset that Layla had snuck away with it.

"I am the most qualified to carry the jewel. I have the lucky talisman, and it will see us through," added Layla.

This new Layla did not sit well with any of the party, including her sister. Kya had never seen Layla like this. Layla was always so respectful and dependable. This Layla seemed reckless and uncaring.

Still, everyone was ready to see the end of this trial, none more so than Abram. He thought an argument about who does what would only slow them down more, so he quickly accepted Layla as the new holder of the jewel.

Layla hesitated at the opening of the cave.

"I can feel the wind at my back," she said excitedly.

Layla broke out in a brisk run.

"Follow me!" she shouted.

The party was forced to run after Layla.

They ran until Abram yelled for them to stop. He raised a question.

"Where's Fleck?"

Chapter 33: Where's Fleck

The party charged in after Layla, but it was only a short while before Fleck fell a little behind.

"Boss! I don't think I can hold this pace!"

Abram didn't hear Fleck's cry, and then something caught Fleck's eye bringing him to a stop.

"Hold on." Fleck said to himself, "A gem!"

Fleck saw a line of gems leading down another turn.

"I suppose the Winds Landing wouldn't mind a little detour." Fleck thought greedily.

Fleck began collecting the gems.

"Oh! A gem! And look! Another gem. And another gem!"

Fleck stuffed his satchel full of gems. He saw something in the middle of a long corridor. A treasure chest!

Fleck ran forward, ignoring the other gems in front of him. The back of the chest faced Fleck. So, he went around the chest to the front.

Fleck had his satchel open and ready to rake in the bevy of treasure that filled the chest.

Fleck opened the chest revealing…teeth?

As Fleck stepped back, the chest bit down, catching the band of Fleck's satchel.

"Chatterbox!"

Fleck tugged on the satchel with all his might. He wanted to get away from the chatterbox but was not ready to part with his newfound treasure.

The satchel's strap broke, and Fleck took off down the corridor trying to outrun the chatterbox. Fleck ran as hard as he could, but no matter what pace he took, the chatterbox matched it. And as he ran further, a strong wind hindered his pace.

The wind became stronger and stronger until the wind lifted him and sent him barreling backwards. The chatterbox jumped and snapped at Fleck, barely missing him. But to Fleck's chagrin, the chatterbox got caught in the wind. The chatterbox barreled towards Fleck, gnashing its teeth, hungry for Fleck.

Fleck looked back helplessly as the chatterbox whooshed closer to him. However, it was at the turn that Fleck first veered off. Fleck collided with something, and before he knew it, the entire party was at the cave entrance.

Layla laid into Fleck.

"What did you do, elf? Are we here because of you?"

Fleck did not care about what Layla was saying. Fleck cared about dying in the teeth of a chatterbox.

"Chatterbox!!! Run!!" Fleck shouted.

Layla turned to the chest.

"What do you mean? This old ratty chest."

Fleck held tight his eyes. He knew Layla was a goner, and he did not want to see the bloodshed. She opened the lid.

"A ratty old chest with nothing but stones in it," Layla said, disgusted.

Fleck was confused. That was the very chest that had chased him down the corridor. Fleck realized something.

"My satchel! The chatterbox bit my satchel and broke the strap!"

Fleck showed the party his broken satchel and began babbling.

"I was following a line of gems. The chatterbox. I thought it was a chest. See the gems!"

Fleck poured out the contents of his satchel, but it contained nothing but stones. Layla was done with him.

"You follow fake treasure when you know our fate lies in finding the Neccrum. I suppose we must go slower to make sure no one else gets left behind!"

Chapter 34: A Giant's Journey Ended

The party went further into the maze and came to an area where the walls were like shiny and reflective glass. Kya was in awe of the cave's beauty.

"Look Layla! The walls are so pretty!"

Layla waved her away. "Pretty walls are of no concern to us. We must keep moving forward and find the Neccrum, bringing it to Aphrodite to lift the curse. We can't stop now!"

Despite her sister's insistence, Kya slowed down, looking at all the beautiful reflections. That is until one reflection caught her eye.

In the reflection, she was…tall! Kya could not believe what she saw. She then looked down and realized she was tall! She was tall!

Not only was she tall, but she was also larger and stronger than ever. Kya did not know how the small tunnel fit a full-size giant like herself.

"Layla! The curse is lifted! We are tall once again! Layla…?"

Kya looked, but her sister was nowhere to be found. Kya fumed.

"How could they leave me here!" Kya groused. "Layla! Abram! Where are you!?!"

Kya became enraged and began punching the walls, shattering the glass. Dust from the ceiling fell and covered her. Then Kya came to the glass where she first saw that she was tall.

Kya stared into the glass. Her face reddened. Her muscles tightened. Anger filled her body and mouth. Kya pulled back her arm and with all her might smashed the glass. When the glass crashed on the floor, the ceiling gave way.

Kya gasped. Large stones pinned her to the ground. No matter how hard she pushed to get herself up, the rubble trapped her. Scarier still, Kya could not breathe under the weight of the rubble. Kya did not know how long she could last being crushed and unable to breathe. She closed her eyes and tried to take one last breath.

"Kya? Kya…? What are you doing lying on the ground?"

The voice was her sister's. Kya's eyes welled with tears.

"I thought I would never see you again, Layla!"

"What are you talking about, Kya? We noticed you fell behind and came back to find you. Now we see you lying on the floor wheezing. What happened to you?"

Kya looked around. There was no rubble. No shiny glass. Everything she had seen before was not there!

"Layla, I think there is something wrong with this maze. I am not sure we should continue."

Layla became irate.

"We have come this far, and we shall not stop now! Come, little sister. We have wasted enough time."

Chapter 35: Leader of the Pack

Layla only grew more impatient. She continued to browbeat the party.

"I will make you all follow, if I have to carry you all!"

Layla turned around to see the rest of the party, but no one was there.

"Is this a joke!?!"

Total silence answered.

"How can I move forward without you? The Winds Landing will blow us back to the entrance of the cave!"

Layla looked at the Winds Landing in her hand. She felt a throbbing in her pocket. She reached in and pulled out the lucky talisman. The talisman beckoned her forward.

Layla looked at the Winds Landing again and then dropped it on the cave floor.

Layla knew she had to follow the pull of the talisman. The talisman carried her to a tiny stream a little way forward.

Layla looked into the stream and could not believe her luck. There was the Neccrum. The talisman commanded her to reach for it, but when she tried to pick it up, she received only strange purple prisms. She reached in, time and time again, pulling hundreds of prisms.

As she pulled the gems, the water became murkier. She no longer saw the Neccrum. Instead, she saw her own reflection.

Layla's skin was now yellow. Her lips, blue. Her eyes, black. She breathed a strange white mist.

Layla pulled her hand to her face. She noticed her nails had turned black, but that was not all she noticed. A figure stood beside her. A beast made of crystal. It had one of its many arms on Layla. She tried to pull away from the beast, but to no avail. She tried to remove its arm, but no matter how she struggled, it would not let go of her.

Layla babbled, "I don't like what I see."

Layla said it repeatedly.

"I don't like what I see. I don't like what I see."

The beast squeezed and shook Layla's shoulder. It spoke with a familiar voice.

"Layla! I've been trying to get your attention. You feel cold, and you dropped the Winds Landing. What happened?"

"Kya!"

Layla embraced Kya. The vision had rocked her to the core. She was uncertain she could continue at first. Then she reminded herself of her duties and retrieved the Winds Landing.

"We should continue on," Layla said meekly.

Kya did not know what to say. So, she said nothing and followed Layla.

The party moved forward and came to an opening with two passages.

"The winds are pulling me to the right," Layla stated.

The group went through it and soon came to a dead end.

"We must have gone the wrong way," Fleck uttered.

"Quite a mistake, my pretties."

Sarai snapped, "Jin! But you're…"

"Dead. You'll find that to be quite untrue, and some other familiar faces have joined me," Jin gloated.

A wall of fire blazed behind the party, trapping them. Through the fire walked Jin. Through the walls walked in Lamund and Showlar. Upon their appearance, shadowy creatures began picking at the quintet.

"Showlar is up to his old tricks and Lamund has the no-magic doohickey, but I think I got this one," Fleck assured them.

Fleck threw a dagger straight for the Tanton, knocking it out of Lamund's hand and shattering it on the ground.

Abram felt the magic welling within him.

"Phantom light!"

From Abram's hand, hundreds of lights sprung. The bodies of Lamund, Showlar, and Jin contorted. When all the lights finished striking, the bodies hung mysteriously limp in the air.

Sarai walked over to Jin, and her jaw dropped.

"Jin is a giant wooden doll hanging from strings, like a marionette. They're all like that."

A figure behind the wall of fire laughed, casting a shadow over the entire party.

"The wall of fire is closing in on us!" Fleck cried.

Layla squeezed the Winds Landing in her hand.

"Please don't be wrong," Layla murmured. She smashed her shoulder into the wall with all her might.

The wall crumbled, caving in the ceiling behind them, blocking their exit, but saving them from the fire.

Chapter 36: The Neccrum Within Reach

Dust filled the air, making it difficult to see. The party was no longer in a cave, but in a room. Layla felt the wind and proceeded forward slowly.

"Wait!" Fleck yelled. "Don't move another muscle. Just slowly step back."

Layla stopped in her tracks and slowly backed away.

"What's wrong, little elf?" Layla said, perturbed.

"I'll have you know I am tall for an elf, and you were about to walk into a living wall," Fleck said plainly.

Layla did not want to admit it, but she was relieved.

"Thank you," Layla said meekly.

"So, this is it. This is our way to the Neccrum! Trapped in a room with a living wall. We seriously need to get rid of the jewel and the compass," Fleck blurted.

"Wait. What is a living wall?" Sarai asked.

"It is a giant wall of ooze that when you step into it, it drags you in and feeds off your body with its acid."

"No, wait, Fleck. There is something inside the living wall…it looks like a sack," Sarai pointed out. "Maybe that can help us."

"Thanks, Sarai," Fleck said sarcastically. "How are we going to get to the sack? The wall will literally burn your skin off."

"Burn…?" Abram repeated.

That gave him an idea. He pulled out his rope, tied one end to himself and handed the other to Layla.

Abram pleaded under his breath, "Oh please. Rings, do your thing."

He put his hand through the living wall and felt the wall slowly pulling him in, but his hand did not burn. Abram walked further into the wall until he was on top of the sack. Abram grabbed it and motioned to Layla to bring him back.

Layla pulled on the rope as hard as she could, but the wall had a hold of Abram and did not want to let him go.

Kya joined Layla to help pull. Then Sarai, and finally Fleck. With their combined strength, they pulled out Abram and the sack.

The sack was heavy. Abram had to hold it with two hands.

"Abram! You amazing man! Do you want to do the honors of opening the bag?" Fleck said, bowing. "It's covered in living wall, and I'm pretty sure if one of us touched it, our skin would burn off."

Abram opened the bag. Inside was a man. A human man was tied and gagged.

Everyone was stunned into silence.

Abram removed the gag and untied the man.

"Air! Praise the stars! Air!" the man celebrated. "Oh, how long my lungs burned for air. Thank you, my champions of freedom. I am eternally in your debt. My name is Kaine. Please delight me with your names so I can thank you properly!"

"You were trapped in that sack!" Fleck said, astonished. "How long were you in there?"

"Six hundred thirty-eight thousand three hundred eighteen years, three months, and sixteen days, give or take a day or two," Kaine laughed.

Fleck looked at Abram.

"He's insane," Fleck said, flabbergasted.

"How could you have lived so long?" Sarai questioned.

"You will find me full of secrets, as I come along with you. I am coming along with you?" Kaine pleaded.

"Well, we are going nowhere because we are trapped in this room," Layla cried.

"Well, that will be no problem," Kaine said boastfully. "Rubble be gone."

And just like that, the rubble was gone.

"How did you do that?" Fleck said, amazed.

"I have a keen ability. With limitations, what I speak becomes truth," Kaine said, striking a dramatic pose.

Layla wasted no time.

"The Neccrum! Can you get it?"

"It is yours for the asking." Kaine said, bowing to Layla, "Open a door to the Neccrum!"

A door before Kaine appeared. He stepped through the door and within a few brief moments, stepped back out carrying the Neccrum.

"I give this to you, finders of my freedom. Your name is?"

“Abram. I’m called Abram.”
“Here you are, good sir!”

Part III:

For The World

Chapter 1: It Is Not Over

"What do we do now, Abram?" Fleck asked.

Abram stared at the Neccrum in his hands. Holding the stone was intoxicating.

"I guess we bring the Neccrum back to…" Abram started.

A blinding light shimmered through the room, and a voice boomed out of it.

"I cannot let you give the Neccrum to anyone."

"Master Hermes! Right on time!" Kaine beamed.

"Yes, Kaine. How long has it been?"

"It's only been a few hundred thousand years. Have all the Gods forgotten me?" Kaine asked.

"Yes, Kaine. They have," Hermes assured.

"Good! Then we can move forward with our plan and find the other Duos Ring. The counter to my ring. Have you any leads as to where it is housed?" Kaine queried.

"No. The Gods will not speak of it. My plan to get you out of the way so the other Gods would talk more freely about the ring did not work. I apologize. Your time trapped in the wall was for naught," Hermes said gravely.

"Worry not, Hermes. We will get the ring. We just have to come up with another plan."

"What are the Duos Rings and why can't you just make a door to them as well?" Sarai questioned.

"The Duos Rings are ancient artifacts imbued with great power. Somehow the Gods have sealed away the location, even to me," Kaine uttered.

"Where did they come from?" Sarai continued.

Kaine expounded, "The Duos Rings are handed down from generation to generation. The exact purpose and extent of their power are unknown. My brother and I were the last two in line to carry the rings. I was chosen for my magical prowess. With just a thought, I could cast magic more powerful than any other mage. My brother was chosen for his physical prowess. He was unmatched by any man or woman. My powers made me something to fear. His strength made him an asset in our simple farming lifestyle. My brother loved me, and I envied him. The Gods somehow knew this and tried to use it to get what they wanted: The Duos Rings. Aphrodite came to me in a vision. She put a taste of hate in me for my brother and instructed me to get his ring. As I walked closer to his home, Aphrodite filled my mind with jealousy until I was blinded by rage. I commanded the wind to blow down my brother's house. I saw him in the rubble. He asked me why I was doing this and said he would not dare fight me. He said he loved me. I told him he would die knowing I did not and brought down a lightning bolt upon him. Just like that, my mind cleared. I was conscious of what I had done. My brother was dead, but the horrors did not stop there.

All manner of creatures swarmed into my village, destroying and killing everything. The beasts pulled at my brother's corpse. They grappled for the ring. Aphrodite must not have been the only God who knew about this unholy night, for the creatures warred over who had the ring. Beasts, scaled and furred. Large and small. Of this realm and others. All descended upon our tiny village. Some turned their attention towards me. But I started a torrent of wind and made my way to my brother. At least, what was left of him. The savage creatures disbanded, one of them with the ring.

However, my plight did not stop there. The Gods themselves came before me. Each one trying to take my ring from me, not wanting any other God to take it. They warred among themselves. The sky ripped with their power. Lesser Gods fell quickly. At that time, I did not know a God could die. The weaker ones, who were smart, steered clear of the battle. The ones that remained tried to crush, burn, and break my body. But no matter the fury poured upon me, I was left standing. The ring made me immortal.

I cursed the Gods and wished devilish things upon them. Strangely, some of what I said took shape. I realized I could now bend reality. I could make the Gods pay. With this power, I hunted lesser Gods. There are actually only a few Gods left thanks to me, with only the ones that steered clear of me and the ones too powerful to touch."

Kaine stared into the distance.

"You almost killed me," Hermes remarked.

Kaine smiled, "Only a little, Master Hermes!"

"I regret to inform you that most Gods are evil," Hermes continued. "Zeus, Ares, Aphrodite, our realm made them evil, and I do not know why they left it for this one. Their hatred of humans pales in comparison to their love of themselves. Hades and I were born in this realm. Hades was good at one point. He found the Neccrum and discovered its use in aiding the souls into the next realm. But something changed, and his hunger for power grew. Abram--- the very item you hold corrupted him. I do not share their ill intent, and I learned very early that I was different. I made it my purpose to become useful to each God. That way, I could get them to divulge their secrets. I've made a fair game of using that knowledge to provoke the Gods into fighting each other and not the humans.

I learned of Kaine and the Duos Rings like you humans do the boogeyman. I was taught he was something to fear. But I wanted to know more. Particularly about the Duos Rings. I found out there were two, that the rings came with unbelievable power and that no God knew what happened when you bring them together.

I knew I had to meet Kaine and help him find the other ring. Leveling the field between humans and Gods was my intent, but I did not know if Kaine served good or evil. I learned he killed his brother, which I found ill. Still, something told me that things would be different.

When I first met him, he tried to kill me. Though I am a lesser God than my father, speed is what I have and what came to my aid. I reasoned with him as he tried to destroy me. My words calmed Kaine's raging heart. He finally put away the gauntlet.

My first step in our venture was to build communication between us. The Gods communicate through channels of thought that anyone with an opening to the Rift can tap into. Gods being the vain things they are, communicate loudly. For some, the amount of chatter is too much. I did not want to break Kaine's mind. So, I slowly opened his mind. The process did not take very long. The trouble then was that Kaine's mind was open to the Gods. At first, I did a fair amount of muting his mind from the other Gods, but over time he controlled it himself. It was then that we delved into what the Gods knew of The Duos Rings.

Kaine first hunted lesser Gods for information. He would threaten them and ask them about the Duos Rings. Though in words they would not betray the other Gods or risk their lives saying the wrong thing to Kaine, their thoughts were free, and their thoughts betrayed them. It was not long before the Gods were talking of Kaine and his search for the other Duos Ring. Eventually, they figured Kaine was able to find the secrets of the Gods through their thoughts.

What happened next astonished even me. The thoughts between Gods stopped. This made things very difficult. Not knowing the intent of every God made it impossible to quell their attacks on humans. Many humans suffered for it. We needed another plan.

I proposed a solution. If we could get Kaine out of the way, things might return to normal. Kaine was on board with it. It was his freedom I proposed to get rid of. So, before the other Gods, we staged a fight that I would win. We fought, I bound and gagged him, placed him into the magic sack, and hid him in an impenetrable maze. With only one hitch, I could not use my power to free him without the other Gods knowing that I had freed him. The aura of my power would have betrayed me.

After the chatter between Gods' thoughts grew, I knew I had to get Kaine out of his trap. I sent many wanderers into this maze. None before you had made it. Your tenacity speaks well of you.

Still, as of now, no God knows the Neccrum is missing, nor where it is, and it must stay that way. We cannot risk any of them finding out where it is. Hades and Ares were using it to fuel an unstoppable army. Ares made armor possessed by the spirits of the dead. Their intent is to kill all life on Earth. But without the Neccrum, they cannot move the army. My father uses creatures to scare humans into being faithful to him. He would no doubt use the armies of Hades and Ares to scare humans into praising him. As for Aphrodite and the other Gods, I cannot guess what they would do with it, but I am certain it would be nefarious."

"That cannot be!" Layla protested. "Aphrodite and Zeus are Gods of the people. Zeus is our patron God. Hades allows souls to pass into the next life. You are trying to dupe us."

"I wish I were, my giant friend," Hermes said, trying to console Layla.

"We have come too far!" Layla cried. "Our people need the tears of Aphrodite to lift the curse on giants! We will take the Neccrum by force if need be. The lucky talisman has taken us this far. It will see the Neccrum goes to us."

Hermes's voice deepened with concern.

"Where did you get that talisman?"

"What does it matter where we got it? We have it now, and we are going to use it!" Layla insisted.

"You don't understand. That talisman is not of this realm. Somehow, a piece of the God's realm has made it here. It may appear to bring you what you desire, but with prolonged use I fear it will bring something more sinister." Hermes warned.

"I am not doing this for me. I'm doing this for my people! Desire will not consume me!" Layla snapped.

"Maybe we should listen to Hermes, Layla?" Kya chirped.

"NO! We take the Neccrum now! Charge, Kya!"

With that, the two giants ran towards Abram. Hermes took no time to get into action. The God waved his hand, and the two giants disappeared.

"I am afraid that will not keep them away forever. With the talisman, they will be drawn to the Neccrum. I do not know what the talisman will unleash if the giants continue to use it."

"Hold on. Hold on. Let me take a stab at where this is going," Fleck scoffed. "We have a rock that you can't touch because it makes all Gods screwy. So, you can be no help with it. We have to hold on to it while keeping it away from Zeus knows what, running until one of the Gods slips where the ring thingy is. We waltz into whatever layer the ring is. Take on the God who has it. Once again while keeping the stone away from all the Gods."

"I am afraid that does sum it up," Hermes admitted.

"Is he for real? We just run with the Neccrum," Fleck said astonished.

"Master Hermes is not one to joke around. If he says run, then we run," Kaine assured. "And I, for one, propose that we run out of this room. If I must spend one more minute in this room, I will go mad."

Kaine stepped back into the cave. With his first step outside the room, a mist sprayed from all sides of the cave.

"Hermes! I think we have a problem."

"Yes, Kaine. What can it be?"

"I can't talk out loud to you right now. I can't talk to anyone right now!"

Abram saw Kaine mouthing something but could not understand him.

"What are you trying to say, Kaine?" Abram questioned.

"He won't be able to tell you, Abram. He won't be able to tell anyone," Hemes explained. "Another God must have put a trap here to stop Kaine from speaking. This would only have been effective in these tight quarters. A keen mind laid this trap. However, this limits what we can do. Kaine will be of no use to you if you can't communicate with him."

"What are we going to do, Hermes?" Abram asked.

"My options are few, but desperate times call for desperate measures. Abram, I told you how the Gods thoughts are open to anyone with the power and know-how. This ability can be granted by a God to any mage. Now, what I say is true. The amount of noise that will travel through your mind at first may be maddening. I would not do this if there were another way. I have made a magical artifact that will ease your mind into the noise. However, your mind will be open for a brief time when I open the channels. The artifact will aid you in hiding your thoughts, and it will be only a matter of minutes before you can select who hears your thoughts. I must make this very clear: when this window is open, you mustn't think about the Neccrum. Are you ready for this, Abram?"

"Have I ever had a choice?" Abram said morosely.

Chapter 2: The Gods

"They have the Neccrum!"

Chapter 3: Let's Find a Good Place to Eat

After exiting the cave, the party made camp and fell asleep. The next morning, morale was low with the banishment of the giants, being placed further away from saving Trow, and on the verge of a God attack. Sarai wanted to pick up everyone's spirits.

"Wakey, wakey, everybody! It's breakfast time, and we have the Bastion's best."

The Bastion was an oasis for the troubled travelers. A night's rest in it was a week's worth of relief. The food and drink from it, though seeming inedible, powered the wanderers through.

"Not a word of disdain from you, Kaine," Sarai said, laughing at her own joke. "I think you are in for a treat. This slop does not look like much, but it tastes like your favorite food. Mine is Candum fruit."

Kaine faked a smile as he looked at the questionable cuisine.

Kaine took a little bite and coughed it up.

"Abram, how do you eat this? It tastes awful! Can we find a town with actual food?" Kaine pleaded with Abram.

"I think it tastes like cucumber," Abram admitted.

"For those of who don't speak with their minds, can we use our words?" Fleck griped.

"Sorry, Fleck. Kaine does not like Bastion's food and wants to find a place that sells food."

"We can ask the compass where the nearest village is," Sarai chimed in.

Sarai grabbed the compass and began talking to it.

"Oh, great compass, where is the nearest tasty food?"

Sarai waited for a moment as the compass dial turned and stopped.

"Look. The nearest town is to the southeast."

"Please let us go," Kaine urged.

The group packed up the Bastion and the rest of their belongings and headed southeast. They travelled three miles to the edge of a village and noticed a group of people collected on the outskirts of town. However, something was not right about the gathering. The people seemed agitated.

"Abram, I am having a disturbing vision." Kaine warned.

Chapter 4: A Snippet of Time

"Let go of me, you murderers!" a captured woman in distress screamed.

"Woman, why do you say such words? We took but a small sacrifice from you." The head captor said calmly.

"You barred me in my hut while you killed my livestock and murdered my family! How can you speak so calmly!?!" shrieked the woman.

"But a small price to pay to our mother Hera. A tribute that anyone here would make. A tribute that I the head priest of Hera would make."

The crowd around the woman murmured their confirmation. Their words sickened the woman and as she cursed, he priest spoke again.

"Have your fields not grown more abundantly? Have not your cattle been fatter? All this made possible by our mother, Hera."

The priest turned to address the crowd.

"Remember how hard your life was before Mother Hera's faithful had come? Remember the small harvests and the sickly animals? Hera has asked for nothing more than a reasonable tribute. However, our resolve was in question, and this year's harvest shows it. A greater sacrifice was needed for the greater good."

The crowd chanted, "The greater good. The greater good."

The woman whipped back at the crowd.

"I praise Zeus! He asks no wicked tribute. He is the true protector of the people."

The priest testified, "This woman has revealed her wickedness and has made apparent why Hera has chosen her. Zeus and Hera were once lovers who sired Hermes. But Zeus cast aside Hera after realizing she would overcome him in strength. The people believe in Hera. Hera is the greater good. Zeus cannot be saved, but this woman can. I give you the seed of Hera. She shall swallow it and become a believer, a vessel of Hera!"

Chapter 5: Travelers at the Edge of Town

Kaine projected his thoughts adamantly to Abram.

"The priest has a seed of Hera. Hera is a hive mind. If that woman swallows that seed, she will become a part of Hera. Then the woman may see me, and we will lose the one advantage we have over the Gods. They don't know that I have been released."

Abram commanded his power. "Phantom…"

Kaine howled, "It's too late, they have surrounded us."

A small group of invisible monks materialized around the party and threw down vials of powder at the feet of Abram and his group. A mist sprang from the broken vials. It was not long before the quartet was asleep.

Chapter 6: Trapped in the Web of Hera

A woman's voice broke the silence.

"Kaine. Wake up, Kaine. I know that powder had barely enough oomph to put you to sleep long, but don't think you will be able to use your magic. The powder weakens the mind so you can't use it."

"Hera. It has been a while."

"Kaine, do you like my latest acquisition? The body of the woman at the gathering. I believe Agatha was her name. Isn't it beautiful?"

"The husk is beautiful, but the fruit is rancid."

"Now, now, Kaine. Is that any way to talk to the God who has your friends? These are your friends? I seem to remember you having none before you were put away."

"Friends? I was going to drop them at the first chance."

"You may get your chance to be rid of them sooner than you think. I will let them go for a price. Come to my Colosseum, take my sigil, and serve me."

"You don't want to force them to swallow one of your seeds?"

"I am afraid my priest only had the one seed, or they would already be mine."

"Well then. I have only one question for you."

"What is that, Kaine?"

"Did you really think your sleeping powder could stop a man who doesn't have to breathe?"

"Don't tell me you intended to fight your way out with your friends still in peril?

"No. I intend to fly!"

Kaine nodded his head, and the four went airborne with no supplies, no wolves, and no Bastion.

"Mother Hera, shall we follow them?" The priest asked.

"No. That will not be necessary. While Kaine pretended to sleep, I fed his friends my mire. Seeds will grow in them, and soon they will be mine."

"What of Kaine? Will you warn the other Gods?"

"I think, right now, I have a juicy secret… This ought to be fun."

The vessel of Hera cackled.

Chapter 7: Unfairly Treated

Over four hundred thousand years ago

Kaine stood by Catnin River. It was where his village drew their water. Kaine traveled farther down the river than anyone else. The river led to thicker woods. No one wanted to travel into the forest because of the wild Dunwi. Unexpectedly, Kaine had a visitor.

"Kaine. Kaine!"

Kaine knew the voice well. The voice belonged to Kara, a girl he was infatuated with as a child and now adored even more as a teen.

Why would Kara travel this far into the forest? Kaine thought. All the villagers are afraid of the Dunwi, and it's not safe even for my brother.

"Kaine!" Kara called.

"Over here, Kara," Kaine responded. "Why are you so far into the forest? Aren't you afraid of the Dunwi?"

"I do not fear the Dunwi while you are around, Kaine. You would not let a hair on my head be harmed."

Kaine knew it was true. He would do anything for Kara.

"What brings you out here, Kara?"

"I must admit, Kaine, I have a crush."

Kaine's heart pounded.

Could Kara reciprocate my feelings? Kaine thought.

"And I must admit you know him well."

This was the moment Kaine had waited for. "Yes. Who is it?"

Kaine knew she meant him.

"It is your brother, but he is always surrounded by other girls. I was hoping you could talk to him and arrange a private meeting. I know that if he met me on my own, he would fall madly in love with me."

Rage filled Kaine.

"I am not my brother's keeper. If you want to speak to him, do it on your own!"

Kaine's response took Kara by surprise. An awkward silence fell between the two. However, a rustling in the woods broke the silence. From the forest came a Dunwi.

Normally, Kaine would fly away from the beast, and the beast rarely followed. They were basically a pudgy mouth on short legs. Despite their appearance, the Dunwi were fast and a bit of a challenge in a fight.

However, today was different. The girl he loved was obsessed with his brother. Kaine did not care about himself or Kara for that matter. Anger powered him now.

Kaine conjured a small ball of lightning between his hands and quickly expanded it to a large raging torrent. The sphere grew bigger and encompassed Kaine. Kaine discharged all the lightning onto the unsuspecting Dunwi.

The bolt of lightning was intense. The lightning rushed through every molecule in its body, exploding it everywhere.

Kara looked at Kaine with fearful eyes. She knew he was a powerful mage, but she did not know how deep the contempt for his brother was.

Kara ran away screaming.

"Kara! Wait!" Kaine pleaded.

But it was too late. She was gone.

Chapter 8: Beware the Dunwi

Abram opened his eyes and found Fleck and Sarai still asleep. Abram was trying to make sense of what had happened. He had been outside a tiny village and now he was somewhere out in a forest. Looking around, Abram saw Kaine.

"Where are we? What are we doing?" Abram blurted.

"Somewhere away from Hera. As for what you were doing, you were having a little nap, courtesy of Hera's henchmen. Don't worry though; the compound they use is mostly harmless. Hera does not wish any potential host harmed."

"Where are the Greymeers and the Bastion?" Abram questioned.

"I am afraid they had to be left behind. I could only take so much."

Abram took a moment to take it all in. Then, a thought came across his mind. "The Neccrum! Hera now has the Neccrum!!"

"Rest assured, she does not."

Kaine reached over his right shoulder and grabbed an unseen object out of thin air. He pulled it down and to the left. Following his hand, a sack appeared.

"I find this sack quite handy. The owner is the only one who can make it visible, and it can only be opened when it's visible. The opening expands to fit any object the owner desires to put in it. When pulling out an item, the sack anticipates the object the owner intends to pull out of it. It will never be full and weighs only a few pounds."

Kaine reached into the sack and pulled out the Neccrum.

"As you can see, Hera does not have the Neccrum. I took it out of your bag after Hermes left. Me not being the best thief, I thought you would have noticed that your bag became lighter."

Kaine placed the Neccrum back in the sack. "I got this sack shortly after the monsters destroyed my village. It came from the hands of a lesser god trying to draw something out of it that could contend with me. I have collected many artifacts in it, and I believe it needs a new owner."

Kaine pulled the sack off and held it out for Abram to take.

"The sack and the Neccrum belong to you, and I will do my best to aid you in getting it where it belongs."

Abram took the sack and was going to thank him, but Kaine interjected.

"Wait!"

A weird sound could be heard.

Chir chir

"Abram, what God were you getting the Neccrum for?"

"Aphrodite."

"This is very important. Did you leave any artifacts behind when you left Aphrodite!?!"

Abram thought for a moment.

"We had masks. We dropped them in her temple."

"They followed you!" Kaine dismayed.

"Who?"

"Not who but what. The Dunwi have followed your scent. We must leave here without leaving a trail."

Kaine reached low to the ground and pulled his arm up. From his hand came a mist that now swirled about him and the party.

"I will pick up your two friends and run with them. Do your best to stay close behind me. There is no point to the mist if you are not in it."

Abram wondered how Kaine could lift his two friends and still run. But in a matter of moments, Kaine had Fleck and Sarai over his shoulder and was galloping away.

Abram sprinted after Kaine. As he ran, he felt his lungs and his legs burn.

How can Kaine keep up this pace? Abram thought.

Kaine pointed to his right.

"There! A cave! We can hide in it!"

The two dived into the entrance of the cave.

Abram gasped for air.

"Abram, I have to insist on quieting your breathing. The Dunwi will follow your scent to find us. When they find they have lost our trail, they will take to the skies. The Dunwi will listen and look throughout the forest. My mist would have been a dead giveaway to our position, but fortunately this cave is here."

"What is the Dunwi, Kaine?"

"A fiendish beast. If a flower could reflect Aphrodite's beauty, the Dunwi would reflect her soul. They are normally solitary beasts, but under the influence of Aphrodite, they amass in great numbers. I could protect us from one or two, but more than that would overpower me in my current state. I am afraid we are going to have to wait them out."

After a little while, Fleck and Sarai woke. Abram went to their side to see if they were okay. Kaine ventured out of the cave.

"I can't hear the Dunwi. They must have moved on. It should be safe to venture out," Kaine remarked.

The three companions crept out of the cave. The sun was high. Shadows flicker across the sun surprised him. He wondered if he had imagined them.

Then a voice became clear in Kaine's mind, "Patience is a virtue, Kaine. But you know that better than anyone."

Kaine shouted into Abram's mind. "Get every…"

A giant owl scooped up Kaine. Before Abram could react, Fleck and Sarai were taken as well. Abram was then ripped from the ground and airborne.

Chapter 9: The Unseen Threat

Abram felt the wind on his face. He saw the owls traveling further into the forest to a gaping hole in the middle of it.

The owls flew above the area and dove straight into the chasm. The descent felt long to Abram. He wondered how deep the chasm was.

Thousands of feet into the hole, the owls stopped near a ledge. They hovered and dropped the four onto it.

Abram could tell that the ledge and the hall were not natural. A voice echoed down the hall.

"This is a great honor. I come this close to the God killer and still live."

"Athena."

Abram was frightened. Kaine's thoughts were squeezed out like a putrid slime.

Athena continued, "You can't talk, Kaine. Is that why you hid from the Dunwi? They should have been no issue for you. Did you hide to save these three? They should have been inconsequential to you. There is no way they can help you in your fight against the Gods."

"Things change, Athena."

"Did Hermes tell you they are special?"

Athena waited for a response from Kaine, but he projected nothing.

"Yes, Kaine. I know about your and Hermes's little pact and how Hermes plays tricks on the other Gods to keep them fighting each other. I also know that you have the Neccrum. Any God with a little insight would recognize that. Fortunately for you, no other God has the wisdom I have."

"Follow me into my temple." Athena ushered the quartet into following her.

Inside the temple, there were men who were more plant than man.

"You might not trust me, Kaine, but know this: I do not seek the Neccrum and the power it brings. I have long since stopped dreaming of pushing my way to the top of the Godly hierarchy. My home is in this forest. I stumbled upon these creatures---the Druids---millennia ago. Their control over the plants and the creatures of the forest captivated me. I have since spent my time with them honing their powers for a chance like this. I do not seek power. What I seek is revenge."

At one point I called Hades my lover. Things changed when he discovered the Neccrum., Though not even the wickedness of the Neccrum could kill our love, Aphrodite is the one who drove a wedged between us and turned his heart cold. Aphrodite has always wanted the Neccrum, and her plans to get it were wicked. She knew my concerns for Hades's wellbeing after the Neccrum started to change him. Every night, she would come to feed him lies---that I was jealous of his newfound power. She told him that she was the only one who knew his true potential. The poison soured our love.

But her wickedness did not stop there. When I was out of the way and she had Hades snared in her trap, she finally made her move for the Neccrum. Aphrodite tried to poison him and take the Neccrum. But his tie to the Neccrum was too strong. Even death could not part them. The Neccrum revitalized him and changed him. Hades's new power made him even more formidable than Aphrodite. He chased her out of his temple. But Hades hid in a realm of his own creation to keep others away from the Neccrum. Why Ares paired with Hades, I know not.

Even now, I can feel the essence of Hades in the Neccrum and the pull between them. Maybe I could have saved him from his cruel fate and salvaged our love. But Aphrodite made that impossible, and for that, I will make her suffer."

"Do you intend to kill Aphrodite? Do you even have the power to do it?" Kaine asked.

"No. I have a more fiendish fate for her."

"How do you intend to do this?" Kaine questioned.

Athena laughed.

"You will just have to stay to find out. Of course, you are my bait, so don't try to escape. My owls would simply bring you back to me."

"Do you have the numbers you need to combat the Dunwi?"

"Kaine. I have everything I need in my Druids. Now it is time to let Aphrodite know I have the Neccrum."

Chapter 10: The Heat of Battle

Two days passed with no sign of Aphrodite.

"I think Aphrodite does not believe you have it," Kaine confessed.

The ominous sound of the Dunwi on the prowl reverberated through the forest.

Chir Chir

In the distance, Kaine saw what appeared to be a flock of birds. But as it came closer, the swarm revealed itself to be a legion of Dunwi.

"There must be hundreds if not thousands of Dunwi. Based on the sound, they are making their way through the forest as well," Kaine observed.

The Dunwi were practically upon Athena's ground.

"If you have a plan, Athena, now is the time to use it," Kaine remarked.

Athena snickered, "Now you shall see the power of my Druids!"

From below the treetops, owls popped up with Druids hanging on their backs. The birds flew headlong into the swarm of Dunwi. Druids sprang from the owls and lassoed several Dunwi with their vine-like appendages. The vines constricted like a vice, squeezing the Dunwi to death. The druids stayed afloat by swinging from one Dunwi to the next.

On the ground, the forest quaked with the stomping of tree-sized druids. The steps of the behemoth Druids alarmed the creatures of the wild. Many of the large Druids had not moved for centuries because never before had they been needed. The goliaths trampled through the forest, smashing the Dunwi under their feet. However, no matter how many Dunwi they killed, there always seemed to be more.

"You can't fight their numbers, Athena. What you are doing here is suicide for the Druids."

"They just have to hold off the Dunwi until she comes."

"By she, do you mean Aphrodite? Do you think she will really come for you?" Kaine questioned.

"She will come. She will take any chance to spite me!"

"Now, I know you and I have no threat from the Dunwi, but what about my fleshy friends?"

"Not a single Dunwi will reach the ground near your friends and remain alive. Even if I must kill every Dunwi that approaches."

Athena pulled a bow from her back and drew arrows from thin air.

"She has no quiver, but she pulls so many arrows. How is she doing it?" Sarai asked.

"It's her Godly magical weapon," Fleck affirmed. "That magic is on a whole other level than any magic item we have. Look at that."

Off in the distance was a small golden light. The light grew bigger, drawing closer to them.

"Here she comes!" shouted Athena as she aimed towards the light and released a torrent of arrows.

While the approach of Aphrodite distracted Athena, the Dunwi pulled in closer.

"This may be a good time to use your magic, Abram. Advise your friends to make no direct combat with the Dunwi. They are too dangerous to fight hand-to-hand," Kaine pressed.

Abram repeated Kaine's warning. Then, he held up his hand and called out. "Holy light!"

The Dunwi around them scattered. Kaine picked off a few with a violent spray of fireballs.

"That is a nice spell, but it is mainly aggravating the Dunwi, and we do not need that. What else do you got?" Kaine instructed.

"Phantom light," Abram admitted meekly.

"Abram, now listen to me!" Kaine instructed. "Your magic leaves a little to be desired. However, in times of great stress, a mage can pull deeper, and new magic will manifest. If it is not clear to you, this is one of those moments."

Abram took a deep breath and slowly released it. He brought his hands together and chanted.

"Phantom Death."

Suddenly all the Dunwi within a short distance fell to the ground dead.

"Incredible, kid!" Kaine cheered. "That spell won't take down a whopper, but that's all we need to take down a few Dunwi."

"Look to the sky, Abram. That must be Aphrodite. I hope whatever Athena has for her works. There would be no chance for me to get you all away from a God," Kaine admitted. "Athena is shelling out arrows, and it has not slowed down Aphrodite."

The light from Aphrodite grew more intense. The mighty God smashed down on the ground before Athena. Aphrodite gripped many arrows in her hand.

"You fight like a common human, Athena," Aphrodite quipped.

"You think so, Aphrodite? Then you won't mind me shooting you this close."

Athena's arms blurred with speed. No matter how many arrows she threw, Aphrodite did not dodge them. Athena panted from her efforts to hit Aphrodite. Aphrodite quickly moved to the exhausted Athena. She gripped Athena's bow hand with her left hand and then brought her other hand to Athena's chest.

"Let me show you how a real God fights."

Aphrodite's voice was bitter. A bright light flashed from Aphrodite's hand onto Athena's chest. The spark sent Athena flying and left an indentation on her breastplate.

Aphrodite stood over Athena with a smug smile on her face. Though bruised and defeated, Athena started laughing.

"What is so funny, Athena? Clearly, I have defeated you and will soon take the Neccrum as my own."

Athena laughed even more.

"You fool, Aphrodite! I knew you would come, and now you are right where I want you. Druids, unleash the trap."

Vines sprang up around Aphrodite, grasping her arms and legs.

"You intend to stop me with thin vines!" Aphrodite huffed. "Wait, I can't move. What have you done to me?"

Aphrodite fell to the ground.

"Poor Aphrodite. Didn't you know that this is holy ground for the Druids? They have protected this land from threats big and small. Even Gods.

I was once in the same place. Ironically enough, I was fleeing Kaine when I stumbled onto the Druids' sacred land. The druids determined I was a threat and incapacitated me in a similar fashion. There is a toxin in these very vines. This toxin only affects Gods. I convinced them I was not a threat and promised to aid them if they helped me with my all-consuming desire, to see the end of you. Although I did not know if their toxin would hold a God of your strength. I also know I don't have the power to end you. I will just have to be content with the thought that I have trapped you here forever."

Athena began laughing again.

Aphrodite's eyes fell on Kaine.

"Kaine, this is your doing. I know Athena could not have concocted this plan alone. You must have used the Neccrum against me."

Kaine rebuked her.

"I had no part in your current state, Aphrodite."

"Lies. I will send a message to all the Gods that you have escaped and now carry the Neccrum. You have painted a target on your own back."

With Aphrodite incapacitated, the Dunwi disbanded.

Athena turned to Kaine.

"Kaine, you can leave the Neccrum with me. I give you my word that I will not use it, and I will snare any God that comes to try to take it."

Kaine responded to Athena's plan harshly.

"And I give you my word that no God shall have the Neccrum! We leave immediately."

Kaine waved his hands, and the party took off into the sky, away from the forest.

"Good luck, Kaine. You have a world against you, and you will need all the luck you can get," Athena uttered.

Chapter 11: A New Friend?

"I think we put enough space between us and Athena. I grow weary. All this power and I still need to sleep. You all must be tired as well. Look ahead. There is a cave that should give us sufficient cover from prying eyes."

The group crawled inside the cave and fell asleep.

In the middle of the night, a mysterious voice and a poking finger woke up Abram.

"Abram. Wakey, wakey."

"Who's there? Who are you?"

"I'm not sure if I should tell you. You may overreact."

"If you are no threat to my friends, then there is no reason to overreact."

"That's the thing. You must promise that you will hear me out."

"If you are no threat to my friends, then I will hear you out."

"I am no threat to your friends. I am Necter, Jin's third lieutenant."

"Everyone, wake up. We are under attack!"

"I knew you would overreact. They can't hear you. This is not even the real you here. These are our astral bodies. Did you really think I would meet you in person? I couldn't harm your friends in this form if I tried. Now will you hear me out?"

"Why would I trust anyone who aligned themselves with Jin?"

"Fair point. Think of me as more of a neutral character. I certainly did not approve of Jin's methods nor his other lieutenants. My relationship with Jin was more of a business relationship. I have certain powers they found beneficial, and they were willing to pay for it. Their being dead cuts into my cash because they can no longer keep me afloat. I need to find another sponsor. I stick only with the powerful, and you, my friend, are one behemoth of a man."

"I still don't see why I should help you."

"You haven't even heard my offer. Abram, you are sitting on a gold mine, and you don't even know it. The Neccrum, you think only Gods can use it. But that is not true with me by your side. I have the skill to master any magical item. Any magical item, including the Neccrum. I can make it possible for you to use the Neccrum like a God can. Imagine how much power you would have and the good you could do with it. No God would be a threat to you. They would all fear your presence."

"I still don't know if I can trust you."

"Let me give you a gesture of my good intent. I have in my hand the Watchdog. If somebody wraps you in it, they can see all your deeds and can teleport to your exact location. This is how Jen and the other lieutenants always knew where you and, in particular, Sarai, were. Watch this."

Necter crushed the Watchdog in his hands.

"No orcs, trolls, or ogres teleporting to your exact location. You are free from the threat of Jin's lackeys trying to make a name for themselves. However, you still have the threat of every God in this world, and I can help you solve that problem. I am not asking you to trust me now. I am asking you to think about it. You can talk to me anytime. Just lay down and say 'Astral projection' then we can talk. Oh, and these astral projections are outside of time. We can talk forever, and not a moment goes by. So, if you are in dire straits, you have all the time in the world to figure things out."

In a snap, Abram woke from his slumber. Something was different about his meeting with the third lieutenant. Jin left him exhausted and frightened. The meeting with Necter soothed his spirit. Abram felt comfort for the first time in a long time.

Could the third lieutenant be trusted? Abram thought.

Abram did not want to alarm his friends. He thought that with the Watchdog gone there was one less thing to worry about. Abram laid back down and fell asleep.

Chapter 12: A Solemn Vow

"Hurry, Kya! We can hide over here!" Layla cried.

On their way westward before they met Abram, Layla and Kya were running away from outraged humans.

The two giants ducked behind a tree.

"Why are they chasing us, Layla?" Kya asked.

"Kya, I know you have only been accepted, but before you were born, humans hounded us. Most humans think all giants are evil because there are few giants that live peacefully with humans."

"But why?" Kya pleaded.

"Because few giants live in a community like us. Most giants are solitary and territorial. Father brought us all together and guided us to a better life, but he is not here. You have to promise me something."

"I would do anything for you, sister," Kya assured.

"You must promise you will trust no one other than me. Humans can appear helpful until they reveal their true intentions. You must promise this for your safety."

"I will do as you wish, sister," Kya assured.

"Come. It won't be long before they search here. Just remember what you swore."

Chapter 13: A Cry for Help

Morning came, and Abram and the others woke up. Everybody in the party seemed more worn down than before they had fallen asleep, everyone except Abram.

The party inched out of the cave.

"What I wouldn't give to sleep a night in the Bastion. I am…" Fleck's eyes looked out into the distance and caught someone familiar.

"Everyone, run! We have a giant problem," Fleck shouted.

Before they could run, Kya fell to her knees, pleading.

"Please wait! Something is wrong with Layla!"

Kaine projected to Abram, "Maybe we should stay. She seems to be in trouble, and one giant would be no trouble for me to take."

Abram agreed, but Fleck was the first to address Kya.

"Come to make another pass on the Neccrum?"

"I need your help. There is something wrong with Layla. I think the lucky talisman has corrupted her."

"What is wrong with Layla?" Sarai asked, concerned for her.

"She has changed. Her skin has yellowed. I can barely recognize her. She has given up her search for the Neccrum and now hunts these purple prisms."

Kya pulled a purple prism from her pouch. With teary eyes, Kya looked at the gem.

"Let's huddle up, guys," Fleck squeaked.

The group stepped into a circle.

"Obviously, this is a trap," Fleck stated.

"I don't know. She seems genuinely distraught," Sarai admitted. "I say we help her."

"Well, bless your bleeding heart," Fleck said sarcastically. "I say we show her how much we appreciate them turning on us and leave her stranded. But I leave this to you, Abram."

Kaine made his thoughts apparent to Abram.

"These are truly odd circumstances. I fear the worst from her description. We should at the very least see what has become of her sister."

Abram spoke to the group.

“We will find out what has happened to Layla and then we shall decide our actions.”

“I don’t like this at all, but I will tell the compass to find Layla,” Fleck conceded.

Chapter 14: A Past Private Conversation

Inside the Bastion, Sarai was watching Abram as he tried to fall asleep.

"I don't even know how old you are," Sarai realized. "How old are you?"

"That depends on where you are. In my village, I'm eighteen."

"What about here? How old are you here?"

"Here I am over four hundred thousand years old."

Sarai laughed.

"You look great for your age!"

Abram smiled. "No, seriously. I am over four hundred thousand years old. In my village, time doesn't move as fast. This pendant keeps me aging at the same speed as the village."

"Yeah, alright, you cradle robber. Obviously, you need sleep more than I thought."

Abram laughed, rolled over, and went back to sleep. Sarai had never felt luckier than at this moment. Sarai pulled in close to Abram and fell asleep.

Chapter 15: Unexpected Detour

"Kya, I don't think we can travel any more today," Sarai acknowledged, feeling tired from the giant's pace.

"We must travel more. My sister is in danger."

"I'm sorry, Kya. We will be no good to Layla if we continue at this pace," Abram agreed.

"If we must," Kya huffed.

"Hey, has anyone considered the alternative? Kaine whooshes us away to Layla," Fleck proposed.

"My power also has its limitations. I cannot fly us forever, and when my magic is fatigued, it takes a long time to recuperate. I would be useless to all of you," Kaine shared with Abram.

Everyone in the party went to sleep. After a little while, something rattled Kaine awake.

"Is that you, Abram?" Kaine asked.

Before Kaine could react, Kya, Abram, Sarai, and Fleck pinned him down. The group spoke in unison.

"Join us, Kaine."

A weird white foam dribbled from their mouths. Kaine was furious.

"Hera! You couldn't have me then, and you will not have me now."

"You couldn't then, but you should now?" Hera teased, "With your power, I would be unstoppable. You must know I have changed and grown since our last meeting. My strength comes from my flock, and I no longer torture them. Instead, I look to building a better world with no other evil Gods pestering humans."

"A world enslaved by you is not a better world! I will not have your heresy!"

Kaine shot off a gust of wind that blasted the others back.

"I am coming for you, Hera."

Kaine levitated the group and took to the skies.

Kaine was uncertain if he could make it to Hera, but something had to be done to save his new companions. Kaine flew for miles until he saw the temple of Hera, but something was different. Hera once worked her minions day and night. Now there was no one. Kaine dismissed the thought and flew into the fortress of Hera.

"Kaine. I was expecting you."

Kaine blurted out, "What have you done with the people that clamor about?"

"I told you, Kaine. I have changed. I no longer work my subjects night and day. They sleep, eat, and care for themselves."

"Subjects. You say that as if these people had a choice to follow you. Your cruelty may have changed, but you are the same. I demand you let my cohorts go."

"I can't do that, Kaine. At least, not for free."

"What are you getting at, Hera?"

"I can let them go, but I have a price. I want you, Kaine. Become one of my subjects and I will let them go."

"So, you can subjugate them again. Never!"

"You have my word, Kaine. I will not take them into my fold now or ever. I am not asking you to decide now. You will have three moon cycles to consider it. For now, I will release them, and you can go on your way."

"How can I know you are telling the truth?"

"You will have to trust me. Don't try to betray me. I will listen in from time to time."

Hera waved her hand and released the party. They became conscious of their surroundings.

"Where are we?" Sarai said groggily.

"Kaine, as a show of my good faith, I will give you supplies for your journey. My Greymeer wolves to carry you and open my temple to you for rest."

Kaine and the party were in no condition to say no. They accepted Hera's offer.

Chapter 16: What Now

The party rode along until they thought they were no longer within earshot of Hera. While they rode, Kaine caught Abram up on the situation. When they finally stopped, Abram broke the bad news to the rest of the party.

"We have three moon cycles to find the Duos Rings. Hera put her seed into us and has released us on a temporary basis."

"That's fresh," Fleck grimaced. "We don't have word one on where the other Duos Ring is, and now this."

Concerned for her sister, Kya broke in.

"What of my sister? Something evil possesses her. We need to find her."

"I guess with no lead on where the other Dous Ring is, we take care of the immediate problem: finding Layla," Sarai conceded.

"Then it is agreed. We help Kya find her sister," Abram stated. "Fleck, get the compass and set a course for Layla."

Fleck reached into his pocket for the compass, but his hand met nothing.

"I don't have the compass. Do any of you have the compass?"

Sarai and Abram checked themselves.

"Nothing," Sarai admitted

"I don't have the compass either," Abram seconded.

"Now what? There is no way we can find Layla without the compass," Sarai sighed.

"I have the lucky talisman," Kya said meekly.

"The same lucky talisman that corrupted your sister?" Fleck questioned.

"Yes," Kya whimpered.

"And how is using it a good idea?" Fleck said sarcastically.

"Fleck, we have no other leads," Sarai urged. "We have to try something. Layla did not become corrupted all at once. It happened over time. Kya has had it for a while. We can each take the talisman for a little, and hopefully that will be enough to keep any one of us from being corrupted. I'll take it first, and we will move on to the next person as we go."

"I should go first, Sarai," Abram said, concerned.

"Abram, this is not yours to decide, and you are the only one who can talk to Kaine. We can't risk losing you. I will go first, and Fleck can take it next," Sarai insisted. "We should get moving. The day is almost done, and we have precious little time to find Layla."

Chapter 17: What luck

After a few hours of travel, the group made camp.

"Sarai, I insist you let me carry the talisman," Abram asserted.

"Abram, I am fine. How long did Layla have the talisman before it corrupted her? Many days, I am sure."

Kaine felt dark energy pulsing from the talisman.

"Abram, I suggest we find a different way to locate Layla. There is no doubt in my mind that the talisman is evil." Kaine interjected.

"What am I to do, Kaine? Sarai has made up her mind. She is as strong as she is stubborn."

"I don't know what else to do," Kaine confessed.

Abram did not respond to Kaine's statement. He merely lay down close to Sarai, who was fast asleep. Concern weighed heavily on Abram, and he was not relieved by what Kaine had to say. Abram thought of what was to come next and fell into an uneasy sleep.

The next day, Sarai was up early and waited for the others to wake. As they rose, Sarai addressed them.

"Woo. I feel good. I think this talisman refreshes your spirit. It definitely does not feel evil."

"I felt it too," Kya concurred.

"I love this talisman," Sarai squealed.

Abram feared for Sarai. She appeared addicted to the talisman.

"The talisman is already affecting you, Sarai. I insist you give it to me or Fleck."

"Don't be a wet blanket, Abram. I am fine."

Sarai's defiance frustrated Abram, but he did not know how to convey his concerns in a way she would understand. Instead, the group continued to follow the path of the lucky talisman. In a very short time, they found Layla outside a dense forest. They were almost certain she could not see them through the forest.

"We should follow her stealthily and when she is not expecting us, we grab her," Fleck whispered.

"I do not concur, elf," Kya said angrily. "Every minute she is like this could mean permanent damage. We do not know if we can reverse the effects."

Sarai spoke at a normal volume.

"She'll be fine. She…"

Fleck quickly placed his hand over Sarai's mouth. Layla stopped for a moment and looked around.

"If you can't speak quietly, don't speak at all," Fleck hissed.

The band silently followed Layla until she reached a cavern. Layla looked around one more time and went into the cavern.

"Perfect. We can try to catch Layla in the cavern, and she will have no place to run," Fleck suggested.

"Let's nab her!" Sarai squealed.

"Inside voices, Sarai. Inside voices," Fleck corrected.

The group crept closer to the cave. Inside the cave was a long and winding tunnel that led to a large open space. When they got to the clearing, they heard Layla chanting. As they slowly approached Layla, she whipped her head around and smiled at them.

"I am very glad you made it here. You can witness Kallos awakening. With his arrival, the Gods will fear once more. Kallos has already destroyed the land of the Gods. With this last crystal, he will be whole once more. He shall abolish all the Gods that remain and everything else the Gods have touched."

Layla placed the last crystal, and beams of purple light streamed out.

Fleck shouted, "We can't allow this to happen. We should try to break some…"

Suddenly, Sarai swung her mace into Fleck's chest, knocking the wind out of him.

Abram stared in horror at Sarai's transformation. Sarai's skin had yellowed, and her eyes were black. Abram cursed himself for not taking the talisman away from Sarai.

The purple prism formed a four-legged crystalline creature. Kallos cried out with a deafening voice.

"As once I have done before, I do again. I will destroy the Gods and everything they hold…"

Kallos stopped talking as if it was in a trance. Light flickered throughout the cavern and Kallos's body. The light centered on a point on the ground behind him.

The force pulling Kallos also tore Layla and Sarai to the same point. They tried to resist, but the power was too strong. Before the party could stop it. Kallos, Sarai, and Layla were all gone.

Abram cried out in agony, "Sarai!"

But it was too late. Abram searched the spot where the three had disappeared, crying in sorrow at his loss.

"She must be here! She has to be here!" Abram fell to the ground in frustration.

Fleck wheezed, "What did we just see?"

Kaine put his arm around Abram trying to comfort him.

"We will find her, Abram. Let us look on the bright side. Kallos is no longer a threat. We should retreat and come up with our next plan."

Abram trudged along as they made their way out of the cave.

"How can this get worse?" Abram thought.

But the worst was yet to come.

Chapter 18: Surprise

As the party neared the opening of the cave, they heard a loud commotion. Expecting the worst, they slowed down and crept to the opening. They peered out into the forest. Waiting for them was the entire Red Army.

The man at the head of the army declared, "Killers of Ren, we know you are in there. We can enter the cave and kill you like cowards. Or you can come out and die as men. Either way, your lives have been forfeited."

Abram turned to Kaine.

Kaine shook his head in defeat. "I can fly out of here with you all, or protect you for a time from their attack, but I can't do both."

Abram wracked his brain for a solution to their impossible situation. Suddenly, he remembered what Necter had said. Abram lay down and closed his eyes. "Astral projection."

Abram's astral self released from his body. He could see his friends huddling at the entrance of the cave and a sea of Red Army soldiers waiting for them. They all looked very far away.

Abram cried out.

"Necter! Necter! Can you hear me?"

"Loud and clear, buddy. It looks like you got yourself into quite a pickle."

"I do not know how they found us, but the Red Army was waiting for us. What am I to do?"

"Abram, listen to me. I have an item that could help you in this instance, but you have to trust me. I can give you an item through the astral plane. It sounds simple, but it is very difficult to do. Think of this like the rings you have. Yes, I know about the rings. The more you trust me, the more likely it will work. Can you trust me, Abram?"

"For my friends, I will."

"Take this trumpet. It has the power to save you, but I warn you. You may not like the consequences. Return to your body."

Abram's body came to life, trumpet in hand.

Kaine stood, astounded.

"Where did you get that horn?"

"That doesn't matter right now. Right now, I must take care of the Red Army."

Abram stepped into the sunlight at the opening of the cave. The leader of the Red Army cried out, and his soldiers roared behind him. Abram blew the horn. All the soldiers simply dropped to the ground. Stunned, Fleck walked out of the cave. He knelt to inspect the soldier.

"He's dead. I'm pretty sure they're all dead."

More death. The death of all the soldiers hung heavily on Abram. He wanted to save his friends, but he had not wanted to kill an entire army of people. Kaine saw the concern on Abram's face and patted him on the back.

"I'm certain the elf is mistaken, but we can't wait for the Red Army to awaken. We must fly away while we still can."

Chapter 19: Morale

Kaine landed them miles away from the Red Army. Abram was still in shock.

"You saved your friends, Abram. That is all that matters," Kaine assured him.

Abram found no comfort in his words.

"Now what?" Fleck spouted. "Layla and Sarai are Gods-know-where. We have no leads and are almost two moon cycles away from becoming the play toys of Hera. What do we do next? Where do we go next?"

Kya murmured, "I have the lucky talisman."

"You have the lucky talisman!" Fleck said, shocked. "How is it a good thing to have the lucky talisman? How did you get it?"

"Sarai dropped it when she was sucked in. I don't know why the force pulling them did not take the talisman, but it is truly the only lead we have."

"Are you hearing this, Abram?" Fleck spouted. "Abram, are you listening to this super bad, super dangerous idea? Abram, are you listening?"

But Abram had his own idea.

"We use the Talisman."

"Are you listening to yourself? You saw what it did to Layla and Sarai. Can we risk losing another member of our party?"

"I will carry it. I've led us this far, and I accept the consequences of my actions. Find Sarai is all that is important to me."

Kaine turned to Abram.

"Are you truly ready for this, Abram?" he questioned.

"For Sarai, I am."

"Hey, Abram, Kaine. We can't hear your private conversation. You aren't doing this, Abram. Right?" Fleck begged.

"Kya, give me the talisman. We move out now."

Chapter 20: A Brother's World

After a day's hike, the party arrived late in a city called Maelor. They decided to find an inn so they could sleep on proper beds.

Abram felt a tug from the talisman pushing him forward, ahead of the others. Abram opened the door of the inn.

Kaine was alarmed.

"Abram wa..."

Abram stepped through the door, and it snapped shut behind him. Ahead of Abram was a flat plain on a giant mountain. Behind him were a cliff and a familiar voice. Abram turned around to see his brother Levi slowly levitating towards him.

"Welcome, brother, to my world. I have created this alternate world using my magic. You are part of a select few who have seen this world. Not even Ares knows about this creation. However, all those who made it here have one thing in common: all their journeys ended here," Levi said coldly.

What do you think of it, Abram? The landscape is a little bleak and dark. I've tried to make it better. I've brought in plants and animals. But the plants slowly wither away, and the animals become ill and die. I guess I am not like you, Abram. You always had a green thumb, and animals always loved you"

Levi landed in front of him. Positioning the cliff behind Abram.

"I am sure you already know why you are here, and you know I am capable of finishing this now, pushing you off the cliff. I could end you and grab the Neccrum from your dead body. However, you have angered Ares, and for that, he wants you to suffer. So, I am here to fulfill his desires."

Levi pulled his sword, and Abram followed suit. Abram's sword did not burn blue. Abram did not know if he could take on his brother in a sword fight. He needed all the help he could get. Not having his sword at full power was a tremendous disadvantage.

Why did my sword fail me now? Abram thought.

Levi stared Abram down. His icy glare gave Abram chills. Levi raised his hand and beckoned Abram to come.

Abram took a deep breath and charged Levi. He thrust his sword forward, hoping to knock his brother's sword from his hand. Levi parried away his advance and flung him to the ground.

Levi closed in on Abram. He tried to rise as his brother approached, but he was too slow. Abram could not defend himself nor stop Levi's attack. He stepped on Abram's sword hand and smacked Abram with the broad side of his sword.

Abram winced. Even with his magical armor, Abram felt the blow to his body.

How can I beat my brother when he is so strong? Abram wondered.

Levi allowed Abram to free his sword arm and roll away. Abram took a different approach with his next attack. He slowly and steadily circled his brother, looking for an opening.

Levi stood firm but did not keep his sight on Abram. Quickly, Abram was at his brother's side and noticed his brother grip his sword. At that moment, Abram struck his brother with an overhead blow.

Levi raised his sword, blocking Abram's blow. While Abram's sword was locked in Levi's guard, Levi pulled back his arm and swung it forward. He landed a crushing blow on Abram's chest. Abram skidded towards the edge of the cliff. His limbs flailed around as he rolled towards it.

Abram felt cuts and bruises all over his body.

Levi started to gloat.

"No matter how much fun this is, I do have to put an end to this, and I know exactly what I'm going to do."

Levi started to grow. His skin turned red. His jowls jutted forward. Horns protruded from the back of his head, and wings grew out from his sides. Before Abram now stood a mighty red dragon.

Abram felt sick in the pit of his stomach. He remembered his vision from the beginning of his journey.

It can't end this way. I need to save my brother. Abram thought, desperate for another way to stop this fight.

"Brother!" Abram yelled. "We have to end this! I do not know what Ares has promised you, but we are family. We must stick together."

"You are right about one thing, little brother. This does have to end," Levi avowed.

A puff of smoke wafted out of Levi's mouth, and flames shot towards Abram. Abram ducked and rolled away. He knew the fire would not hurt him, but he did not want his brother to know that.

As the flames ceased pouring from his mouth, Levi snapped his tail at Abram. The blow knocked Abram dangerously close to the edge of the cliff.

Abram did not know how much more punishment he could take. Every blow was excruciating. No magical armor could protect him from Levi's advances. Abram tried to catch his breath. His mind racing. He knew what he had to do. Abram gathered all the strength he could muster and threw himself towards Levi's chest. Abram rushed to strike the final blow, but Levi laughed and swatted him back to the ground.

"This is futile, little brother."

Levi pinned Abram in his claws.

"This is the end for you, brother." Levi declared, "I am going to crush you with my hands."

Abram felt a sinking feeling as Levi pressed him, but an unusual calm soon replaced it.

"Brother, we can share magic," Abram said meekly.

"What was that, brother? Are you pleading for your life?" Levi reveled in the moment.

Abram shouted, "We can share magic!"

Abram exploded in size, knocking his brother back. Before Levi was a behemoth blue dragon.

"How did you grow so large?" Levi questioned. "It matters not! I will destroy you just the same!"

Another plume of smoke leaked from Levi's mouth, followed by a rush of flames. A volley of ice shards met Levi's attack.

Levi winced from the pain. He felt something surrounding him. Abram wrapped his mighty arms around Levi and bit one of his wings, ripping it off.

"There is no escape for you, brother," Abram cried. "Take my help and break your ties with Ares!"

"Never!" Levi exclaimed.

It was at that moment Abram noticed the sigil of Ares on his brother's back. Abram placed his hand on the sigil and used his icy touch to freeze the mark on Levi's back. He ripped off the frozen flesh.

Levi shrieked in pain. Then began shrinking until he returned to his human form and fell to the ground. Abram returned to his human form as well.

"Brother! I am here for you!" Abram vowed. Abram lifted Levi onto his lap.

"Abram," Levi said weakly, "I wanted none of this. I never wanted to hurt you or Aleese. I made a deal with Ares to save my life after the succubus left me to die. All I could do was watch in horror at all the atrocities."

"Don't speak, brother. Save your strength. We will get you help, and you can come back to Trow," Abram pleaded.

"Abram, I knew," Levi coughed, "I knew one day you would surpass me. I am just glad I got to live to see it."

"Brother, you are speaking nonsense. We need to get you out of here and get help," Abram cried.

"Abram, you must know. The Duos Ring… Zeus has it. It is the only way you can defeat the Gods. Ares planned to take them from Zeus and Kaine and use them to ensure his supremacy. Now go! This world will collapse soon, and you will be stuck if you stay!"

A door opened at the cliff's edge.

"Levi, I have to take you with me. We can get the rings together."

"Abram, go…"

Abram felt his brother's breathing stop. With tears in his eyes, Abram laid his brother down and made his way to the door. Abram looked back at Levi.

"I will find you, brother. I will take you home…"

Darkness fell over Levi's world. Abram looked back one last time and stepped through the door.

Chapter 21: Everyone Has to Pay

Three men gathered, and for the first time, they did not fear retribution.

"He's gone. He's really gone," stated Lamund. "It is finally time to step out of his shadow and make a name for ourselves."

"Make a name for ourselves? This is a time for vengeance. We owe him a lot. Abram and his crew must pay."

"Don't be like that, Showlar. Think of the opportunity before you. Jin kept us in a trash heap, hiding from the Gods, never getting what we rightfully deserve," Lamund remarked.

"I can't believe you are so callous. Maybe we had to hide a little, but we were kings among peasants. Everybody who knew us feared us," Showlar retorted.

"You have been quiet this whole time. What do you think?" Lamund asked Necter.

"I think everyone pays for their actions, and this is no different."

Chapter 22: The Edge

Abram was shaken to the core. His brother was truly dead, and the power he gained from Levi passing was immense. His entire body tingled. The only thing keeping him alive was the pendant.

He had returned to his own world, in front of the inn in Maelor. Everyone noticed a change.

"Abram, you are seething with magic. What happened?" asked Kaine.

"My brother and I could share magic. When he passed, I gained his power."

"You're not looking so good, Chief," Fleck noted. "Are you alright?"

"I think I'm going to be alright. The only thing holding me together is my pendant."

Kaine offered him a hand for support.

"Let's get a room in the inn."

The four travelers spoke to the innkeeper and wearily trudged to their rooms.

Abram laid down.

"Astral projection."

"Necter! Necter! Are you out there!?!"

"Abram, I am here. I see you got an upgrade of sorts."

"That doesn't matter right now. What matters now is what will become of the Neccrum."

"I don't understand. What is your plan for the Neccrum?"

"In the fight with my brother, I was lucky. I could share his power, and that is the only reason I was able to best him. Maybe with the Gods, we will not be so lucky. We need an edge."

"I'm still not following you, Abram. What is it you want to do?"

"I want you to give us the power of the Neccrum."

"Now you have come to your senses! I can do that. All you have to do is give me the Neccrum."

"If I do that, do you promise that you'll give us the power of the Neccrum?"

"I am a man of my word. I will give you what is coming to you."

Abram reached for the pouch holding the Neccrum and slid it over to his chest. Abram removed the Neccrum, and he hesitated.

"Abram! You have a magic pouch! You are full of surprises! Now give the Neccrum to me," Necter insisted.

Abram did not move. After a moment, He gave the Neccrum to Necter.

Necter started laughing.

"Are you really so gullible? You think I wouldn't repay you for killing Jin and the others? Why any of them fell to you, I don't know. But I'm with Hades now," Necter gloated. "The Red Army outside the cave was a plant. They were a small price to pay for your trust and the Neccrum. The look on your face when you killed them all. Priceless! That's right. I saw it. I never destroyed the Watchdog on you. The only thing I was missing was a way to get the Neccrum out of your pouch. I couldn't get close enough to it without warning you of my intent. You had to hand it over. However, I will not leave you empty-handed, Abram."

Necter threw a scroll to Abram.

"This is a magical map. If you want the Neccrum back, you must prove yourself through a series of trials. This map shows the way from one trial to the next. It will only reveal the current trial to you and nothing further. The longer you take, the harder the trials will become. If you survive them all, you'll find me. Don't worry about me telling anyone that you no longer have the Neccrum. I am enjoying every God chasing you down."

Necter snapped his fingers, and Abram shot back into the physical world. Sharp pains shot through his body. It was all too much. As Abram returned to his physical body, he passed out.

Chapter 23: Where Am I

Abram slowly became conscious of the world around him, and a familiar voice rang through.

"Abram. Are you okay? You were moaning in your sleep. We could not find out what was wrong, but you seem to be alright now."

"Levi?" Abram stammered. "You died."

"To the contrary, Abram. I am quite alive, but I was not the only one who worried about you. Sarai barely slept a wink thinking about you."

"Sarai…" Abram said, disoriented.

"I'm here, Abram," Sarai bubbled. "We think the Bastion saved you."

Abram came to suddenly and remembered everything.

"The map!! We have trials to find Necter and the Neccrum."

"Who is Necter and what is the Neccrum?"

Abram sat up and faced Levi.

"What happened to Trow?"

"What happened to Trow? What an odd question! It is never better. Trade is good. Our village is thriving."

"What are we doing out here?"

"Seeking glory, of course! A merchant with a map came. He was too afraid to seek the treasure himself. He was happy to give us the map if we cut him in on the treasure, and we were plenty fine to do that."

"Are Sarai and I still married?"

"Ha, ha, ha. Abram, you are a strange bird today. Of course, you are married and trying to have children."

"I thought mages can't have children."

"Mages! Now I know you are mad. Mages. That is funny, Abram. Now, let us stop this crazy talk and get to the matters at hand---finding the treasure at the end of this map. We can't be far now."

Abram did not know what to think. He had everything he wanted. Levi was alive. Trow was not in trouble, and best of all, Sarai was beside him, and they were trying to have a family. Still, something seemed wrong.

Levi pressed on past Abram. Sarai pulled forward and wrapped her arms around Abram. He, for a moment, forgot what was wrong, and reveled in peace and happiness.

"Maybe this isn't so bad," Abram admitted to himself. "I have everything I could ever want."

"Look ahead!" Levi shouted, "A crumbling castle! That must be where the treasure is hidden."

Levi took off in a sprint towards the castle.

"Come on, Abram," Sarai interjected as she took off running.

Abram got caught up in the excitement. He began running as well.

In the castle, Abram found Levi covered in jewels and gold.

"What luck, Abram!" Levi said giddily. "All this treasure left unguarded! We are fortunate indeed. I found an ancient artifact. I do not know how old it is."

Levi turned around, grabbed the object, and presented it to Abram. Abram paled.

"Abram, you do not seem well. Are you alright?"

Abram cleared his throat.

"That's the Neccrum."

"Abram, you were on about this earlier. What is the Neccrum?"

"It's the artifact Hades uses to control the spirits of the dead."

"Hades? You are talking awfully strangely. Are you sure you are not sick?"

Abram closed his eyes and turned his attention inward.

"This isn't real. This isn't real."

When Abram opened his eyes, he was back in the astral plane. Abram realized he was in a losing game.

Chapter 24: What Is Next

Alone, he waited there in the astral plane. A moment of clarity struck Abram.

"I need to save my friends."

Abram closed his eyes and did not open them until he heard familiar voices.

"Abram. Where are we?" asked Kaine. "Wait! I can speak here. What manner of place is this?"

"What did you do, Abram?" Fleck added.

"This is the astral plane. I brought you here because Necter has taken the Neccrum. We must get it back. He has tasked me with following a map to him. I fear we will never get to him if we follow these trials. But I feel I know a better way."

Abram shut his eyes and when he opened them, he was in another realm and Necter was before him.

"Abram! You sneaky man. I would never have guessed that you would find out how to pull another person into the astral plane and I have no idea how you used it to skip realms. That is some impressive stuff. Despite that, you are too late. I've already given Hades the Neccrum."

As if they were conjured by Necter, Hades and Ares appeared behind him.

"I've aligned myself with new friends. And I made a deal with them. If you had somehow made it through my trials, they would have finished you painfully."

At Necter's words, Hades laughed.

"Why do you think we would align ourselves with some sniveling little cur?"

Necter retorted, "You're making a mistake, gentlemen. I can make your people so much stronger."

The two gods just laughed.

"Pappy always said keep a trump card," Necter said glibly. "Kallos. The name may be unfamiliar to you, Hades, but I know Ares knows it well. Kallos was crafted in your world to destroy everything. It was a magical weapon. The strongest magical item I've ever seen... And now it is part of me. Don't think you can zap your way out or fight with your magic. Kallos nullifies all powers of the Gods."

Kallos materialized in front of Necter. A deafening cry echoed from it and light welled up in Kallos mouth. A beam of energy sprang from Kallos towards Ares and Hades. The Gods did their best to dodge the beam, barely getting out of the way in time.

Kaine made his thoughts known to Abram.

"Abram. We can't allow him to control Kallos. He is not looking at us. We must get to him before he turns his attention to us."

Abram ignored Kaine's words because he had just seen something more important to him.

"Sarai!"

Abram ran to Sarai's unconscious body but quickly found he could not get to her. There was an unseen force keeping him at a distance. Out of the corner of his eye, Abram saw Kya charging towards him. Layla lay limp beside Sarai.

Kya struck with all her might, smashing into the field blocking her from Layla. She bounced off the mystical force. The giant jumped up and pounded on the bubble with both her hands, crying out Layla's name.

Suddenly, Layla and Sarai snapped up and, in unison, called out, "None can control Kallos."

Sarai and Layla screamed and charged towards Necter. He was busy fighting Hades and Ares and had no time to protect himself as Sarai smashed her mace on his chest, killing him with one fatal blow. Kallos let out a roar of pain and collapsed into a small ball of light. At its smallest and brightest, the sphere exploded in every direction.

The blast lifted Abram off the ground and his friends as well. He resigned himself to his fate of being smashed to death on the walls of Hades' realm. Instinctively, Abram felt his magic return as Kallos effects dissipated. He blinked himself and the rest of his party into the astral plane.

Kaine was the first to speak.

"Is everyone alright?"

"Not everyone is alright. Sarai and Layla are unconscious!" Fleck added.

"Sarai!" Abram said, alarmed.

Abram dashed to Sarai's side.

"You must wake up!"

Sarai slowly opened her eyes.

"Where am I?" Sarai said meekly.

"You are safe," Abram wept with tears of joy. "This is the astral plane. It is a space unlike any other. Through it, we can go anywhere."

Kaine broke in, "I think we should put that to our advantage and go straight to the Duos Ring!"

"There is something wrong," Abram admitted. "I can't see where it is located. Something is blocking my sight in the astral plane."

"Do you think Zeus knows about the astral plane, Abram?"

"It would appear so, Kaine."

"Let me sum things up?" Fleck cracked. "The Dous Ring, we need them, but Zeus has it, Gods-know-where. We need Zeus out of the way so we can find it, but the only thing that might do away with a God, the Duos Ring, is in said God's hands. We may be able to trade for it. However, the only bargaining chip we had, the Neccrum, is in the hands of Hades and Ares. I am sure they will not be letting go of it any time soon. In short, we have nothing."

A twinkle sparked in Abram's eye.

"Maybe we have more than you think."

Abram blinked away from the astral plane late in the morning. The morning became the afternoon. The afternoon became the evening. When late evening arrived, Abram reappeared.

"Abram! Where have you been?" Fleck said, startled by Abram's return. "And what do you have there? How did you get the Neccrum back?"

"I didn't," Abram said flatly. "It is a decoy. Come with me now. We must get into place."

"Where..." Fleck started talking as he was blinked away, "...are we going?"

"We must be quiet," Abram warned. "Zeus's forces will hear us."

"Hear us?" Fleck said, looking about. "Is that Mt Olympus I see? With an army of Zeus's men around. Abram, I said you were my lucky charm, bringing me wealth beyond my greatest dreams, but now I see you are the one that will get me killed."

"Keep it down, Fleck," Abram restated. "I have a plan, and I have this."

"You have the Neccrum."

"A facsimile. Yes," Abram said snidely.

"And this plan. Are you going to tell us what it is?"

"Nope," coughed Abram.

"And this plan will happen when?"

"Six days from now. We wait here at the very edge of Zeus's forces…and hope Hades and Ares aren't faster."

"Can we vote for a new leader? I am allergic to dying by a maniac."

"Trust me."

Chapter 25: The Sixth Day

The group rested on the morning of the sixth day while Abram kept watch. A sound in the distance woke them all.

"Horns!" Sarai gasped. "That's the sound of an oncoming army. Who would be foolish enough to go against the forces of Zeus?"

In moments, Zeus's army was ready for war. Fleck pointed into the distance.

"I see the forces of Hera coming from the west. What is she doing attacking Zeus? Her army could push Zeus's men back, but they would not let her followers near Zeus's fortress."

Abram smiled.

"Look to the east!"

"Giants and elves! A union I would have never expected!" Fleck said, astonished.

"Now look to the south!"

"It's the people of Aulmad with their moving carts. But they are facing the wrong way," Sarai observed.

"They are our backup, and hopefully we will not need them," Abram assured them. "Now we must make our way up Olympus. While Zeus's forces detained, we should be able to slip up the path to his stronghold."

"We're going to pull this off, Abram!" Fleck said, astonished.

"Fleck, I need your keen eyes taking point. Layla, Kya, I need you bringing the muscle. And Sarai, I need you watching our backs. I don't foresee any of Zeus's men coming after us, but we need to be prepared. Kaine, I know you know your role. Let's move."

Chapter 26: Betrayal

Earlier:

"Hermes!" Abram shouted.

"How did you find me, and what manner of travel did you take? This realm is my own, and I thought only I was privy to it."

"I travel through the astral plane. I think it links all realms, but despite its power, I cannot pinpoint the Duos Ring. We need the ring. Hades and Ares once again have the Neccrum. Their army marches towards Zeus's fortress. Hades and Ares are coming for the ring, killing everything in their way. Hades becomes stronger with every person they kill. We know your father has the ring, and we believe it is in his fortress. We have plans to distract his men with an army of our own and slip into his fortress undetected. Can you lend us aid?"

"I cannot give you direct help without possibly pulling Zeus into the fight, and I have little in the way of an army. But I have been preparing for this moment. I have a troop of blacksmiths who have been minting armor and weapons in the event I must go to war with my father. It pains me it has come to this, but I fear my father will not give up the ring until it is too late, and Hades and Ares's army will have swallowed everything in its path. If you bring your army, I can outfit them well."

Chapter 27: Moving Mountains

Abram flashed out of the astral plane before a group of giants

"Giant folk! I'm looking for Valadameer. I felt him near, but I do not see him."

One of the older giants spoke.

"You have found him, or at least his final resting place."

Abram cursed his luck. Without Valadameer's influence, Abram risked enraging the giants with his plot against Zeus the way Hermes angered Layla and Kya.

"Then you must carry my message. An unstoppable army bears down on Zeus's fortress. Without reinforcements, they stand little chance."

Abram's story did not convince the old giant.

"What power can rival the force of Zeus?"

"I seek not to offend you. I am merely carrying out the will of Hermes. He tasked me with raising an army. Valadameer trusted me to save his people in Millet. Now, in our time of need, I seek the aid of the giants. Valadameer entrusted me with this gold coin."

One of the younger giants spoke in astonishment. "The Hienick."

"Stranger, allow me the care of that gold coin and you will have an army."

Chapter 28: Time in the Sun

Abram now sought the aid of the elves. Not wanting to repeat his mistake with the giants, Abram materialized away from the elven camp.

Abram walked up to the encampment.

"I seek the right hand of the Hessin."

"Careful, human. Mentioning the Hessin will have some elves wanting to torture you and more still wanting to kill you where you stand."

"I mean no offense. I merely speak on behalf of Ardan. I know he served as the right hand, and I look for his kin."

The elves at the edge of the camp whispered to each other. Abram did not know if this was a good thing or not, but he readied himself for a quick jump. The whispering elves beckoned Abram to come into the tent in the center of the huts.

The elf leading Abram approached an elder and whispered in his ear.

"Here you are, human. You can speak with our elder."

"You speak on behalf of Ardan, I see. Strange how many speak in the name of Ardan. So many of them make war in his name as well. Tell me why you are different."

Abram cleared his throat.

"I seek not to create war, but only to warn all of a war that comes for them. Ares and Hades have created an army that need not eat, not sleep, and will not stop. It is bent on killing all life on Earth."

"And you expect that the few hundred elves that you can dupe into this war of yours would make any difference?"

Abram tried restating his word, "Fleck would…"

A woman's voice broke in from the back of the tent, in the darkness.

"STOP! You were one of the humans imprisoned by the Hessin. With you, Ardan defied his will."

The woman came out of the shadows and revealed herself to be Katanna, Fleck's mother.

"You put into motion a cataclysm that has fractured the elven people, and now you come asking for elven help for this war."

Katanna paused. Abram felt her eyes cutting through him.

"Tell Fleck he will have his army."

Chapter 29: Gathering Arms

Abram blinked to the wall of Aulmad. Abram furiously banged on the gate.

"Sault, Sault. I seek an urgent meeting with your council."

"Abram. What's the matter?"

"War is upon us, Sault, and we need more troops!"

On the walk to the inner circle, Abram got Sault up to speed.

"You wait here, Abram, and I will brief the council."

Abram waited, and waited, and waited for Sault's return.

"Abram, they wish to speak with you."

Abram stepped into the room as it fell silent. The leader of the high council addressed Abram.

"You have ruffled many feathers here today. Talk of an undead army, tales of how Hermes is willingly betraying his father. We must say, much like Hermes, we too have prepared for a day like this, but we can't risk these instruments for mere skirmishes between Gods. The council would like to know what effort has been made to take out the source of the army's power. What if we were to circumvent the army and go straight for the Gods themselves? What power do they wield?"

Abram felt hysterical. The Gods had been alive for hundreds of thousands of years, if not millions. Abram only knew of one thing the Gods feared, Kallos, and Abram watched it implode. He knew the vines in the Druid's sacred forest could slow them down, but would that work to stop an army of undead with two Gods leading it? In frustration, Abram spat out the first thing that came to his mind.

"They enslaved my brother!"

"I'm sorry, Abram. Can you repeat what you said?"

"They twisted my brother. Made him do evil things. They enslaved Levi!"

"Abram, in light of this new information, if the good in Levi could be snuffed out by these Gods, I feel I can speak on behalf of all my council members. The Gods are a threat we cannot weather. To take them head-on would be foolish, and to wait for them to knock on our wall would be disastrous. We will approve the use of all our arms. You designate the time and location, and we will be there."

Chapter 30: Playing the Fool

Abram phased back into the astral plane. Until this point, Abram had been successful in pulling together the troops he needed. However, this next jump posed a great threat to him, and he did not know what to expect. Abram braced himself for the worst and materialized into his realm. Waiting for him was a shocked Goddess.

"You have quite the nerve barging into my domain, human."

Abram had never seen this God, but he knew it was Hera.

"You smell of my own and I recognize you as one of Kaine's acquaintances. Have you come to beg for your life?"

"On the contrary, I have come to serve you."

"That is an interesting trick. Please continue."

"We have learned that Zeus has the other Dous Ring. We have also learned of his treachery, using beasts to scare humans to his flock. There is only one God who truly represents us humans, and that is you, Hera."

"This is true. But what is it you need, and what will you give me for it?"

"We seek to pull a ruse on Zeus so we can infiltrate his fortress and take the other Duos Ring. We need soldiers at the ready to lure his men away. As the true protector of humanity, we promise you much in return. Kaine has agreed to become one of your flock, and I promise myself as well."

"You make a tempting offer. Kaine and the Duos Rings would ensure my superiority. I will give you the soldiers you need, but if you betray me, I will take you over and make you destroy your friends."

"Your terms are fair. We won't disappoint you."

Abram blinked back into the astral plane.

Chapter 31: Matters at Hand

The party was halfway up the path to Zeus's stronghold.

"Look alive, people! We got stone statues, and they are getting a little movey! I think we have a pair of golems, and there are more all the way up the path!" Fleck shrieked.

Fleck pulled behind a rock, preparing for the worst. Everybody except Layla and Kya followed suit.

The giants unleashed a cry and charged the golems. The statues' eyes glowed and fired a beam of light towards Kya, knocking her back. Layla pressed forward, grabbing one golem and throwing it into the other golem. Layla addressed her sister.

"Kya! Are you alright!?!"

Layla rushed to Kya's side to check if she was still breathing.

"Kya is still alive, but she is hurt badly. I don't think we are forcing our way up there."

Kaine began working his way up the path with the fake Neccrum in hand.

"Kaine, you are going to get blasted off the side of the mountain," Fleck warned.

But Kaine did not turn back.

The stone statues up the path kept Kaine within their sight but did not attack him. Kaine quickly made his way to the opening of Zeus's fortification. Inside they found Zeus anxiously waiting for Kaine.

Kaine shouted out with his mind, "Zeus! We have come to make a trade. The Neccrum for the other Duos Ring."

Zeus laughed.

"Kaine, your boldness and arrogance will be your downfall. I will take the Neccrum!"

The doors into Zeus's hall slammed shut.

Kaine looked sternly at Zeus.

"You can try, Zeus! You can try!"

Kaine threw up his hands, and a gust of wind swept up Zeus, throwing him violently.

Zeus grinned, "You think a little wind will stop a God that controls the elements?"

Wind swirled about, lifting every loose item, including Kaine. Zeus pushed all the items into Kaine. Kaine barely had time to conjure a sphere of protection. The items thrown at Kaine shattered upon impact.

Kaine tried to go back on the offensive. He reoriented himself and hovered in the air. He pushed his hands forward, and immense fireballs sprayed from his hands. Zeus braced himself. The raging fire impacted him, but the force barely pushed Zeus.

Zeus chuckled, "Come on, Kaine! Is that the worst you've got?"

Kaine floated back to the ground, swirling his hands around. Zeus fell through the floor. Kaine loosened the ground below Zeus and hardened it, trapping Zeus up to his elbows in rock.

"Kaine, you know this is a mere setback. I will get out of this trap, and when I do, I will make good on my promise to take the Neccrum."

Just then, one of Zeus's soldiers burst into the hall of Zeus. The sight of Zeus trapped in the floor alarmed him, but he had an important message he had to deliver.

"Zeus, a sea of masked soldiers makes its way from the south. I fear we don't have the troops necessary to fight them."

"That is Ares and Hades' army, but they cannot move them without the Neccrum. Kaine, you don't have the Neccrum, and this is interesting. The way you pulled the protective sphere to guard yourself. Why would you...? Wait, you don't have the Dous Ring either. This is quite a revelation. Move the soldiers to guard the fortress from Hades and Ares."

Chapter 32: Pushing Forward

One last favor before the raid on Zeus's fortress.

"Kaine, I brought you to the Astral Plane for a request."

"Abram, you only need to ask."

"I need the Duos Ring."

"That is quite the request. May I ask why?"

"If we stand a chance, one of us needs to distract Zeus while the other looks for the ring. The person who looks for the ring needs to carry the other Duos Ring. If they are kept separate, we risk becoming mortal. Zeus could kill one of us and take the ring from the one who falls. I am not sure if I can distract Zeus, but I know I can become invisible. My power hides my physical form but does not hide my magical aura. However, if we approach Zeus and I hide behind you, he will be none the wiser of my presence. Our way in is you holding our fake Neccrum. I think it will be too tempting a prize for Zeus."

"Alright, Abram. We will move forward with your plan."

Chapter 33: Warring Outside

"Look, Fleck," Sarai pointed. "Zeus's troops are moving to the south. Do you think they are moving against the Aulmad troops? Aulmad will be outflanked if Zeus intends to attack them. Look what Aulmad is up against. There are more soldiers in Hades and Ares's army than can be counted."

"Still, Aulmad must already be engaging Ares and Hades's army with some serious firepower," Fleck observed. "I don't see any mages among their ranks, and I don't know how they are attacking from such a great distance. Hades and Ares's army must be more than three miles away. How are they doing that!?!"

Chapter 34: Aulmad's Assault

"Sault! The combat vehicles have engaged Hades and Ares's soldiers. What is your next order?"

"We shall fall back when the enemy approaches and act as bait while Hermes and Hera's soldiers flank Hades and Ares's army."

"What do we do about Zeus's soldiers?"

"That's the hitch. We must hope they see Hades and Ares's army as the bigger threat and move against them. Zeus's soldiers are foolish if they think they can take on an army of that size alone."

Chapter 35: Herme's Army Private Talk

"Katanna, how do they expect to coordinate this army and flank the enemy? Most of these people have no experience fighting. I heard there are so many soldiers against us, we stand no chance of flanking them."

"We may be marching to our death, but it is not our choice whether or not we fight. Our place is to hold back this unstoppable force and nothing more. We must put our faith in Fleck and his friends. Now, no more talk of dissent. We fight with honor until the last of us."

Chapter 36: Zeus's Forces

"General, sir. A small army has engaged Hades and Ares's army. They seem to have a power stronger than our army. It may be wise to destroy them and then fortify our position to prepare for a three-pronged attack from the army from the east and west, as well as Hades and Ares's army."

"We will be lucky to survive an attack from Hades and Ares's army on our own, let alone a three-pronged attack. We shall hold and fortify our position and hope the armies to the east and west attack Hades and Ares's army. Our only chance is that the armies take out enough soldiers that we can finish the rest."

Chapter 37: Hera's Plan

"The chosen are in place. Now we hold our position."

"But Lady Hera, aren't we supposed to flank Hades and Ares's army alongside the army to the east?"

"I will not risk my flock in this battle. We will allow Hermes and Zeus to expend their troops, then we will attack what's left. Our main objective is to get the Duos Rings and nothing more."

"As you wish, Lady Hera."

Chapter 38: The Beginning of the End

Zeus laughed.

"Kaine, did you really think I didn't plan for this eventuality?" he gloated. "You should have kept the ring. You would have spared your life. Now you forfeit it!"

Zeus removed his arms from the stone and kicked his feet to free his legs.

"Kaine, this is the beginning of the end for your party. I have a trap waiting for your friend with the ring. The rest of your party is stuck fending off the golems. And now, I am going to finish you."

Zeus's hands sparked as they charged with lightning. Kaine closed his eyes, anticipating the end of his very long life. As Zeus discharged his lightning, a blur of light knocked away his hands, redirecting the bolt away from Kaine.

"Zeus! You will not harm a hair on Kaine's head."

The outcome shocked Zeus and Kaine.

"How could you side yourself with these uncouth humans!" Zeus exclaimed.

"Master Hermes! Your timing is impeccable."

"Now that you know my allegiance, Father, there is no point in continuing the ruse. You will not hurt another human."

"You know you are no match for me, Son."

"Master Hermes, he is right. I no longer have the Duos Ring. My ultimate power no longer feeds you."

"Worry not, Kaine. Abram had already planned for this. Now, Father, I am going to stop you."

Hermes charged towards Zeus, striking him with his shoulder, bringing both Gods to the ground. Hermes flipped on top of Zeus and released a barrage of punches on him.

"Son, you may be stronger than I am, but your touch to the Rift doesn't compare to mine."

Zeus brought his hands up to Hermes's head and discharged an enormous blast. The force of the lightning threw Hermes through the wall.

"Where were we, Kaine? Ah, yes. I was going to electrify you. However, Hermes's attack made me realize I can do a more excruciatingly painful death. I'm going to slowly crush your head with my bare hands."

"You will do no such thing, Father."

Hermes grabbed Zeus by the shoulder and smashed his other fist into Zeus's stomach. Zeus stumbled, winded. A second blow sent Zeus flying, smashing him into his throne, turning it to rubble.

"Son, you have grown stronger, but you cannot defeat me."

Zeus released a flurry of lightning bolts. No matter how many bolts Zeus fired, Hermes dodged them. He moved so fast that he became a blur.

"Father, it is time to end this."

"What can you do to me that will end this fight?"

"I got a tip courtesy of Athena!"

Hermes quickly wrapped Zeus up in the vines from the Druid's sacred forest.

"What manner of treachery is this, Hermes?"

"These vines have a paralyzing effect on Gods. You are trapped. Admit defeat, Father."

"This is far from done, son."

Zeus's hands sparked and glowed brighter than before.

"Father, you should know by now you can't touch me with one of your lightning bolts."

"Ha, ha, ha! This is not meant for you, Son!"

Zeus moved his arms towards Kaine.

"Kaine! No!"

Hermes shot into a position in front of Kaine, absorbing the brunt of the bolt. It sent him flying through the wall of Zeus's fortress.

"Ha, ha, ha! I win, Kaine! Soon enough, my troops will come for me and untie me from these vines. Then, I will make good on my promise to crush you."

"Master Hermes, please be alright," Kaine prayed.

Chapter 39: The Beginning of the End: Part 2

Abram quickly wound his way through the fortress and entered the room with the other Duos Ring. He was shocked to find that no guards or protection was set up to prevent someone from taking the ring.

Abram stood at the entrance, prepared for an assault. He crept towards the ring, and when it was almost within grasping distance, the floor beneath him collapsed.

The pit in the floor was deep. Abram tried to use the ring. However, when he tried to speak, he made no sound.

Abram noticed gems surrounding the top of the hole. He thought they must be the items preventing sound in the hole, but it was the least of Abram's worries. The chasm began to fill up with sand. Abram knew that without the ability to talk and cast magic, he soon would be trapped in sand with no chance of being saved.

Abram was up to his waist in sand, and he was still unsure what to do. This seemed to be the end of his journey. But when he felt most helpless, a rope dropped down, wrapped around him, and pulled him up.

When he got to the top, he saw no one, just a rope attached to an unseen person. Abram thought he knew who it was.

"Fleck! You amazing elf. You saved me."

But a familiar voice proved him wrong.

"Not quite."

The mysterious person pulled back the hood, and then there was no question who it was.

"Sarai!" Abram exclaimed. "But how?"

"Fleck and I were trapped by the golem. When all seemed lost, Fleck gave me his cloak and told me to get to you. He ran out into the open to distract the golems. I don't know if he made it."

Sarai began to cry. Abram pulled her close.

"I'm sure he made it, but we must not waste his brave act. We have to get the ring."

Abram turned to the Duos Ring, jumped over the pit and reached for the band. But then Abram's arms went limp, and his eyes were empty.

"And now Hera wins! Ha, ha, ha!"

Abram was now a puppet of Hera's. He grabbed the ring and disappeared.

The

End

Chapter 40: Not Really

Abram slowly came to and found himself floating in a void surrounded by stars. In front of him was a giant, older gentleman busily placing more stars in the void.

"Hello, Sir. Where are we?"

"Oh! You startled me! Who are you and how did you get here?"

Abram thought this gentleman was not accustomed to visitors, but at least he was extremely friendly.

"Abram is my name, but I don't know how I got here. The last thing I remember is reaching for the Duos Ring. Then I blacked out. How did I get here? And who are you?"

"Why, Abrem, you amazing creature! I am…well…do you believe I have never been asked that? Ever. You can call me the Creator. I feel it is obvious how you got here. You brought together the Duos Rings and were teleported here, to the center of the universe, with me."

"Teleported to the center of the universe?"

"Yes. All the planets and stars revolve around this place. But the only way to get here is by combining the Duos Rings!"

"What are planets?"

"Have you not figured out telescopes yet? Surely my guardians guided you in celestial gazing by now."

"No. I was trying to fend off the Gods from my home. They seek to dominate it, and they rule with no concern for any of the creatures on their land."

"Gods? I put no Gods on Earth. I put guardians on Earth to guide your people. They were chased out of their realm and came here seeking protection. They agreed to lead you humans to a greater existence. You see, I made you in my image. You are made to grow over your generations, reaching higher and further with every iteration."

"I don't know of any guardians, but if they are the Gods, they have only twisted the world."

"I must see this for myself, Abrum."

The Creator waved his hands and blinked them to Earth.

Abram and the Creator hovered over Earth. The sight blew Abram away.

"Is this Earth?"

"Yes."

"And it's a planet?"

"Quite astute of you to notice."

"It's so round!"

"It is indeed."

"Are there more of these?"

"More than you can count in a lifetime!"

"And are there more humans on all of them?"

"Only on the planets I love. But I must see what my guardians have done to this planet."

Abram and the Creator pulled in closer to the Earth. As they flew over the planet, the Creator became more and more concerned.

"No, this is an abomination! The guardians were supposed to lead you to science. I never intended for them to open a rift to their realm and pull on the power within it. These creatures. They are all twisted and abnormal. This will not do!"

At that moment, Abram snapped to and remembered his friends were in danger.

"Creator! We must go to Mount Olympus. My friends are at war with the Gods, and I fear for their lives!"

"Then we will make haste there."

The Creator teleported them to the site of the war. He saw Hades and Ares's army and was disgusted.

"What a misuse of the spirits of the dead!"

The Creator waved his hand, and the spirits disappeared, leaving only the fallen armor. The Creator looked at Hera's army, and with a wave, he freed all the enslaved minds.

"Creator! We must find my friends! Sarai, Fleck, Layla, and Kya!"

"An simple task, I assure you."

The Creator waved his arm, and all of them appeared in front of Abram.

Abram was overjoyed to see Sarai. He rushed to her, embracing and kissing her. But then he noticed Fleck lying on the ground.

"Fleck!" Abram and Sarai cried as they hurried to his side. Abram was devastated. Fleck's armor was destroyed, and he was covered in burns. Tears filled Abram's eyes.

"Fleck. Please, no…"

Fleck coughed. "I may look a little less pretty, but don't count me out…"

Abram pulled Fleck close and hugged him as tight as he could.

"Come on, Abram. Burns! Burns all over."

The Creator spoke up.

"I think I can take care of these burns."

The Creator waved his hand again. Fleck was lifted to his feet, and all his burns were healed.

The Creator spoke, "Now I must take care of my guardians. Guardians, appear before me, and return to your realm."

The Creator formed a hole in the realms. Before the Creator appeared all the guardians: Zeus, Hera, Hades, Ares, Hermes, and many others. They trudged through the hole back to their own realm, all but one. Hermes knelt before the Creator.

"I must beseech you to stay here among the humans. I know them better than my kin. I betrayed my own kind to protect the humans. Please let me still walk among them."

"Abrom. Is this true?

"Yes, Creator. He speaks the truth."

"Then I allow you to remain, but I must tell you. I am severing the tie between your two realms, and you will lose the power from it."

"If it must be done, it must be done."

The Creator turned to Abram.

"I leave you now. I must look after the universe."

Abram spoke up.

"Without the guardians' magic and leadership, what will happen to Earth?"

"I suppose humanoids will become humans, creatures will become animals, their magic will slowly fade from the land, and you will have to lead yourselves. It looks like your line will make fine leaders."

"My line? I have become a mage and can't have children. How will I have lineage?"

The Creator smiled.

"That's for me to know and you to find out. You are going to have a hard time, however, convincing her that you can't have children. Well, I must be on my way. Abraham. Sarah. Fluck. If you ever need me, you simply have to bring the rings together."

The Creator then disappeared.

"Fluck! That guy was a piece of work," Fleck remarked snidely.

"I don't know. I kind of like Abraham."

"And I like Sarah." Sarai added.

"Are you sure we can't sell you on Fluck?"

"*Fluck?* NO."

Chapter 41: Home

After the battle, Layla and Kya parted ways with the group to go back to their home. Abram and the others were given Greymeer wolves to speed up their travel.

"Where to now, boss?" Fleck asked.

"Home to Trow!" Abram exclaimed.

Abram pushed the wolves and others as hard as he could. But when he arrived at Trow, it was nowhere to be seen.

"It's gone," Abram said, morose. "I'm too late."

Abram dropped to his knees and wept. As his tears touched the ground, something unexpected happened.

The ground rumbled, and from the desert off in the distance, mountains erupted. Before him, exploded the forest around Trow. From it came a slew of Tangfu as if they were waiting for him the whole time.

The Tangfu greeted the group with arms wide open. They hollered and cheered as Abram made his way through the forest. The cries of joy did not stop during his whole walk through the forest.

On the other side of the forest, waited some Tangfu to help them up the mountain. When Abram reached the other side, he broke out into a sprint and coaxed the others to follow.

"Come on, guys, you have to meet my family!" Abram yelled, elated.

Abram ran into the house shouting.

"Alesse, Mom! I'm home!"

From her room, out walked Aleese, sleepy-eyed.

"Why are you making so much noise so early, Abram?"

Abram ran and embraced her.

"Friends, this is Aleese! Aleese, this is Fleck and Sarai! Sarai is my wife!"

"Why are you talking so crazy, Abram?" Aleese laughed.

"Grandpa! You have to meet Grandpa!"

Abram pulled Sarah and Fleck along to Grandpa's house. Abram blew open the door.

"Grand…"

Abram stopped mid-sentence. Before him lay his Grandpa next, to a fallen chair by the table. It was obvious that Grandpa was writing a letter before he fell.

Abram ran to Grandpa's side.

"No, this is not how this is supposed to happen!"

Abram rolled Grandpa over and there was no mistaking it. He was dead. Tears welled up in Abram's eyes.

Abram got up and grabbed the letter. He began to read it.

"Abram,

I fear my time is short. I feel the surge of power and I am led to believe one of the twenty has passed. With my final moments, I will have done two things.

I have put all the villagers into a deep sleep and hidden the village. You must already know the village will reappear and the villagers will awaken upon your return.

Second, without me casting my magic to extend the lives of our village, the people of the village will age at the same rate as the rest of the world. To prevent them from aging, I have taken the chalice on the table and imbued it with my magic. You can fill the chalice with water and place a pendant in it. The pendant will be enchanted and will extend the life of the wearer. Unfortunately, this magic will fade away over time.

Abram, I know I am not your real grandfather, but know I have loved you and your family more than anyone in my life. Also, know that I have lived a full life because of you.

Love,

Grandpa"

Abram wiped the tears from his eyes and stood still for a moment. Sarai approached and put her hand on his back. Abram squeezed her, knowing none of this would have been possible without Grandpa.

Abram looked at Sarai.

"Grandpa is the first person to die in my village."

"I know, Abram. But he gave us a future here in Trow," Sarai consoled him.

"He would have wanted that." Abram admitted, smiling. "We should go back and tell the others."

The
End

Perhaps.